Her Hidden Smile

PROTECTOR'S OF JASPER CREEK
BOOK TWO

CAITLYN O'LEARY

To Drue Hoffman. Thank you for always being there for me.

Has Life Ripped Away Her Ability to Love?

Renzo Drakos' job has taken him to every corner of the world, and he's loved every minute of it. The freedom has helped him bury many demons from his past. But as he's watched his huge family start families of their own, he feels like something is missing. He wonders if his wanderlust will allow him to stop long enough to find a woman who will capture his heart.

Millie Randolph has struggled all her life. As a child, she barely survived when her family home burned to the ground and she lost her beloved parents to the flames. Her aunt and uncle reluctantly took her into their family where she shut down. Emotionally and physically scarred, she feels flawed and knows she'll never be loved again. Years later she finds herself at her parents' farm, trying to fulfill their vision. What others say can't be done makes her even more determined to achieve what has now become her dream.

When Renzo meets Millie, he finds the missing piece of his broken soul. Knowing this gentle woman has been through so much, he refuses to be another person who lets her down. Will Renzo be able to see that living in one place is not a cage, but with Millie, it's a home? And will Millie open her heart to believe that love is possible, or has life taken away her smile forever?

Prologue

TWENTY-FIVE YEARS AGO – LIMA, PERU

"Get up!"

I grunted. That was my first mistake. But I couldn't help it. Izan's kick wrenched me out of a dream where my grandmother had made me a little plate of ceviche. It was the first time she gave me grown-up food.

"Ha! You don't like being kicked, do you, you lazy piece of shit?" He kicked me again; this time it was in my backbone. I was careful not to make a sound. Any time I did, he just kicked me more and harder.

"You are such a slacker. You did nothing yesterday. I don't know why Luis lets you have any food."

I scrambled up from the piece of cardboard I'd been sleeping on. The cold bit through my thin shirt, and I shivered. I saw that the old, ratty wool coat that I'd found in the trash was over on Izan's pallet. It stung when the wind slapped my long hair against my frozen cheeks.

I started toward Luis' makeshift house. He was our leader, and his cardboard leaned up against the bridge wall and a tarp covered the entrance. If Luis woke up, then Izan would stop hurting me.

Fire shot down my arm as Izan slammed me into one of the concrete pillars that held up the bridge we'd been sleeping under.

"Lay off the kid," Jorge yelled out. "We need him. He's no use to us if he's hobbling around."

"I don't know. Won't they feel more sorry for a cripple?" Izan laughed.

"Shut up, all of you. Renzo, get over here." Luis had flipped back the tarp and must have seen me cowering away from Izan.

I shot Izan a dirty look as I scurried over to Luis. He'd been my protector ever since we'd escaped from the orphanage. If it hadn't been for him, I'd probably be working for the gold-toothed pimp who forced everyone to work in Miraflores. Izan was always telling me that one day he would sell me to that man, but I knew Luis wouldn't let him.

I was shivering when I stood in front of Luis. Lima was cold in the mornings.

"Here." Luis handed me his jacket. It was his Cristal fútbol club jacket. I couldn't believe it. "If you do good today, you can keep it."

"I can?" This was better than any Christmas or

birthday with my grandmother. This would be the best thing I'd ever gotten in my whole life. I fingered the blue and gold material.

"Only if you do good," Luis warned. "Today is Fiesta de Las Cruces. There are going to be a ton of tourists. We're depending on you to lure the marks. Do you understand? We're down to our last sols."

"We are?"

"We only have enough for beans and bread tonight."

My stomach growled. I was so sick of beans I was going to throw up. I wanted sweet Chançay bread like my grandmother made me, or even better, that pork roll sandwich we once stole from the bakery. That'd be good.

"Are you listening to me, Renzo?"

I wasn't, but I nodded.

"We got to find Americanos," Luis said. "They have the most money."

"Yeah, they're rich and stupid," Izan sneered. He yanked at my jacket and glared at Luis. "You're too soft to lead. Renzo doesn't deserve this jacket. He's just a baby. We should get rid of him."

"Shut it," Jorge barked. He came up behind Izan and slapped him upside his head. Jorge looked more like fourteen, but he was only ten. He could crush Izan like a bug, and Izan knew it. But Izan had a knife. Last month when I saw it, Izan threatened to slice me up if I told the others. I worried he would use it on Jorge one day if Jorge kept hitting him.

Luis shook his head at Izan. "Renzo isn't a baby. He's almost seven, and he's smart. He's perfect at distracting the tourists. We need him."

Izan gave an ugly laugh. "That's bullshit. I can lure the tourists better than he can."

Luis and Jorge laughed in his face. "Nobody would trust you. Just thank the saints that you run fast," Jorge scoffed.

"Enough. I have a little food left over; we need to eat. It's going to be a long day." Luis pulled some bread out of his pack, along with the dreaded can of beans.

"Them," Luis pointed at the man and lady coming out of the toy store. "Just look at them, Renzo. They act like they own the world. Shitty Americanos who buy everything and don't even think about the homeless and hungry."

They look happy.

"Is Izan going to steal her purse?" I asked.

Luis looked down at me and stared. "Does it matter?"

It mattered. Izan didn't just take the ladies' purses, he made sure that he pushed them down. He liked it when he hurt them. There was something wrong with Izan.

"Look, Jorge is at the parade. He's picking pockets, so yeah, Izan is going to grab her purse while you distract her. It'll be easy because the man is carrying all those shopping bags."

I eyed the lady and the man. I watched as they came out of another shop with another bag of stuff they didn't need. The pretty lady was laughing up at the man. He had his arm around her waist.

Did they like each other?

My grandmother said that my mama and papa had loved each other very much. Did these two Americanos love each other?

"Go!" Luis shoved me so hard I fell forward, but I caught myself before my face hit the cobblestones. There had been little to share for breakfast, so we were all hungry. That made even Luis angry. I knew my job. I had to distract the yellow-haired lady while Izan came by and grabbed her purse. But still, I had to protest. The lady wasn't just holding her purse, it was over her shoulder. Every time Izan grabbed a lady's bag from her shoulder, she was for sure getting hurt.

"Can't we choose someone else?" I begged. "Look at her purse. Izan's going to hurt her for sure."

Luis grabbed me by my shoulders. I winced as he squeezed the bruise I got from Izan this morning. "Look at all those shopping bags. She's rich. We need the money. If you don't do this, I'll let Izan at you."

I could see by the look in his eyes, he meant it.

I twisted out of his grip. "I'll do it," I promised.

"Wait," Luis muttered. "Give me the jacket. You look too good wearing it." He grabbed the collar and yanked it off me.

I didn't flinch, even though it really hurt my shoulder again.

"Now get going."

I saw the man and lady were heading toward the cathedral. That was good. There were some beggars already there. I would be just one more. Out of the corner of my eye, I could see Izan. He was near the far edge of the cathedral stairs. All I had to do was get them talking to me, then Izan could come up behind the lady and take her purse. It's what we always did. We'd been doing it since I was five, after we escaped from the orphanage.

I walked a little funny as I rushed up to them. The last kick in the back that Izan had given me had really hurt, and now I couldn't walk straight, but at least I hadn't made a sound. When I was almost to the lady and man, one of the older beggars tripped me. I slammed to the ground, my chin scraping against the cobblestones.

"That wasn't nice," the pretty lady said in Spanish. "You should be ashamed of yourself."

Who was she talking to? How did she know how to speak in Spanish?

Soft hands helped lift me up. I saw that she'd put her purse on the ground.

Good. Izan wouldn't hurt her now.

"What's your name?"

Her eyes were really pretty. I'd never seen somebody in real life with blue eyes.

"Honey, can you talk to me? Can you tell me your name?"

I eyed her purse again, then scanned the plaza to see where Izan was, but I couldn't see him. I was finally standing, and she was trying to brush the dirt off my clothes, but that would never work. I'd been wearing the same clothes for over a month.

"Sharon, honey," the man interrupted, "we need to go."

"He looks hungry." She turned back to look at me. "What's your name, sweetheart?"

Where was Izan? He never waited this long.

I looked up into her pretty eyes. "Renzo. My name is Renzo," I mumbled.

I needed to get away from them.

"Renzo what, honey?"

I shrugged my shoulders and winced. Where was he? I looked behind her, but all I saw was the big man's legs behind the lady.

She squatted down, her flowery skirt flowing around her so it was touching the ground.

"Don't be afraid. Are you lost? Where's your Mama? Where's your Papa?"

She brushed back my long, greasy hair from my grimy forehead and I forced myself not to cry. The last time someone touched me so nice had been before I was forced into the orphanage. Back when my grandmother was alive.

She turned her head and looked up at the big man. "I don't think he's lost, Christos. I'm worried he doesn't have anyone."

I looked up at him, too.

"Sharon, we can't save everyone," he said in a kind voice.

"But we need to at least get him something to eat. Maybe a—"

Izan slammed his head into the nice lady's side, and she actually lifted up before she crashed down onto the cobblestones.

"Sharon!" the big man yelled as he slid on his knees to cradle her in his arms.

I looked over and saw her purse was gone. My job was done. But I couldn't leave her. She was bleeding. I stood over her.

The man looked up at me. "Get the police. We need an ambulance."

I nodded my head without thinking.

"Renzo!" It was Luis shouting. "Time to go."

The big man's eyes darkened with fury. He realized what I'd done.

"Policia!" he yelled. A couple of tourists stopped, but they would be of no help. I knew where the policia were. I ran like my feet were on fire and found the two men who guarded the other side of the cathedral. I told them what happened. They were talking on their radio for an ambulance as they followed, then passed me by to get to the lady and the man.

When I almost made it to them, I was grabbed so hard by my arm, something popped in my shoulder. I looked up, expecting it to be the man, but it was Izan.

"You rat. You're going to turn us all in, aren't you?"

I was so scared, I couldn't speak. He swung me by my useless arm. I couldn't stifle my scream. He punched me in my face, still holding me by my arm so I couldn't fall to the ground. He punched me again. Then he pulled out his knife.

"We don't have time," Luis muttered as he pulled me away from Izan. "If you kill him, then they'll come after us. They won't pay any attention to a street rat, but a dead street rat they might do something about."

"I," Izan dropped me to the ground.

"Don't," Izan kicked me in the face.

"Care," Izan bent down with his knife.

"You better start caring," a man bellowed. His fist was as big as my head, and it circled Izan's wrist. He held Izan a foot off the ground.

"Here he is. This is the kid who hurt my wife." The big man shook Izan like he was a puppy. I couldn't see Luis or Jorge. One of the policia that I had brought to help came over and grabbed Izan.

"We're going to need another ambulance for this kid," the man said as he squatted over me.

"They were probably in it together," the second policia said, then spit on the ground.

The big man looked at me for a long time. "No, I don't think so. He was just a beggar who was at the wrong place at the wrong time."

I hadn't cried since the first week I'd been sent to the orphanage. The jailers beat you if you were a crybaby. But my face scrunched up, and I felt tears leaking out of my eyes. It wasn't the pain of Izan's beating. It was the fact that this man was being nice to me. Nobody was nice. Nice stopped being a part of my world the day my grandmother died.

I heard a man rumbling in English. I understood a lot of different languages. It helped me to survive. English, French, German, and some Japanese. I tried to listen to what the man was saying, but his voice was too low. I opened my eyes, but then closed them again. The light hurt.

"Christos, lower the blinds. The light is hurting Renzo's eyes."

It sounded like the lady near the cathedral.

"Mom, not another brother. There's already four of us," a boy whined in English.

"I raised you better than that, Jase." It was the man talking again. "If you're not careful I'm going to give him your Big Wheel when he comes home with us. Got it?"

I opened my eyes just a bit. I wanted to see where I was and who the kid was who was talking.

"Got it, Dad."

"I'd like another brother," another boy spoke up. He was looking over at me and smiling. He was even darker than I was.

Both of the boys were around my age. Maybe a little older. I really couldn't tell. I really wanted to know what a big wheel was.

"You're right, Malik, another brother would be good," the pretty lady said in English. "His name is Renzo, and according to the police, he doesn't have anyone, so your father and I are going to ask him if he would like to go home with us."

"Where did he come from?" the girl asked.

I turned my head and saw a girl who looked just like the lady.

"The police think that he's one of the homeless children here in Lima. Sometimes their parents have died, and sometimes they just kick their children out of their houses."

The girl who looked like the lady gasped. "They wouldn't really do that, would they?" She was looking at the big man. He went over and put his arm around her.

"I'm sorry, Elani, but it's true. We're going to have to wait for Renzo to wake up before we'll know what happened to him."

"He's awake."

It was the boy who had complained about me coming home with them. He was tall. Jase. That was his name.

The lady came to stand over me. Once again, she pushed the hair off my forehead. "Are you awake, Renzo?" she asked in Spanish, her voice soft.

"Yes," I answered her in Spanish. I didn't want anyone to know I spoke English. I needed all the help I could get. Them not knowing I could understand English would help me know if they were lying.

"Renzo, can you tell us your last name?"

I shook my head. That was a stupid thing to do. It made my head hurt even more than it already did. I thought about telling her my last name was Carera. But if I did, the police might send me back to the orphanage. The beatings were bad before I ran away; I knew they would be a hundred times worse if I went back after I was captured. I shuddered when I thought about the cattle prod.

"Are you cold?"

"No, señora."

"But you shivered." She pulled the blanket up higher so it reached my chin. It was the softest blanket I had ever felt.

"Really, I'm not cold." That was when I remembered Izan hitting her with his head. "How are you?"

She put her hand to the back of her head. "I just have a bump."

"But you were bleeding."

"Just a scratch. I didn't need an ambulance. No stitches. I'm fine," she said with a smile. "Are you sure you don't know your last name?"

"I don't," I said again. I shoved the arm that didn't hurt under the blanket and crossed my fingers. The other arm was in some kind of sling.

"Sharon, don't pester the boy. He's been through a lot," the big man said. He came up to stand next to the lady with the yellow hair. He put his arm around her shoulder, just like he had the girl. "Why don't you take the kids to the cafeteria and let me talk to Renzo."

I shivered some more. I wanted to beg the pretty lady not to leave me. Not with the man who knew what I had done. He might be nice in front of her, but I knew he was big and mad. If Izan could hurt me this bad, this man could kill me for sure.

He must have seen my fear.

"It's okay, boy. We're just going to talk." He smiled, but I didn't trust him.

The lady looked up at him. She was frowning, but she must have seen something in his face, because she smiled, then looked down at me. "It's going to be okay, Renzo."

She turned to the two boys and the girl. "Come on, let's get something to eat."

She made them leave the room, then turned back to me and smiled. "I'll come back soon, Renzo." Then she followed the kids.

The man grabbed one of the two chairs in the room, dragged it over to the bed, and sat down. He was still higher than I was and I had to look up at him. His eyes were darker than Luis'. Darker than Izan's. They were black like Jorge's.

"Renzo, my name is Christos Drakos. I want to thank you for getting help for my wife."

I sucked in a deep breath and held it. He couldn't really be thanking me.

"You know what I did." Even I could barely hear my voice, but he nodded. "Then why are you thanking me?"

"I know what it's like having to go against people meaner and stronger than you are. It's tough. Sometimes it's the toughest thing you'll ever have to do in your life. But you did it, Renzo, and I'm grateful."

I wanted to bawl like a baby, but I didn't. The big man. Señor Drakos. He seemed to know. He hurried on.

"You know your last name, don't you?"

Looking at him, I knew I couldn't lie. "Yes."

"Is there a reason you don't want to tell us?"

"I'm never going back to the orphanage. Never." My hands hurt, and I realized I was holding them in tight fists.

He nodded. "All right then. I have a proposition for you."

"Huh?"

"I have an offer for you."

I didn't like the sound of that. Luis had had an offer for me, too. It had been only a little bit better than the orphanage. Of course, it was a lot better than the pimp.

"What offer?" I finally asked.

"Become a part of my family."

Again, that was what Luis had said. He said that the four of us would be a family. He said we would all look out for one another. I just stared at the big man. We looked at each other for a very long time.

"What are you thinking?" he finally asked me.

"The boy who beat me up was supposed to be my family, too."

"Ours will be better. You can talk to our other children."

"Was the boy in this room supposed to be part of my family, cause he doesn't want me. It won't be good."

Señor Drakos chuckled. His laugh didn't scare me like a lot of grown-up men's laughs scared me. "You're pretty smart, Renzo. Jase is one of my sons, but he is all bark and no bite."

"What does that mean?"

"He's like a junkyard dog that barks a lot, but when you go up to him, all he does is lick your hand. He is like my wife. All of my children would welcome you into the family. I would welcome you into my family."

"Why?" It seemed too good to be true, I didn't trust him.

"I believe in your goodness. You proved it yesterday."

"But why? Why bring another boy into your family?"

He reached out and picked up my fist. He gently pried it open and took my hand in his and squeezed.

It felt good.

Like he cared.

But that was impossible. Right?

"I'll tell you why we want you as part of our family. When Sharon first saw you, and realized you had no one, she wanted you to be part of our family." I didn't say anything. I just listened.

"My wife has a big heart, so you're probably not surprised that she would want to take you in, are you?"

I nodded, then shook my head. I didn't know what I believed. How could that nice, pretty lady want me to be part of her family? It made no sense. Señor Drakos seemed to understand what I was struggling with.

"My son Jase is adopted. So is my son Malik. But they are my sons, the same as if Sharon and I had made them ourselves. We have three more girls and two more boys at our villa. We're heading back for the United States next month. Sharon and I both want you to come with us and be part of our family."

It was getting stranger and stranger, and my world felt like it was spinning out of control. "Is everyone adopted?"

"All except Elani. You met her. She's the spitting

image of my wife."

When the room stopped spinning, I took a deep breath. The lady was a good lady, and so was this man. They adopted children. I had to tell the truth.

"I help steal things," I whispered.

"I know," he whispered back. It was like his dark eyes could see into my soul. Like he was a priest or something.

"Then why do you want me?"

"When I realized you were in on it, I was furious. I wanted you punished."

I bit the inside of my cheek. *I will not cry. I will not cry.*

"So, why do you want me?" I asked again.

"Then you brought the police, and when the medical personnel were helping Sharon I saw that asshole beating you. I heard what he was saying. You put your life on the line to help my wife."

I didn't say anything. What could I say? He was right. I had to save her. She mattered, not me.

Slowly I squeezed his hand in return.

"Is that a yes? Will you give us a chance?"

I wasn't sure.

But what did I have to lose?

I slowly nodded my head.

The big man looked down at me, his eyes gleamed with pride.

"I promise you Renzo, you will not regret this."

I prayed he was right.

Chapter One

When did I become the Good Samaritan of Jasper Creek?

Just because I helped Bertha, Aza, and a few others on the mountain, didn't mean I was going to help everyone. Yeah, okay, so I worked on repairing the rec center. But everyone did that. That didn't mean that I should be the one who Irving Monroe called when he was sick and needed something to be done for some helpless woman who owned an orchard.

For that matter, why in the hell did I let Jase talk me into coming here in the first place? Oh yeah, I needed a place to lay low. A place to hide.

I sighed as I tapped the steering wheel to the beat of "Ring of Fire." Nothing better than Johnny Cash.

I rolled down the windows of Irving's old truck and grinned. I loved this clunker. It reminded me of working in South America. Manual transmission and no electronics. You actually had to turn the crank to roll down the window. When I did, the brisk air shot into the cab and I grinned. Okay, there was a lot to like about Tennessee.

And, on the plus side, there had been the little problem Trenda had a couple of weeks ago. That was something that got my blood pumping. Working with her man, Simon, had reminded me of my brother Jase. I guess all that SEAL training made them pretty similar.

I looked down at my phone. *Two miles to go, better keep my eyes peeled*. I took another deep breath of the cool, fresh air. Yeah, maybe big brother wasn't full of shit. Sending me here to rest and recuperate might have been one of his rare strokes of genius.

There was something about the look, feel, and the people that made it really relaxing. Being a hermit on the mountain had been just the trick for the first two months. Then gradually reaching out to some of the mountain folk... well that had been a kick.

I looked down at my phone one last time. I slowed down. The Randolph farm should be coming up on my left pretty soon, and I didn't want to miss it. I crested one more little hill and there it was. I pulled over to the side of the road and stopped the truck. I had never seen anything this idyllic. There was the white farmhouse, the obligatory red barn, a greenhouse, and then there was the orchard. In the distance I could see a pond.

I wondered what the orchard would look like when the trees bloomed.

Irv Banks had explained to me he had been working as the orchardist for Randolph Farms back when Millie's folks had been alive. Back then, he'd just made some suggestions about what and where to plant. Like any new parents of an orchard, the Randolphs needed a lot of help. They needed to know where and when to plant and how to irrigate. Then he taught them how to ensure the trees were pollinated by bees. Later in the season, he taught them how to spray for insects and inspect the trees for disease.

The first three years, the trees didn't produce fruit, so the Randolphs didn't need to harvest. It was right after the fourth year that there was the house fire that killed Howard and Felicia Randolph. Their fourteen-year-old daughter, Millie, had survived. Irv had been working the orchard on Millie's behalf until she was nineteen and moved back to Jasper Creek. The deal was that he took all the profits from the harvests while Millie lived with her aunt and uncle. Millie had been back for the last five years, but Irv had stayed on as the orchardist. He still took the majority of the profits. He offered to pay me to go out and check on Millie and the trees, but I had refused. I figured this was the same as checking on people up on the mountain.

"Hell, I guess I am a Good Samaritan."

I shook his head in disgust.

"Should know better than that by now."

Irv warned me that Millie was skittish around new people, so I'd have to go in soft. That wasn't going to be a problem. I had seven sisters, four of whom had been adopted from bad situations and I'd had to coax them into being comfortable around me.

I've got this.

I took one last look at the beauty, drinking it in, letting it soothe my soul, then I started up the truck and went down to the farm.

When I took the left into Randolph Farms, I meandered down a gravel drive. There was a fruit stand set up about fifty meters from the house. It had plenty of space for people to park. I imagined during apple, pear, and peach season; Ms. Randolph did a brisk business with the folks of Jasper Creek. What I didn't understand is how she would have a fruit stand if she was averse to having people in her space; that didn't track.

When I got close to her home, I was met with a white picket fence. It was a lot higher than normal, six feet, and it had a professionally installed electronic security gate. I wondered if it was electrified. If not, it wasn't much of a deterrent. But maybe it was just to keep the people at the fruit stand from coming to visit.

Who knows?

When I got within ten meters of her electric gate, it began to open. I don't know if she had a sensor set up or if she was just looking out the window, waiting for me. I parked in front of her porch. I didn't see any vehicle, but it might be in the garage.

The front door opened and a woman walked out. She was petite. Maybe five-two. I couldn't guess her weight. She was wrapped up in layers and covered it up with some kind of ugly shawl.

I got out of the truck and walked up the stairs. With each step I took, she took a half step backward. When I got to the top, she was back in her house, looking at me from behind the threshold of her door.

"You're Millie, right?" I asked in the same tone I'd used with my four previously fragile adopted sisters. "My name is Renzo Drakos. Irv Monroe sent me to help you. He's got bronchitis and the doctor and his wife are worried it might turn into pneumonia. He said you'd know that your normal workers are in Florida about now. What he didn't have time to tell you is that he's arranged for some horticulture students from Walters State Sevier County Center to come help with the debris left by the storm. Their professor is giving them class credit for assisting you."

"He is?"

Her voice was no more than a whisper. I nodded.

She shook her head. "Only Irving could wrangle something like that."

"He said you might be a little too shy to give them their assignments?" I posed it as a question so I wouldn't offend her.

Millie gave out a harsh laugh. "Shy, huh? I guess that's one way to put it."

"I'm sorry. I wasn't trying to upset you."

She studied me as I apologized, missing nothing. She was also taking in my demeanor and expressions as she tried to determine my emotions. On the last one she was out of luck. I had my emotions locked down, tight as a drum.

"I didn't know Irving was that sick," she said, changing subjects. "I wouldn't have called him for help if I had known. Maybe I should make him some soup. I could leave it on the porch for his wife to pick up."

I didn't bother to comment on that, instead I turned to the matter at hand. "I saw the broken branches; how would you have taken care of them yourself? Some of them are pretty high up."

"A ladder."

"Using a ladder without a spotter isn't safe, as a matter of fact it is downright dumb."

She winced.

"But you know that already, don't you?" I persisted.

She nodded.

"Are you telling me you're so bent on not taking other people's help that you'd risk injuring yourself and not being able to call for help?"

"I'd take my cell phone."

Finally, a bit of backbone.

"And what if you were unconscious?"

"I'd wake up, and then call for help."

Now her backbone had taken a turn to stupidity.

"Now you're just being contrary."

"Look, Mr. Drakos—"

"Call me Renzo."

"Mr. Drakos, I don't need your help." She stepped back from the threshold and started to close the door.

"Hold up." She stopped closing the door and looked at me. "Are you always this stubborn?" I asked her.

"I'm not stubborn," she protested. "I just like working with Irv. I've been working with him for years."

Irving was an older man. Small but wiry. I could see how he wouldn't be intimidating. Meanwhile, I almost topped six feet, and I was built on the larger side. Muscular. And if it was a concern to her, like it was to some people, I was half Peruvian and half Caucasian, so that meant I was brown skinned. I couldn't be more different from Irving than a hummingbird was from an ostrich.

"Miss Millie, Irving has already arranged for the kids from the college to come and help. They're going to be here in a little less than two hours." I'd worked on and off in the Southern states. I knew the vernacular. You always went with Miss Millie or Mizz Bertha, depending on the age of the woman you were talking to. Hopefully, addressing her as Miss Millie would put her more at ease. I hated seeing the look of panic that suffused her face.

"They can't be. I can't possibly supervise the workers. That's just not doable. What's more, I don't have lemonade and cookies ready for them."

I couldn't stop from grinning.

Cookies and lemonade?

"Can't you send them away when they get here?" she pleaded.

I could, but I wouldn't. She needed to get those trees cleaned up. Hopefully that was the last windstorm and frost for the year, but we still weren't done with March, so who knew what was going to happen. She needed this done.

"Miss Millie, these kids are counting on this for their grades." I knew that any woman who made lemonade and cookies for the men and women harvesting her fruit would be a soft touch for the college students.

I watched as she bit her thumbnail.

"Irving told me a little about what needs to be done. I can supervise them," I assured her. "Throughout the day I'll probably need to ask you some questions, though. Is that all right?"

I was pretty sure she nodded, but hell, maybe she flinched.

"Was that a nod, yes?" I forced her to answer.

"Yes," she whispered.

"Then I'm your best bet, without Irving, right?"

She didn't just frown, the corners of her lips turned down and she looked sad. Then she nodded.

"Miss Millie, you can just tell me how you want your trees trimmed, can't you?" I pulled my iPhone out of my back pocket. "We can Facetime, and you can tell me what needs to be done on each tree. How does that sound?"

"I don't have a phone that does Facetime," she admitted.

"That's okay. I'll take pictures and text them to you. If it's really complicated, I'll come up here and we'll go over the pictures together. Okay?"

Again, she barely nodded.

"Are the ladders in the barn?"

"Yes. So is the cherry picker."

I took a minute to process what she was talking about, since we're talking about peach, pear, and apple trees, but I realizes she was talking about the mini truck with an extending ladder that hooks to a basket on top that somebody stands in. That way, they can reach the tops of trees.

"I'll go check that out before the students get here."

"But you and the students won't know what to do."

"Their professor will be with them. I should hope since she is a horticulturist, that she knows how to prune trees after a storm, right?"

Millie sighed. "Yes," she whispered. "The workers

understand I stay inside and they work with Irv, but the professor will think it's odd."

I heard the sadness in her voice and I hated it.

"I'll tell her you're baking cookies for everyone. How about that?"

She took a deep breath. "I know I'm being ridiculous."

"I'm not here to judge. Four of my sisters feared strangers when they were first adopted, so I get it. Zuri is still pretty shy."

The door opened two, maybe three inches wider.

"But not like me, I bet."

I laughed. "Well, you *have* taken shy to a whole new level, Miss Millie."

"You understand, I don't enjoy being this way? Right? And I'm not always."

"I told you, Miss Millie, I don't judge. My sisters had their reasons, and I respected them. I respect yours."

She nodded again. I hated to see the downward turn of her lips, but it was what it was.

"Why don't you get started on those cookies, and I'll go see what you have going on in the barn. Deal?"

She pulled her shawl up higher. It might have hidden her slender shoulders, but nothing could hide her high, prominent cheekbones. I wondered if she just naturally had those, or if they might be from not eating enough. Maybe I could bring her groceries and drop them off. I'd definitely include chocolate. Polly, Angel,

Elani, Zuri, Indah, and Nia all loved chocolate. That just left out Sandy. She liked jellybeans.

"Okay," she mumbled. "I'll get you the key." She shut the door and I could hear her lock the door.

Yep, definitely skittish.

She came back in less than a minute. I had to stifle a laugh. Only Zuri could put her hands on a key that fast because she was just that organized. The rest of my sisters would have to hunt for the key, especially Angelica. Hell, she'd take thirty minutes, then call me in to help her find it.

Millie bit her lip as she considered how to give me the key. For a moment, I thought she was going to have me back up and then put it on the porch and close the door. When she held out her trembling hand with the key in her palm, I practically cheered.

Thata girl!

I slowly reached out to pluck it out of her small hand, doing my best not to touch flesh. She immediately pulled back her hand. I could see her entire body was shaking. It was time for me to go.

"How about after I walk out, you close your fence? I'll direct the kids and professor to the barn and we'll get started. When would you like me to come for the treats?"

She sighed in relief. "Can I call you?"

I took my phone out of my back pocket. "Give me your number and I'll just log it into my phone, then I'll text you and you'll have my number."

She gave me her number. She wasn't whispering anymore, and I took that as a good sign. I put it into my phone, and then I shot her a text. We could both hear her phone ringing from somewhere inside her house.

"There you go," I said with a smile.

She nodded. "I'll start on the cookies. Thank you, Mr. Drakos."

"That's my father's name. I'm Renzo."

"Thank you, Renzo."

I nodded and turned to jog down her steps. I heard the door close before I cleared the first step. I even heard the door lock. She might've been skittish, but by God, she'd handed me the key. She'd been brave today.

When I was halfway to the barn, I heard the electronic gate close.

Chapter Two

I shut the door and leaned against it. My body wouldn't stop shuddering. He'd touched my hand. It was only for an instant, but our flesh had connected. I never should have handed him the key. I knew better. But for once, I wanted to be brave.

Why can't I be brave all the time?

Shoving off my door, I forced myself to my desk and sat down. I was flapping my hands and blowing on them before I even realized it. The temperature was sixty-eight inside, but that wasn't going to handle things today. I got up and went to the thermostat then set it to seventy-three. Hopefully, I would warm up soon.

When I pulled up the diagram of the orchard, I closed my eyes. I remembered when the trees were planted. It was so exciting when Mom, Dad and I would go out to see their progress.

Dad had listened to Irving and planted the trees far enough apart to allow them to grow and not get in each other's way. At that time we'd only had thirty-five trees. Dad had left acres and acres of room to plant other apple trees, pear trees, and peach trees. I didn't realize it at the time, but the peach trees would only last seven to fifteen years, whereas the apple and pear trees could live fifty years.

I remember Dad teasing Mom for wanting to plant peach trees. He said that they weren't as economical and profitable in the long run as pear and apple trees. Mom had insisted because she liked the smell of the peach blossoms. What's more, she knew how much Dad liked peach cobbler. Dad had laughed at her silliness, but he'd planted them. I remember how she had hugged and kissed him and whispered in his ear. They did that a lot. I'd always wished for that one day, but now I knew it would never happen for me.

The first time they bore fruit, we were practically jumping up and down. Mom even let me have a little glass of champagne, even though I was only fourteen. I'd felt like such an adult.

I hoped Renzo or the professor wouldn't tell me that any of the trees were too damaged and had to be cut down. I couldn't tell from when I had walked the orchard last night. There had been a lot of debris, but it didn't look like any of the trees had been uprooted.

I got up from my desk and looked around the living room. When I spotted the fire extinguisher over the couch, some of the anxiety I had been feeling after touching Renzo, eased. The extinguishers always made me feel better.

Turning around, I headed down the hall to the master bedroom. I went straight to the massive closet that they'd built for the new house. It was only a tenth of the way filled up. I pulled out Dad's old, brown, leather jacket and shrugged it on. It was huge on me, but I didn't care. I loved it.

It was still charred from the fire. It was the one thing that I had that was left after the blaze that decimated my life. I stroked the charred spots. This jacket was my savior. After spending time in the burn ward, I knew I got off way easier compared to so many others.

When I awoke in the unit, I was alert enough to understand I now belonged to Aunt Marge and Uncle Phil. Aunt Marge was my dad's mom's cousin. I'd only met them when I was little, but they were who Mom and Dad had given me to if they died.

The nurses let me have Dad's jacket in the room with me. It was covered in plastic, but it was in a spot where I could always see it. It was after Aunt Marge told me she and Uncle Phil were going to take me back to Des Moines, Iowa to live that she picked up Dad's jacket. She told me she was going to have it repaired before I was transferred to a hospital in Iowa. I screamed at her. I don't know who was more shocked, her or me. It was the first time I had said anything since the first day I'd been admitted to the burn unit in Nashville. At that point, I'd been there four weeks.

It was a year later that I found out that they were the only people who would agree to be my guardians if Mom and Dad died.

Other people from Jasper Creek came to visit me. Some from school, but I hated that. Even my two best friends Harriet and Jenny came, but I couldn't stand for them to see me either covered in gauze or with my burned flesh uncovered to supposedly help me heal. I hated seeing the horrified look on their faces.

Other people who knew my mom and dad came too. But somehow seeing them was even worse. They acted like Mom and Dad would have. People like Ms. Pearl and Mrs. Draper. I couldn't even look at them when they came to see me, so they stopped coming.

But there was one little person who got through to me. Maybe because I always thought that she would be how my grandmother would be if I had one. So, she was the one person who it didn't hurt to see. She could make me feel better. It was Little Grandma Magill. She came with her daughter and granddaughter. I couldn't handle it until Lettie and Patty left. When it was just me and Little Grandma, she brushed back my singed hair and held my hand. I cried. She described heaven to me and I cried harder. She promised me that's where my mama and daddy were.

She promised.

When she held my hand, the burns on my hip and

leg didn't hurt as bad. I never spoke to her, but she knew what to say to me.

After six weeks in Nashville, they said I could be transferred to the burn center in Iowa City, a two-hour drive from Des Moines. Uncle Phil had already left. Aunt Marge explained he was an important executive at an insurance company. I didn't care. She said that she was a financial planner, and she was doing her job from the hotel in Nashville. She made it sound like it was a hardship. I wanted to tell her to go home, but the words stuck in my throat, so like normal, I just turned my head and looked at the wall.

The last time Little Grandma Magill came to visit, we both cried. I finally spoke to her, and I begged her to let me stay with her. She explained it couldn't happen. She explained that Aunt Marge and Uncle Phil were fine people who lived in a big house and would take good care of me.

"But what about the farm?" I whispered. "What about the trees? They're our babies."

"The people of Jasper Creek will figure out something. I promise."

I was still thinking of Millie when I got to the barn. I saw that it was even more organized than my brother Malik's garage. Damn, I wouldn't have thought that was possible. She even had built-in cabinets. Who had that in a barn?

Is that a Stanley tool chest?

I went closer to check it out. It was. And not just any old tool chest, it was their top of the line. When I opened it up, I saw it was fully loaded. Hell, somebody could rebuild an entire car engine with that set of tools. But if they had, they sure as hell had cleaned them up good. These babies were pristine.

I looked over at the ladder wall. It couldn't be called anything else. She had eight. No wait. She had ten ladders and two cherry-pickers.

What the hell?

The outside of the house looked almost brand new while the barn didn't. But inside, it was kitted out with nothing but the best equipment. Irving told me he was still taking a large amount of the profit, and he was planning on paying me far too much for a couple of day's work. Millie must come from money; it was the only thing that made sense.

She had two top-of-the-line cherry pickers. As a matter of fact, I'd only worked with a mobile elevating platform picker on one job. Normally, you'd need a truck to haul them around. I jumped inside the cab and there was no sign of the keys. I checked out the other picker, same thing. I'd have to go back to Millie sooner than I promised.

I'd wanted to get a feel for operating one. I really didn't want one of the kids operating one of these things. We could have a liability issue. Speaking of which, I needed to talk to the teacher and make sure that the kids had all signed a waiver. The last thing that Millie needed was some kind of lawsuit. Hell, maybe she already had a waiver written up.

I pulled my phone out of my back pocket.

"Hello?"

I smiled. She sounded like a different woman. It was as if having the barrier of the phone between us allowed her to be more confident.

I like it.

"Hi, Miss Millie, it's Renzo. I have a couple of questions. First, do you have the keys to the cherry pickers?"

"Yes." I waited for her to continue. "Come on by, and I'll give it to you. Is there anything else you need?" she asked. Yep, this was definitely a different woman.

"I'm going to ask the professor if she had the kids sign any kind of waiver to come work here for the next day or two. But I wondered if you had some kind of worker's liability form that you had people sign when they worked for you."

"Oh. I hadn't thought about that." Again, I waited for her to keep talking. "That's a really good point, Renzo. Thank you." I could almost hear a smile in her voice, and if it wasn't a smile, I at least heard gratitude. "I should have thought about it. I have a liability waiver that I used once. Let me get that updated so they can sign it. Usually Irv takes care of it because the workers work for him."

"That makes sense. Remember, I should too."

"You should what?" I heard the confusion in her voice.

"I should sign the waiver, too."

"Why, are you planning on getting hurt?" she teased.

I barked out a laugh.

"Are you teasing me, Miss Millie?"

"I was, wasn't I?" She sounded bemused.

How adorable.

"I just like the thought of you being protected," I explained.

I heard her huff of laughter and smiled.

"Hopefully I'll have the paperwork completed before the first student arrives," she said. "How much time do I have?"

"Now? About an hour and a half."

"Okay, I'm on it. Talk to you soon."

I smiled. "Bye."

"Bye." She hung up. I knew the OCD woman was probably already at her computer, just waiting for me to get off the phone so she could start working on the waiver. I shook my head, still smiling.

I turned back to the barn.

"Shit."

I pressed in her number again.

I definitely heard a smile in her voice when she

answered. I wondered if I would actually see one on her face. "You need the keys, right?"

"You're a mind reader," I answered.

"Yep. I'll leave them outside the door."

"You're not going to hand them to me?"

"I've got a waiver to write."

Damn. I felt disappointed.

"Okay, be right there."

I jogged over to the house where the gate was open again. I found a keyring taped to her front door, with two keys. The ring was meticulously notated *cherry pickers*. The keys had numbers written in indelible ink, one and two. Yep, definitely OCD. I needed to introduce her to Angelica. Maybe she could teach my sister a thing or two.

I was in the barn when I noticed that one picker had a number one stenciled on the side, the other a number two.

"Of course." I rolled my eyes.

I grinned as I used the key with the number one to start up the number one picker. I looked at the manual transmission and laughed. I wondered what college kid knew how to drive a stick shift.

I got her going and was pleasantly surprised when I wasn't inhaling the perfume of diesel smoke. Yep, Millie had definitely gone top of the line. Maneuvering the vehicle out of the barn was a breeze.

For me.

But I'd been dealing with every kind of

construction equipment out there. Hell, I'd even worked with the world's most MacGyvered excavator known to mankind. The guys and I were trying to repair it with a few rubber bands and some barbed wire because we couldn't find baling wire or duct tape. It wasn't doing the job until Gus pulled out his Fixodent to keep his dentures in place. Damned if that didn't do the trick.

Yep, there was no way I was letting any of the students drive this thing. I got out of the cockpit and examined the basket. I liked the harness set-up. No matter how far someone leaned out, there was no way they would fall to the ground, as long as they were harnessed in properly. And I'd see to that.

But it'd sure be nice if we could use both pickers. I ran my fingers through my hair and thought about the men I'd met since landing in this town. I still wasn't sure if I wanted to do anything as drastic as putting down roots, so I was renting Simon Clark's drafty cabin way the fuck out of town. I could always call Simon to help out, but he was busy repairing the house he was sharing with Trenda Avery.

Still, he should know someone.

I pulled out my phone.

By the fourth ring, I was about to hang up and text him instead. I hated leaving voicemails; personally I never listened to them, but I always read my texts. Then I heard Simon answer.

"Yeah?"

"Simon, it's Renzo."

"I know. How you doing?"

"Pretty good."

"You staying in touch with your mother?" Simon chuckled.

Bastard.

"Yes, I just talked to her and Dad last week."

"Good man."

"How about you? Everything going well with Trenda and Bella?"

"Except for a little damage to the roof, we're doing fine. How did the cabin fare?"

"Really well. I was surprised. I'm over at Millie Randolph's orchard. She has a lot of trees that need tending to. Broken branches. I don't think any of the trees were uprooted. She got off easy that way, but still if the branches aren't handled now, it's going to be an issue come harvest time."

"How do you know so much about orchards?"

"I've kicked around a lot. Worked more than just construction in my travels," I laughed. "It's been fun."

"Huh."

I could almost hear the former SEAL commander's wheels turning. "How can I help?"

"I don't want to take you away from what you're doing, but do you have any idea who might be up for driving a cherry picker?"

"It's the truck with the basket up top, right?"

"Yep. I've got a bunch of college students who are

getting credit in the horticulture class to help out, but I don't trust any of them to operate the picker."

"I wouldn't either. Trenda's brother and sister-in-law are in town. Probably just landed a couple of hours ago and are settling in at Evie and Aiden's place. Bella always loves to ride herd over her little cousins. I'll send Trenda over there. That way, Drake can head your way."

"I'd appreciate it."

I hadn't met Drake Avery, but I had heard many stories. I had no doubt that the SEAL could operate the cherry picker, but he might end up being just one more kid I'd have to supervise. Then again, he could surprise me.

"I'll call you when I've got it all sorted."

"Thanks, Simon. Say hello to Trenda and Bella for me."

"Hold up. Bella heard me talking to you. She wants to say hi."

There was a moment of silence.

"Hi Mr. Renzo!" Bella chirped. "Mom's going to bake homemade lasagna this week. You should come eat some. You know you like it."

I chuckled.

"You're just trying to get me to swear so I can pay you money."

"I'm too old for that. I have little cousins. I'm the oldest now."

Her prissy little voice made me laugh harder. "Are

you telling me that if I say 'hell' you're not going to ask for a dollar?"

"Well...maybe you. And Daddy. And Uncle Drake and Uncle Aiden because all of you should know better by now. If you think about it, I'm really just trying to help you become better men."

I damn near dropped my phone I was laughing so hard. "Are you sure you're only eight years old?"

"I'm eight-and-a-half. Daddy says I'm a chip off the old block. I think he means I'm like my mama."

"Well, I'll come over, because I can't resist your mama's homemade lasagna."

"Don't forget to bring a dollar. You said H-E-double-toothpicks."

"I'll remember my dollar, you little swindler."

"What does swindler mean?"

"Ask your daddy. Now give him back his phone. He needs to make some phone calls for me, okay, Cariña?"

"Okay, Mr. Renzo. I'll have Daddy call you when it's lasagna night."

"Thank you, Miss Bella."

"Good-bye, Mr. Renzo."

I was still chuckling when I put my phone in my back pocket.

Chapter Three

I had all the waivers printed out and sitting in my outbox beside my computer. I had the second batch of cookies in the oven, and I just needed to get one phone call done before I could worry about my orchard being invaded by strangers.

I set the timer for the peanut butter cookies, then pushed in the number for Ginny G's personal assistant and put the call on speaker so I could multitask. Rebecca had assured me that today would be a good day to call.

"Hi, Millie, you called at the perfect time," Rebecca said as she answered the phone. "Ginny just got done putting Erica down for a nap."

"How does she get everything done in a day?" I asked.

"I have no idea," Rebecca laughed. "Let me get her for you."

"Hello. This is Ginny."

For just a moment I was nervous. I was such a fan of this woman. I'd been listening to her music since I was sixteen, and here I was talking to her in person.

Get it together!

"Hi Ginny, I'm Millie Randolph. I'm calling from the International Burn Alliance. I really want to thank you for taking my call."

"Rebecca researched you and said you were on the up-and-up."

"I'm glad. I wanted to tell you a little bit about why this charity means so much to me. I lost my parents in a fire when I was fourteen, and I was badly burned in that fire. If I hadn't been able to get to the Burn Center in Nashville so fast, my injuries would have been much more catastrophic. The people there were wonderful, even if I didn't think so at the time."

"Aw, hell, Millie. That must have been rough."

"I know you know, because one of your band members also sustained burns last year."

"Yeah," she said softly. "It was terrible. We all miss him."

I knew he had been free-basing cocaine and caught on fire, then died from his injuries after a week in the hospital.

"You and I know I'm playing on your sympathies because of Garth, and I'm going to go even further. Arkansas only has a pediatric burn center; it desperately needs an adult burn center. That is something we are currently working with UAMS to get built."

"So, you're hoping because I grew up in Arkansas I would be willing to donate, huh? Not a bad pitch."

The timer went off.

"Hold on, I have to take my cookies out of the oven."

Ginny laughed.

I took out the second batch of peanut butter cookies and slotted in some chocolate chips.

"What kind of cookies?"

"Some college students are helping me out at my orchard, so all kinds. Right now chocolate chip and peanut butter," I answered.

"Good choice. Can I ask you a question, Millie?"

"Sure."

"I donate money every year, and I've set it up with my attorney. Why didn't you just go through him?"

"Honestly? I did my research. You're bringing in twice the money this year from last year, and before your attorney came to you with charity suggestions, I wanted to bring this to you."

Ginny laughed. "You know, this is exactly the kind of polite forcefulness that I used to get my first record deal."

This time I laughed. "You believed in yourself, just like I believe in what I'm doing. When you believe, it's easy."

"You've got that right. I'm all-in on donating my

extra monies to your cause this year. Let me talk to Shep and I'll have him give you a call next week. If, for some reason, you don't hear from him in five days, call me back. We're going to make this happen."

I'd been putting the warm cookies onto a plastic platter with a spatula, and as soon as she said that I threw up my hands in excitement and the cookies went flying through the air, landing on my living room couch.

"Thank you so much, Ginny. This means the world to me, and it will make miracles happen for so many people. Please know that one of the things that we do for donors is let them know exactly how their money is being spent and then provide stories of patients, as long as we get their permission."

"I appreciate that. I'll let you get back to your cookies."

"Thanks, Ginny. Goodbye."

As soon as I hung up, I jumped up and down. Then I went and picked up the broken pieces of the cookie off the couch. As I did, I saw the first two cars come up the drive. Renzo was there, and he motioned for them to head toward the barn, just like Irving always had the farm workers do during harvest season. After five cars drove by, I went to my bedroom where I had the best view of the barn and watched as Renzo stood in front of one of the cherry pickers with his legs spread and his arms crossed over his chest. It was clear he was in charge. A Prius and a double cab truck with an extended bed drove up at the same time. A strawberry-blonde woman in khakis, who also had an air of authority, got out of the Prius and a gigantic man with a big grin got out of the truck. He'd be scary if he wasn't smiling.

Renzo walked toward both of them and shook their hands. After the introductions were made, he motioned to my house, and I knew I was visible in the sliding door to my patio and I waved. That's me, always good at a distance or on the phone.

They all waved back, then turned their attention back to Renzo. Soon the woman, who was obviously the professor, was handing out paperwork to all the students. Renzo and the large man went into the barn, and soon Renzo came out, followed by the second cherry picker driven by the big man. I watched as everyone headed out to my orchard. That was my cue to head to the kitchen and continue baking.

Hours later, I jumped when there was a knock on my door.

What in the world?

I knew I'd closed the gate. I went to the door and looked out my speakeasy peephole.

It was Renzo. I unlocked and opened the door a couple of feet.

"How did you get past the gate?"

"I jumped it."

I frowned. I looked past him to the gate. Then looked back at him. "You can't jump it, it's too high."

"Jumped up to the top then climbed over, would be more accurate," he grinned ruefully.

I looked at the gate again. "Nobody else has ever done that."

"Nobody else has been promised cookies. Do I smell snickerdoodle cookies?"

I nodded. "Chocolate chip and peanut butter, too. My men don't eat many of the snickerdoodles, so I rarely make many of those, but I saw that half the students were girls, so I made a third of each kind."

"See, you offered an incentive for me to climb over the gate."

I scowled at him. "Are you always so impetuous?"

He laughed. "You think I'm impetuous, huh?"

"Absolutely. Impetuousness could get you into big trouble. You should be more careful."

"The last time I was called impetuous was when my mom and dad caught me dating a college sophomore when I was still a junior in high school."

"That doesn't make any sense. Why would a college freshman want to date someone so young?"

"I had a friend who got me into all of his fraternity parties. When Kathy and I met at one of those parties, I convinced her I was a college senior."

"How were you able to do that?"

"I looked old for my age."

"That old?"

I loved the way her eyebrows scrunched together as she frowned.

"I was on the football team. I was big for my age." I grinned.

"How did she find out that you were still in high school?"

"After one of our dates, I was dropping her off at her house in my dad's car. What I didn't realize was that her father worked with my dad and he recognized the car. He called my dad."

I winced. "That must not have gone well."

"That's an understatement."

"Dad came over to Kathy's house and apologized to Kathy's father. When he got me home, he read me the riot act for drinking and partying with college kids. I felt awful because I'd left Kathy in tears."

"How long had you been dating?"

"Six weeks. But it seemed so much longer. At that age, you think that six weeks is a lifetime. Later, Mom came to talk to me. I really liked Kathy, and she really liked me. She was the first girl I'd ever kissed, and I was broken up. I felt even worse that I had hurt Kathy. Mom called me impetuous for playing games of the heart. It was a hard lesson to learn, but I learned it."

"I don't think climbing a fence is in that category. What happened to Kathy?"

"A week later, she was dating Eric. That was my friend who got me into the fraternity parties. I guess she wasn't as upset as I was about our break-up."

"How long did it take before you were dating someone?"

"Seven months."

"Wow. You really were broken up," I whispered. I couldn't imagine the powerful man in front of me as a heartbroken boy. It was then I noticed my door was wide open, and I had my hand on the doorjamb and I was leaning forward.

I jerked backward.

"How are you going to give out the cookies?" Renzo asked.

My bottom lip hurt, and I stopped biting it. "Normally, Irv comes inside and carries the platters outside. There are bottles of cold water in the barn fridge."

Renzo nodded. He must have peeked inside.

"Everyone can help themselves," I added.

"How many platters are we talking about?"

"Six. They're good-sized plastic ones that I bought off the internet."

"Will you be okay if I come inside?"

His tone was soothing, like he was trying to calm a wild animal.

I hate this.

"Yes, you can come inside." I heard my petulant tone, and I hated that, too. The only people I really enjoyed having in my home were Little Grandma McGill, her daughter, and her granddaughter. Other than that, I could tolerate Irv. I was a mess.

I hid behind the door as Renzo stepped inside.

Renzo realized what I'd done.

"Cariña, what do I need to do for you to relax? Do you need to stay in that corner and watch me pick up the platters from the dining room table? Or do you need to move even farther away, so you know I won't get close to you?"

I considered his words. I moved to the living room behind my couch. I felt comfortable beside the fire extinguisher that hung on the wall. It was silly, but it made me feel safe.

I felt Renzo watching my every step. When I turned to look at him, I thought I would see mirth in his eyes, but I only saw understanding. Maybe he really *did* have sisters who were neurotic like me.

"I'm taking the chocolate chip and snickerdoodles first," he said with a grin and a wink.

"How come I get the feeling you want to save the snickerdoodle cookies for yourself?"

"Because you're a smart woman, Millie Randolph."

He picked up four of the platters. One in each hand, and one resting on each forearm. "I won't be able to climb the fence, so you'll have to open the gate this time."

"I think I can manage that. As a matter of fact, I'll even open the front door for you."

Was that me? Was I actually teasing this man?

He moved to the door, but well away from the doorknob. I appreciated his consideration. "I'll be back for the other couple of platters later. I'll put these on the hood of the truck. The kids will love these. Thanks for this."

I nodded. I was out of words for the day.

"By the way, the professor got all the waivers signed."

"That's good," I mumbled.

"I'll be back for the other two trays, then I should be out of your hair for the rest of the day. Does that sound good?"

I nodded.

I pushed the button that opened the gate and watched him walk out. The way his shoulders and back flexed as he balanced the trays was captivating.

Hmm, that was weird. I only thought that way about men on the TV.

Two hours later, when Renzo came back for the last two trays of cookies, we did the same process and I watched him once again. This time, I was ready for the show. I was glad he was wearing a light-gray Henley shirt that fit him so well. When I got back to my computer, I was still thinking about how he looked. I had to shake my head to get back to the business at hand. What I was working on was important and required my full attention. I didn't have time for stupid daydreams.

~

"Don't tell my wife, but these cookies are much better than hers," Drake Avery said as he snatched up one from each tray.

I shook my head. "Leave some for the students."

"They're already leaving for the day. Their professor said that they've done enough to get the extra credit that they needed. We won't see them again."

"I see some of them still out there," I protested.

Drake laughed. "The football players. They need *extra*, extra credit."

"Yeah, they do seem to be working their asses off. All the more reason not to eat all of their cookies."

"Renz, there's plenty left. Your woman baked up a storm."

This time, it was my turn to laugh. "You do know who you're talking about, don't you? This is Millie Randolph. She's closed up tighter than a bug in a rug. She doesn't belong to anyone."

"Really? The way you were going back and forth to her house, I was sure there was something going on between the two of you. Is she nice?"

I nodded, then I grabbed a peanut butter cookie and took a bite so I wouldn't have to answer any follow up question he might have. Drake gave me a knowing look and waited for me to wash down the cookie with some water.

"What does she look like?"

"Big violet eyes, creamy white skin, and hair the color of teak. Beautiful."

"What about who she is? Do you like her?"

"Like I said, she's closed off, so I haven't got a bead on her yet. And what's with you, anyway? I heard a bit about you from your sister, Trenda. She never told me you were a matchmaker."

He barked out a laugh. "Fuck no, I'm not a matchmaker. It's just that I'm deeply in love with my wife. I've seen some of my sisters and teammates pair off. I believe in love, and I like to see other people find it. Sue me."

I stared at the man. "Are you for real?" I finally asked.

"Straight up. I like seeing good people finding their other half."

Good people. Hmmm.

"And you think me meeting Millie today means I've found my other half?" I asked.

"Stranger things have happened." Drake took a long pull from his water bottle, then finished off the other half of his snickerdoodle cookie.

"Well, Trenda was right about one thing. You *are* a nut."

"I know my sister. Guaranteed she said I was smart, loyal, and loveable too," Drake flashed me a grin.

"Amazing you could fit your head through the barn door."

"Nah, barn doors are easy. It's normal house doors that are hard."

I laughed. This guy was a mess.

We watched as the last three college students headed toward their cars. We returned their waves with chin tilts. Then I looked over at the orchard. From what I could see most of the branches had been taken care of, but there was still work to be done.

"Break time's over," Drake said as I was standing up.

I nodded.

We didn't finish until dusk. Drake and I made four trips from there to Irv's place with the tree waste. Since Millie's folks had died in a fire on this land, I totally understood why she wouldn't want the branches held at her place. I'd go back to Irv's tomorrow and take the branches to the Sevier composting facility.

"It was nice working with you, Renzo," Drake said as we unloaded the last of the branches. He held out his hand and I shook it. "Don't be a stranger. Trenda and Simon told me all you did for them a while back. Karen and I are going to throw together a dinner. We'd love to have you come."

I nodded, not committing to anything. Drake knew I hadn't said yes.

"Say hello to Jase for me."

"Have you worked with Jase?" I asked. "I thought that East and West Coast SEAL teams didn't mix."

"We do, sometimes. We've trained together. Good guy. A little nuts, but a good guy."

Talk about the pot calling the kettle black.

"I'll tell him you said hello," I promised. He got into his truck and drove away.

I pulled out my phone.

"Hello," Millie answered.

"Your orchard has been cleaned up, and all the debris has been delivered to Irv's place."

"To Irv's?"

"Yeah. I'll be taking it over to the composting facility tomorrow."

"Renzo, why are you doing so much? The least I can do is pay you."

"Nope. I was just happy to be of help."

"But you'll end up spending two days doing this. I don't want you to use your vacation time just to help me."

"I didn't. I'm between jobs right now. This helped to fill my time. Anyway, you paid me in cookies. Done deal."

"But—"

"Seriously, Millie, if you bring up money again, I'm going to be pissed."

"Oh. Well, in that case, thank you."

"You're welcome."

I hung up the phone with a smile.

Chapter Four

MAY, JASPER CREEK

"You're going to have to shit or get off the pot."

I shook my head. My brother sure had a way with words. "I take it Bonnie and the twins aren't home."

"I'm over at Gideon's place. They'll be over a little later," Jase chuckled.

"How long have you wanted to say that to me?" I asked.

"About as long as the rest of the family. Seriously, Renz, you have been jonesing to move back to the States for the last three years, why don't you just face the facts?"

"What do you mean, move back to the States? We hardly lived in the States, not with Dad's job taking us all over the world."

"That's bullshit. Every time a job was over we came back home to Springfield and Grandma Maureen. The house on Westchester Avenue was home. Hell, you know Sandy did her best not to show it, but she was bummed that her wedding had to be in Duluth and not in Springfield."

"Yeah," I sighed. "Peter was a douche for insisting on Duluth. What, he had seven relatives and four friends up there?"

"And it was fucking cold!"

"Are you still bitching about the cold?" I asked Jase.

"Damn right I am. How long before she's going to dump his ass?"

"I'm just praying she doesn't get pregnant. I heard from Elani that Sandy's put off having a family until douche-boy keeps a job for longer than six months."

"That's our girl." I heard relief in Jase's words.

"Still, it was fun to have the whole family together, even *with* you bitching the entire time about how cold it was." I laughed.

"Yeah, it really was. It would have been better to have Grandma Maureen there. I know she said she didn't want to fly, but Angelique said she could arrange a private plane for her. Hell, I offered to drive her up there."

"So did I."

"So did Malik." Jase chuckled.

"She still wouldn't go. I hate to think of her getting older. But she is in her upper eighties."

"You wouldn't guess it when she's around her great grandkids. She'll get right down on the floor and start playing with them." I heard the smile in Jase's voice.

"Have you taken Bonnie, Lachlan, and Amber to Springfield yet?" I asked.

"Yeah, the kids won over everyone, and Dad said Bonnie was a keeper."

"Of course, he did."

"What about you? Is there more keeping you in Jasper Creek than just Simon's dilapidated cabin and the Southern cooking?"

I thought about Millie and everything Drake had said. She and I had traded a couple of texts, and I'd coaxed her into taking a few phone calls from me.

"Renzo? You listening to me?"

"I am. So, is there a wedding in your future?"

"Damn right there is. I swear to God, Amber wants to be the wedding planner, but she seems to be most interested in the wedding gown, the cake, and the flowers. Lord save me from seven-year-olds that are smarter than me."

"Isn't the cake, flowers, and dress everything?" I wanted to know.

"Fuck if I know. I asked Bonnie if we could have it in Springfield and she was all for it. It's set for October. You're going to be my best man, just so you know."

I sat up in the cabin's shitty recliner. "What? I don't do that kind of thing. Ask Malik to be your best man."

"I'm asking you."

"You're *telling* me, and I'm saying ask Malik."

"No can do. You're my man."

"What about one of your teammates?"

"You do realize this is supposed to be an honor, right?"

I cricked my neck and looked up at the ceiling. "Yeah, I know, Jase, and I *am* honored. But I suck at making toasts and holding onto rings and fitting into tuxes. You know that."

"That's a load of bullshit. I know better. I saw you escort Angelica on that red carpet deal, two years ago. She had you looking like a movie star."

"I didn't have a choice. I'd just beat the shit out of her asshole boyfriend and threw him out of her condo. She needed a date at the last minute."

"Renzo, what's the real reason?" Jase asked quietly.

Aw, shit. He was making me think and be honest with myself. I didn't like it. It forced me to feel.

"You know where I come from. Occasionally, not too often now, I can still smell the stink of the streets of Lima still on me. I want you to have the best possible man standing up with you. Choose Malik."

"Well thank God you said occasionally, otherwise I'd tell Mom and she'd be hauling a counselor or a priest down to JC to talk to you so you'd get your head on straight."

"You threatening to tell Mom is beneath you."

"It sounds like you have most of this figured out. Why not all of it?" Jase asked.

I rubbed the back of my neck. "The thing with Angelica, that was Hollywood, and that didn't mean anything. Standing up with you in a church, that's sacred. You know I spent two years as a thief."

"Yeah, what were you, five?"

"I was six when I stole from your mother and your father caught me."

"*Our* mother, and *your* father. You were six years old. Younger than Amber and Lachlan. So if they were living on the streets in fucking Lima, Peru, would you hold it against them if they were pickpockets? Hell, would you hold it against them if they were having to sell themselves? Fuck no! You wouldn't care what they did as long as they survived and we could find them and help them. I don't want to hear shit about you still having the stink of Lima still on you. You were a kid who was surviving. Get your ass over to Virginia and spend time with my kids, and you'll see."

I thought about the red-headed rascals and I couldn't help but smile. I'd kill anybody who harmed them. Hell, there was Bella too. Any of them. They were kids. Just kids. I kept judging myself through the eyes of an adult, and I needed to get over that shit.

"Please tell me that your silence means that you're actually thinking through what I had to say."

"Yeah, you're getting through," I admitted.

"Then you're my man. You're my best man."

"When's the wedding?"

"September in Springfield, Bonnie and the sisters are still trying to figure out a venue."

I laughed. The idea of all those women working together made my head spin.

"Oh, and Renzo?"

"What?"

"Bring a date."

"I'll work on that."

It was time to call Millie again.

When my phone rang, I was hoping it would be a finalization of Luxton Corporation's donation. They'd been putting me off for a week, and that was always a bad sign. But I'd put a call into Regina Weatherford, who was the chairman of the board's sister. Regina knew everyone and saying she was tenacious was putting it mildly. She was tenacious like a honey badger. I grinned. She'd never heard of a honey badger, so I sent a link to a video called *Honey Badger Don't Give a Shit* on YouTube. She said she hadn't laughed that hard in ages. Since then, she'd been solidly in my corner. \

Yep, Luxton Corporation should be calling me real soon.

I found my phone in the kitchen and when I saw that it was Renzo Drakos, I was even more excited than if it *had* been Luxton.

Get a grip.

"Hello?"

"Hi, Millie. I was wondering if you would take pity on me and bake me some cookies."

Huh?

I was confused, but halfway to a laugh.

"That's how you ask for favors, you just blurt them out? No warmup? No niceties ahead of time."

"Hi, Millie, what are you up to today?"

I looked around my living room and grinned. It smelled and looked like spring. "I might have gotten carried away and picked a lot of peach blossoms and filled every vase I owned."

"Only your vases?"

"You got me. Maybe I filled up my pitchers, my watering cans, my mayonnaise jars, and my orange juice bottles."

"Now this I have to see. And smell. I bet the scent of snickerdoodle cookies would blend nicely with the peach blossoms."

Damn, he's right!

"Maybe."

"Can I ask you a question?"

I frowned. "Sure."

"Why are you so much more comfortable on the phone than you are in person?"

"Caught that, did you?"

"I'm observant, what can I tell you. So why?"

"I handle gifts and grants for the International Burn Alliance."

"You're not a newbie, are you?"

I twisted my hair, then answered. "No."

"How long have you been doing this?"

"I've been working for them since I was seventeen. I got my masters in nonprofit administration online, while I kept working for the NBA. Eventually I worked my way up the food chain."

"How far?"

Ouch!

I let go of my hair.

"Director," I admitted.

"How much money do you bring in each year?"

I definitely wanted to sidestep that question. "Let's talk about you. I hear you have a degree in architectural engineering from University College in London."

"Been asking around about me, have you?" I could hear the satisfaction in his tone. He sounded smug.

"People around here gossip."

"I thought you didn't go into town."

"I have to get groceries, and sometimes I order food from the restaurants, so I talk to people. I hear things. Speaking of which, are you going to stay and work for Harvey?"

"He and I are talking about things. Right now I'm doing some work for him, and that's fine. But staying on and working with him is a whole other thing. So far, we still haven't got things hammered out so that we're both happy. It's a work in progress."

"I heard that he's chomping at the bit to bring you on. Trust me, you have the upper hand."

Renzo chuckled. "That's how I see it too. Millie, you explained to me why you're confident on the phone. That makes sense, but why so skittish in person?"

Fuzzbucket! Nope, this requires fuck!

I really didn't know how to, or maybe didn't want to, answer the question, so I was silent.

"I threw you a curveball, didn't I?"

"Yeah," I whispered.

"My brother just asked me something earlier today. It was one of those introspective questions that didn't just make me think, but made me question my feelings. He really put me on the spot, and he was my brother. It was out of line for a stranger to do this to you. I'm sorry, Millie."

"Thanks for understanding." I wondered if he could hear my whisper.

"You're welcome," he replied softly. "Now, about those cookies."

I grinned. "I don't know, what have you done lately to *deserve* cookies?"

"Hold on, I can think of something."

He paused for a long time, and I knew it was just to mess with me.

"I agreed to be best man in my brother's wedding."

"That should be fun. Why does that deserve cookies?"

"I have seven sisters and nine brothers. Do you know how much pressure I'm going to be under to toast Jase and Bonnie? I'm going to get so much shit, especially from Malik and Bruno. It's going to be hell. I won't be able to return the tuxedo because of the sweat stains."

I couldn't stop the laugh that popped out.

Sweat stains?

"It's worse than that, then there is Grandma Maureen. She is going to be giving me the stink eye because I won't have a date. She tells me I'm not getting any younger, and I have to be carrying on the Drakos lineage, even though everyone but Elani is adopted. She hates it when any one of us brings up that we're adopted. She insists we're all Drakos, and it is up to all of us to carry on the Drakos name. Which is kind of funny, because one of Dad's Greek uncles stopped talking to him after he adopted Malik because he was black. Luckily the rest of his Greek family didn't feel that way."

"I'm not sure I could ever keep up with all the players."

"Actually, I have an idea. You can really help me out."

"I know, you want cookies."

"Nope, you can be my date for the wedding. I'll start showing you pictures of everybody today when I stop by for the snickerdoodles, and that way you can start putting names to the faces."

"Have you lost your mind?"

"Nope. My minds still intact. My single brothers

would be so envious if I showed up with you as my date. You'll do it, right?"

"Absolutely not."

"Do you have cream of tartar?"

"Huh? Yes. Why?"

"Then I'll see you in two hours."

He hung up.

Cream of tartar?

Oh yeah, for the snickerdoodle cookies. The man was so far out in left field, he was in the bleachers.

Chapter Five

I looked around my kitchen and considered if I had all the ingredients for snickerdoodle cookies, and I did. Almost every part of me didn't want him to come over, but there were a couple of parts that would be okay if he did. Not happy, but okay.

I shoved the phone into the charger and strode over to my desk and pulled up my calendar. Yep, it was clear. Tomorrow was going to be hellish, but this afternoon was free. I needed to be ready for Luxton to call, but I had all of my notes memorized. It wouldn't be a problem.

Should I let Renzo inside?

My eyes rested on the fire extinguisher again and I winced. I really needed to stop looking at that. When they built this house, they made it as fireproof as possible and I did my part too. I made sure that on a twenty-yard perimeter, there was only grass, so no trees or shrubs could catch fire. The roof was metal, the siding was decorative cement and the windows were tempered. There were doors on all four sides of the house for easy escape. The fence was built with metal. My God, whatever they could think of to make me feel comfortable, they did it. It cost a small fortune, but with the way Uncle Phil had forced my parents to over-insure everything and then the way Aunt Marge managed my money, I had way more than enough to build the house I wanted, with tons left over.

I forced my attention away from the extinguisher and brushed my fingers over the soft peach blossoms that were decorating my desk.

Okay, make a decision. How do you handle Renzo?
Easy.
Pretend he's a work problem.
Yeah, like that's going to work.

What work problem ever looked like him? Sounded like him? That accent. I melted every time he spoke. What work problem ever flirted like he did? because that was flirting. And nobody ever tried to invade my space. Nobody. Not even Little Grandma Magill; she always called before coming over.

Renzo called.

Really? Really? Now the voices in my head were on Renzo's side? What was up with that? I brushed my fingers against the peach blossoms again. I looked around and saw I was caressing the blossoms in the orange juice bottle.

Dammit! How'd I walk into the kitchen without realizing it?

"Guess I better start making cookies. I can worry about Renzo showing up later."

I pulled up to her gate but she didn't open it for me. So that was the way it was going to be, was it? No matter, she knew I was able to jump it, so I would jump it. Looking over into the back cab of my truck, I spotted my backpack. I hadn't intended to lug that into her house, but I'd need that to carry the box of chocolates. The only reason I told her I would take two hours was that I knew I would want to go to the candy store in Knoxville. The store was one where I could hand select the chocolates that would go into the box. I'd been going there for each of my sisters' birthdays, except Sandy's.

Little Grandma Magill filled me in that Millie liked dark chocolate and loved soft centers and was especially fond of caramel. They'd even wrapped the box in their blue foil paper, so hell no, this box would not be thrown over the fence.

After I shoved the chocolates into the backpack, I got out of my truck, pulled on the pack, then jumped the fence. I was at her door in seconds. Even from outside I could smell the cookies and I grinned. There was no way she could send me away. I knocked on her door.

She undid the locks then opened the door halfway.

"Hi, Renzo," she whispered.

Darn, I'd been hoping for a smile. I'd heard her smiling earlier when she'd been talking to me, but I really wanted to see one in person.

"Hi, Millie," I smiled at her.

"Here you go."

I looked down and saw she had two Tupperware containers in her hands.

"What's this?"

"Your cookies."

She had a stubborn look on her face and her chin was jutted out. She was adorable.

"You do realize you're giving me mixed messages, don't you?"

Her chin jutted out farther.

"I'm not. I realized that I had some free time and baking cookies sounded like a nice way to spend the afternoon. So here are some cookies for you, and I'm hoping you will give this other container to Irv."

"I'm pretty sure he likes chocolate chip," I lied.

"He likes snickerdoodles." She didn't even blink.

"How can I eat these without milk?"

"Go to the store."

"But they're warm from the oven. The best time to eat them is now. I need milk now."

I saw her eyes begin to sparkle.

"Knock on my neighbor's door."

"I bet she's not as pretty as you."

"Kevin's handsome, he'll like you."

I lost it.

I started laughing.

She didn't.

Dammit.

But her eyes were dancing.

"I came bearing gifts," I coaxed.

"I remember reading something about how I should beware of Greeks bearing gifts."

I laughed again.

I pulled the backpack off my shoulder and pulled out the box wrapped in shiny blue paper. "I think this is too small to be hiding an army inside."

"Hmmmm."

"We could trade." She lifted up the containers. "Then you could leave."

"I drove all the way to Knoxville for this. I made sure to get your favorites. Are you really going to send me away?"

She squeezed her eyes shut, then opened her eyes.

And the door.

"Fine, come in. I'll pour you some milk. But if I find one nut in this box of candy, I'm throwing you out."

I like her like this.

I like her a lot.

How many people really got to meet the real Millie?

As I followed her to the dining room table, I inhaled the powerful scent of peach blossoms and relaxed. Grandma Maureen always liked cherry and apple blossoms. Jase, Malik, Bruno, and I would go around the neighborhood at night and sneak into some of the neighbor's yards and cut small branches of the flowers and put them on Grandma's doorstep. If we'd give them to her in person, she'd give us hell and make us go apologize and take back the flowers. This way she would keep the flowers.

I was careful to keep my distance. I knew better than to crowd her. So, when she went into the kitchen, I propped my elbows on the island that separated the kitchen from the rest of the space.

"Take a seat." She waved her arm. "I'll get you a plate for your cookies."

"It's okay, I can just eat it straight from the container."

"No, I have more in my cookie jar."

She waved to a Hello Kitty-shaped jar.

Cute.

"The only other person I know with a cookie jar is my Grandma Maureen. Hers is a leprechaun. Mom got it for her."

"That's darling. Your mom is Irish?"

"Yeah, she's Irish. She has the red hair and the temper to match."

Millie frowned. "Was she harsh with you when you were growing up?"

"She'd read us the riot act if we crossed a line, that was for damn sure. But we always knew she was more bark than bite. But we hated disappointing her, so we'd work harder not to get caught the next time."

Millie let out a laugh as she got the milk out of the fridge. "It didn't occur to you to behave?"

"Where was the fun in that? Anyway, Malik, Jase, and I always had to be the big brothers to the younger kids and help out. The way we saw it, we deserved to act out sometimes."

"I bet you were hell on wheels."

She slid over the plate of cookies and the glass of milk.

"Aren't you going to have any?"

"I had a couple of spoonfuls of dough. I'm good."

"I hate to eat alone. Can't you at least eat one cookie with me?"

Millie rolled her eyes. "How can you sweet-talk the way you do, when you mostly spend time on construction sites?"

"Ah, you forget. Not only am I working with construction crews, I have to deal with a lot of different inspectors, architects, engineers, state, county, and city officials. Trust me, man or woman, sweet talking is a necessary skill set. Why? Am I doing it wrong?"

"I guess not. I'm getting a glass down for my glass of milk, aren't I?"

She sounded disgruntled. It was cute. I watched as she poured herself a glass of milk then set it down across from me.

"Well?"

I lifted my eyebrow and grinned. "Well, what?"

She put out her hand, "Gimme."

My grin turned into a wide smile.

"What have you done to deserve your box of chocolates?"

She reached across the island and pulled back my plate of cookies. "Ever hear of quid pro quo?"

I started to get up to get the box of chocolates when her phone rang. She held up a finger, indicating I should be quiet, then answered it, putting it on speaker as she left the kitchen and walked over to her desk that took up a good-sized portion of her living room.

"Hello, this is Millie Randolph." She infused her voice with a professional smile.

"Hello, Ms. Randolph, this is Chuck Reston from Luxton."

Before she sat down in her office chair, she looked over at me and gave me a huge grin and a fist pump. I'd never seen her so animated.

"Mr. Reston, please call me Millie. I hope you're calling me about my proposal for a donation from your company."

The man chuckled. "All right, Millie, please call me Chuck. I have to say, I've never received such a comprehensive proposal from a charity before.

Normally charities just explain what and why they need money and request a donation. Instead, yours looks like a business plan."

"That's exactly what it is."

Milly crossed her legs and looked out the window toward her orchard. I was surprised that she wasn't looking at her computer.

"I have some questions. Seven years seems like a long time to commit to one charity. Normally we diversify who we give our funds to."

"I realize that. However, I was able to access the amount of money you spent on lobbyists last year and the year before. It was ten times the amount of money you spent on charities."

"How did you find that out?" Chuck sounded incredulous.

"Not from anyone in your corporation. I have sources in Washington D.C. who help me gather that information. Don't think that I just called up your lobbyists and asked how much Luxton spent, instead we have a database that tracks all lobby money."

There was silence on the phone.

"I would be very interested in looking at that database," Chuck said. He was more than just interested, I could hear the greed in his tone.

"I'm sorry, that is confidential. I would be breaking my NDA." I watched as Millie crossed her fingers on her left hand. I wondered whether Millie had a hand in gathering that information.

"All right. I do get your point. However, we have vetted and believe in the charities we are currently supporting. I would hate to stop allocating funds to them in order to provide you with the amount of money you're asking for."

"Chuck. I've attended your last three quarterly earnings calls. You've had spectacular results this year. What I am asking for is less than a quarter of a percent of your net increase for the first two quarters of this year. If you allocate monies to us, you'll receive a substantial tax deduction to offset the increase in revenue."

"I'll go back to the fact that seven years is a long time to commit. I have no idea what our earnings will be like for the next seven years."

The man is smooth.

"If you set aside one percent of your net increase for the first two quarters of this year, and put it in a high yield savings account, it will fund the seven-year plan."

Shit. My girl knew her stuff.

Chuck paused, then changed his tack. "What kind of publicity would we get from the International Burn Alliance?"

"Each time one of our new centers in Africa, Asia, or South America goes live, we will be highlighting this in our newsletter and on our website. Our newsletter reaches over one-hundred-and-fifty thousand readers and goes out monthly. We will work with your marketing team so that they can link these articles to your website and newsletters. We have a half-yearly publication that we send out to our seventy-five-thousand person mailing list; all of the accomplishments made with your donations will be recapped in the publication."

"Will we get top billing?"

"No. Each donor will get articles based on the projects that their money has accomplished."

Damn, she has an answer for everything.

"If you want to send a Luxton representative to any of these locations in order to do a photo shoot, that has to be coordinated through IBA. Have I answered all of your questions?"

"Yes. You have. I'll still need to think about this."

"Why? You just said I answered all of your concerns."

"It's still a lot of money," Chuck answered.

"One percent of your net earnings for the first two quarters of this year is a lot of money?"

"You know it is," Chuck said in a condescending voice.

"Chuck, I assume you were planning to do a lot of buybacks with this money. I realize that's good for your stockholders, but the last time you did that, you were written up in the New York Times, Wall Street Journal, and Time Magazine for being one of the greediest companies currently traded on Wall Street. Imagine if you had a story that could spin that around. A story that talked about how you tripled your charity donations due to your increased earnings. Every time someone talked about your buybacks, you could talk about your company's generosity."

There was silence.

"That would be a good story to tell," Chuck admitted.

"So, you agree to this plan?" Millie pushed.

"Let's make it a five-year plan."

"It needs to be seven. You read the proposal. Most of your money will be working in third world countries, which are the same demographics most of your subsidiaries are expanding into. Those countries need seven years to get up and running. This tie-in will allow these communities to see how invested your subsidiaries are in giving back to them."

I could hear his sigh even from where I was sitting.

"Do I have your agreement?"

"You do," he sighed again. "You're right, this makes sense on every level, and our PR department will love it. I'll have our social responsibility director email you and set up a call. We'll have something set up by the end of next week."

Millie jumped out of her chair, then almost collapsed as her left leg gave out. She dropped her phone and gripped her desk. I was off my stool in a nano-second and had my arm around her waist and picked up the phone and put it on the desk.

Good, she was still connected.

"Are you okay?" Chuck asked.

"The phone slipped off my desk," Millie answered. I saw she crossed her fingers again. "I want to thank you for your time, Chuck."

"It's been interesting. Are you sure I can't get a peek at that database?" He cajoled.

"I'm sorry, you know about those pesky NDAs." She laughed.

Chuck didn't hear the pain in her laugh.

"Call me back if you run into any problems. Here's my cell phone number."

Millie leaned over with me still holding her around her waist and grabbed a sticky note and pen. She wrote down his number.

"Thanks, Chuck. I really appreciate this."

"You're welcome, Millie. I'll copy you on my emails to my marketing team, my legal department, and my social responsibility director."

"I look forward to seeing it. Again, thank you for your time."

Chuck chuckled again. "I have a couple of openings for sales managers. Is that something you might be interested in?"

This time Millie chuckled. "I'm going to have to pass. But I'll keep you in mind in case I ever considering a career change. Good-bye."

"Good-bye, Millie."

As soon as she ended the call she gasped in pain.

Chapter Six

Even the jubilation I felt over getting the Luxton donation couldn't offset the pain and embarrassment I was feeling over having my leg collapse. I slammed my eyes shut, willing the tears back.

"What do you need?" Renzo asked, his voice filled with concern.

I opened my eyes. "I already got it. Didn't you hear? I have Luxton on board to donate for the next seven years." My grin turned into a grimace as shards of pain shot up from my knee to my thigh all the way up to my hip.

I needed a prescription pain tablet, maybe my heating pad, but preferably a hot bath where I could massage my damaged flesh and hopefully stop the nerve pain.

Renzo moved my office chair in such a way that my

butt could plop down, but the idea of bending made me whimper. Renzo heard me.

"Fuck it," he growled.

The next thing I knew he'd swung me up into his arms. He stalked over to my sofa and gently set me down. He grabbed my three throw pillows and put two of them under my head.

"Do you need this one under your leg?" His gaze was intense.

"Yes. That would help." I whispered. I didn't tell him that it would only help a little bit.

Again, he gently lifted my left leg and slipped the pillow beneath it before lowering my leg on it. "Now what?"

I bit my lip. My eyes were still burning. It hadn't been like this in a while. Of course, normally I wouldn't show off by crossing my legs in my office chair. I knew better than that.

Idiot.

"I usually take one pain pill and do heat and massage." I left out the bath part. The last thing I needed was him carrying me into my bathroom.

I frowned. Why wasn't Renzo making me more uncomfortable? The reason I was so itchy around people was all the poking, prodding, and lack of privacy that I had endured during my time in the hospital. Then Aunt Marge and Uncle Phil only reinforced it. They were the opposite of my parents. It took months before Aunt Marge even tried to hug me, and by that time, I'd shut down. I'd cringed away from her embrace. But here I was, allowing Renzo to carry me without feeling like I was going to throw up or pass out.

How is this even possible?

"Where are your pills?"

I tried to sit up. "I can get them."

Renzo frowned. "Millie, what are you talking about? You can't walk. Tell me where they are, and I'll go get them."

"Can you get me my cane? It's in the hall closet."

"Millie. What the hell?"

I couldn't tell if he was angry or frustrated. Probably both. Well, good, because I could feel the heat making its way up my neck to my face. I probably looked like a Red Delicious apple.

"Just tell me where your goddamned pills are."

"They're in my nightstand. *Top drawer!*" I finally admitted.

"There. Was that so hard?"

"Yes!" I shouted.

"What the hell?"

"Just get me my damned pills and a glass of water," I demanded.

He stalked down the hall to my bedroom and I waited. And I waited. And I waited. When I didn't hear any laughter, I didn't know what to think. Renzo came back with a prescription bottle of pills and my bottle of ibuprofen.

"Are you allowed to take both at the same time?" he asked.

I nodded. I couldn't get any words out. He had to have noticed all of the romance books in my nightstand. Why didn't I just have them on my Kindle like a normal person? Why did I have to like actual paperbacks? I prayed to God and my Mom, not my Dad, that he hadn't opened the bottom drawer and seen the little plastic case that contained my clit stimulator.

Please.

Please.

Please.

He handed me the bottles and went into the kitchen to fetch me some water. His expression hadn't changed at all from when he had gone into my bedroom, and when he came back from the kitchen, he just looked concerned. Was it because I was the poor woman who lived alone with only romances and a vibrator to keep her happy?

"It's from the burns, isn't it?"

"Huh?"

"Your pain. It's nerve pain, right?"

"How do you know?"

He crouched down beside me and handed me the glass of water, then looked at each bottle. He shook out one pain pill and two ibuprofens.

"Here you go."

I took the offered pills, then downed them with a

sip of water.

"Finish the glass."

I frowned at him.

"You need to drink all of the water with your medicine."

I huffed out a breath, then finished the glass of water. He took it from me.

"I need to get you something to eat. Definitely something more substantial than chocolates. I peeked in your fridge. It looks like you have the makings for a sandwich, but there are a lot of containers in your freezer. I'm thinking you like to cook comfort food," he teased.

I stared at him. He wasn't going to give me any grief for the romance books? I thought all men thought those were silly.

"Uhmm."

"Cariña?"

I squinted at him. "What does that mean?"

He smiled. "It's just an endearment."

"Yeah, but what does it mean?"

"You sure don't take anything at face value, do you?"

Just then, my leg seized. I cried out as a debilitating cramp fired from my knee to my eyes. An inferno of agony shot through my whole left side.

"Millie. Where's the pain? Your leg? Your—"

I grabbed my thigh through my jeans, cursing the denim. I needed to push in on the different parts of my thigh until I found relief, but I couldn't press hard enough.

"Cariña, Millie, what are you trying to do? How can I help?" He sounded calm and comforting. In a world of agony, his soothing tone was a blessing. I tried to get the words out. His strength could help with the percussive massage that I needed, but I was beyond speech.

His hand eased mine aside, then pushed down, again and again, at different spots. He never kneaded, he just pushed.

"Harder," I pleaded.

"Like this?"

"Yes," I hissed. "But not there. I don't know where. I'll tell you when you've found it." I gasped the last words. It was as if I'd run a marathon.

I closed my eyes until he finally found the spot that brought some relief. It was where the cramp was hitting the nerve, and with the massage, it was releasing the cramp so that it wouldn't surround the nerve and torture me. Plus, I thought the pain meds were doing their work.

Renzo continued to massage my thigh, but now he was doing it lighter, which was perfect. My body was more relaxed and I wasn't crying anymore. I couldn't keep my eyes open. The last thing I remembered was Renzo putting a blanket over me. I thought he kissed my forehead, but that was just a dream.

I woke up to the smell of meatloaf and macaroni and cheese. I didn't want to get up, I was so comfy, and I was in the middle of the nicest dream. Renzo Drakos was actually in my house, and I wasn't all agitated. In fact, I'd enjoyed his company.

And he'd kissed me! That was such a good dream!

Only on the forehead. Yeah, I didn't care how good the food smelled, I wasn't going to open my eyes. I started to roll over, and that was when I realized I was on my couch.

Huh?

"Sleeping Beauty, are you awake?"

It wasn't a dream.

"Renzo?" I sounded hoarse. I cleared my throat and tried again. "Renzo?" I shook my head and everything came flooding back. "Why are you still here?"

"I told you that you needed something more substantial to eat than chocolate, but then you decided to do the sleeping beauty act on me. You've been asleep for a little over two hours. I was about ready to wake you up for dinner. How are you feeling? Nauseous?"

I did a mental check. Actually, I was feeling pretty good. My thigh and hip weren't hurting; well they were only aching and that was definitely a win. And my head didn't have a marching band playing in it anymore. Usually after such a bad cramp that went up to my head, I'd end up with a headache from hell, but not this time.

"I'm starving," I admitted as I sat up and swung my legs over the side of the couch and started to rise.

"Hold up," Renzo said as he bolted from the kitchen. "I don't want you walking by yourself quite yet. You almost took a header the last time you tried that, remember?"

I could feel my face turning red.

I nodded.

"How often does that happen?" he asked as he hovered over me.

"Never."

"How about you tell me the truth?" Renzo said as he watched me stand up on my own. I scowled at him.

"When I say never, I mean never. You saw how I was leaning on my desk. I would have sat down on my own until it was safe for me to stand up again. I work with a physical therapist online every week. It's not medically necessary anymore so he's not covered by my insurance, but I work hard with him to make sure that I stay limber and my leg and hip will always be working to their peak capacity."

"So what happened today?"

Gah! I could tell that Renzo was not going to stop questioning me until I told him. Well, I'd tell him part of it. But I sure as hell wasn't going to tell him that I was showing off for him!

"I crossed my legs when I was sitting in my office

chair while I was talking to Chuck. I didn't even think about it, I just did it. I was feeling like a hotshot because I was going to get this big donation. For once I felt like I was really one of the big dogs, and I was doing what I thought all those women in the corporate world would be doing in their offices."

"Seems to me that you are hot shit. How much was that donation worth? Five million?"

I laughed. "Multiply that by ten."

Renzo's eyes got wide. "Are you kidding me?"

"Nope. Luxton has deep pockets, and they need to pay after what they've done."

"Why, what have they done?" Renzo guided me to the dining room chair and I sat down. He'd set the table, and even found my cloth napkins and had them folded at my place setting.

Impressive.

"Luxton has one arm of their company that does paper products; their money maker is diapers. When we had the big supply chain problem because of Covid, they had to raise their prices by twenty percent."

Renzo nodded. "It was the same in the construction business. Everything went up."

"But then it went down again, didn't it?"

"Yep. We were on all of our suppliers to get us our supplies at the pre-Covid pricing."

"Exactly. You were large and savvy customers, who could have taken your business elsewhere. Unfortunately, Luxton's subsidiary held forty percent of the diaper market here in the US, and when the supply chain problem went away, they didn't lower their prices to the pre-Covid pricing. They figured if people were paying that price, they could continue to ask for it. When other smaller companies saw what they were doing, they followed suit."

"Why? They could have undercut Luxton and taken more of the market share."

"They were after those same easy margins. Now there were one or two who tried reducing their prices, and when they did, Luxton acquired them. It was easy. Come to think of it, I probably should have asked for a much higher donation."

"I'm not sure I'm as hungry as I was ten minutes ago," Renzo admitted.

"Wait til you taste my meatloaf, you'll get your appetite back. If you like my cookies, you'll love my meatloaf."

Chapter Seven

A week later and I was still savoring my time with Millie, but I couldn't stop worrying about her. Luckily, I had an ace in the hole. It was the little lady who basically ran the diner in town called Down Home. Somehow back in March she'd found out through the little town rumor mill that I had been helping clear out the orchard debris for Millie. She'd grabbed onto me the next time I'd gone to eat at her diner. For a woman over one hundred years old, she had a hell of a grip.

"You been over to Millie's place?"

"Yes, ma'am."

Her eyes squinted as she looked me up and down. "She let you in?"

"Yes, ma'am."

"That's good. That's real good."

She kept holding onto my wrist like I was going to fly away or something.

"I need you to promise me something."

I looked around the diner and saw that I had every patron looking at us. I lowered my voice. "I can't promise anything until I know what you're asking."

"You keep going over there. Don't stop. You need advice, I'm your woman. She needs friends. You push, but you be gentle about it. You hear?"

A slow grin took over my face. "I hear."

"Now go on along. Patty cooked brisket today. There's also some cheesy potatoes to go with it. You can't go wrong. Boy like you needs to keep up his strength." She let go of me and her granddaughter motioned me over to a table. I started toward her.

"Oh, one more thing," Little Grandma yelled out. "Millie likes dark chocolate. Especially with caramel centers. No nuts."

I turned and saluted. "Gotcha."

I smiled at the memory. It was definitely time for another visit with Little Grandma, but first I had to go talk to Harvey.

I nodded at Harvey Sadowski as he explained for the third time what I was supposed to accomplish in my meeting with the new client in Nashville. I knew it was a meeting he wanted to do himself, but his daughter's boyfriend was coming over to talk to him. Harvey hated the guy, and he was worried that the dumbass was going to ask permission to marry Harvey's daughter.

"I'm going to kick his ass out of my house!" Harvey had been saying all week. It was a regular riot, since everyone knew he pandered to his daughter.

So that was the reason I was going to meet with one of the suburban school boards outside of Nashville about building an elementary school. Harvey was shitting kittens. His company had made it on the shortlist. He was dying to get the job, but he was worried he wouldn't make a profit on it. I'd been over the plans, the subcontractor bids, and our labor costs three times. We were going to make a very good profit if we met the timeline. That's where Harvey's team often failed, and where I came in. He was using my name and credentials to help shore up his company's reputation, and then he was depending on me to get his shop in order so that they met their goals. If we got this job, I would have a two-year commitment to Jasper Creek.

"Are you listening to me, Drakos?"

"Why should I listen when you're repeating the same thing you said yesterday and the day before yesterday? Seems to me I'd be better served trying to remember all the school board members' names, concerns, and any affiliations they may have toward other construction companies."

Harvey damn near turned purple.

"What are you talking about? Are you saying some

of the school board members have friends with construction companies who are bidding on this project?" The big man was always turning red and looking like he might have a heart attack. It had taken me a week working with him to find out that was his standard operating procedure.

I chuckled at his bluster. How Harvey could bellow that question with a straight face, was beyond me. He and I both knew that winning a bid was half how good your bid was and half who you knew.

"Are you saying you never benefited from knowing someone on a project you were bidding on?" I finally asked.

He opened his mouth.

"Be honest," I added.

He closed his mouth, then started again. "Maybe once or twice," he admitted.

"Exactly. So, there are five board members. Edna Fairly's brother-in-law has a construction company in Nashville that is three years old. They need this project, so my guess is that she'll be advocating hard for them to get it."

"Gotcha. You can win her over, can't you?" Harvey asked me.

I shook my head. "But I should be able to win the rest over. Leave it to me, boss, you go kick Tina's boyfriend's ass."

Harvey lowered his shoulders and shook his head. "Tina is going to be the death of me."

Wasn't that the damned truth?

He must have given her everything she wanted as a kid and made her into the spoiled, entitled woman she was today.

Harvey clamped one of his big paws on my shoulder. "Is there any way I can get you to take a minute and talk to Jenny Brooks? She's over at Wiley Plumbing Supply and she wants to talk about the bid Junior gave us."

"Who's Jenny?"

"She's Beckett's daughter. She just came back from some college on the West Coast. Supposedly, she's good with numbers and according to her daddy, she knows every kind of estimating and accounting software there is. He tried to get me to hire her, but..."

"But what?"

"A California college?" Harvey made a sour face.

"What about it?"

"Who knows what kind of kooky ideas she might have learned out there?"

I laughed. "How about me? I went to University College London. The UK has socialized medicine."

"It does?"

"Yep."

"Well, geez. But you don't believe in that kind of shit, do you?"

"Harvey, you're getting off track. Why do I need to talk to Jenny?"

"She says that something's off with the bid for the elementary school."

"Shit," I muttered. At least it wasn't too far off. They only came in seven percent lower than the next bid I'd considered. It would hurt if we got the job and we had to go with the other plumbing contractor, but we could suck it up.

"I'll call her on my way to Nashville."

"Good."

I looked Harvey in the eye. "Anything else?"

"I think that's enough, don't you?"

"It's easier than having to tell Tina that you kicked her latest boyfriend to the curb."

Harvey let out a deep laugh. "Ain't that the truth? The only way this is going to work is if I find her a man. Are you sure you don't want to go out with her? You know I'm going to want to retire, eventually."

"Harvey, we've been over this already. I'm more than happy to discuss partnering up, but I'm not looking to marry into your business."

He pulled off his Stetson and scratched his head. "I'm not looking for a partner."

"That's what you've said, and I'm okay with that. Especially since you'll be cutting me in on the profits for the elementary school job if we get it. But I've got to consider my long-term future, and I'm not so sure that Jasper Creek is where it's at."

"With all that you've done, we'll get the bid," Harvey grinned.

"Maybe."

"And when you get it for us, Renzo, then you can get licensed to work as an architect here in Tennessee."

"Yep," I agreed.

"Then afterwards, the sky's the limit for Sadowski Construction."

I looked at my boots.

"Come on, boy, you know you don't want to leave here, Jasper Creek is growing on you."

I knew Harvey was hoping that I would work as his company's architect, but that wouldn't be happening unless I was a full partner.

"Let's talk about this later, Harvey. I don't want to be late."

"Tell me what you're thinking," Harvey pestered me.

"Look, I'd like to be working here in Jasper Creek after I get my license, but you and I both know there's a couple of places in Gatlinburg and Knoxville where I could work on bigger projects. Hell, I might just move to Nashville."

"Now let's not get too hasty."

"I don't intend to. I'm just exploring all of my options. Now, I've got to get a move on if I want to arrive a couple of hours early."

"That's what I always do. You want to be there for the coffee and pastries and start making friends," Harvey grinned. "Don't forget to call Jenny."

"I won't." I gave him a nod as I left the

construction trailer and headed for my truck. When I finally got on the road out of town, I used my truck's Bluetooth to place a call.

"Hi, this is Millie."

"You didn't check who was calling. I got your professional voice," I teased her.

"Renzo. I should have known it was you."

"Hey, you make it sound like I'm some kind of stalker. I've only called you every two or three days."

"You made my point."

She was a feisty little thing.

"I was calling to talk about the wedding. Bonnie still hasn't figured out if it's going to be indoors or outdoors."

"The wedding in September? Your brother Jace's wedding? The wedding you invited me to? The wedding I told you that there wasn't a chance in hell I was attending? That wedding?"

I had to stop myself from laughing. "Yeah, you're going to love it. I can't wait for you to meet my brothers and sisters, but especially my parents." When she didn't respond, I really wanted to laugh. It took everything I had to keep it together.

My Millie was funny.

"I can't wait for you to show me the photos."

"I'll come over tonight. I saw you have some chicken parm in your freezer. We can thaw that out. I'll bring some wine and dessert. Then we'll FaceTime with Jase and Bonnie. Hell, maybe Jase can talk Amber and Lachlan to join the call. It'll be a riot."

"Now why on earth would I want to do that?"

I was getting to her. Yeah, she sounded exasperated, but I could hear a little bit of laughter in her voice.

"Don't you want to feed me? Come on, you're a great cook. Don't chefs want to feed people?"

"You're a goofball, you know that, don't you?"

"I've been called worse." I pulled onto the highway toward Nashville. "I'll be at your house at five."

"Six," she countered.

"Okay, six."

I was making headway.

Damn good headway.

"I've got to go. I've got calls to make," she told me.

"Go rustle up some money, Hotshot."

"That's the plan."

Chapter Eight

I'd opened the gate at five o'clock. Then I'd dithered on what to wear for forty-five minutes. Since Renzo had come over the last time, I'd foolishly bought some pretty clothes online. It was foolish, but now I was grateful. I had three pairs of slacks that I could wear, with four cute tops and two really nice sweaters. Plus, I'd purchased two form-fitting dresses that hit me mid-calf. I wouldn't have been able to pull those off if I hadn't had some curves. Not much, but some. Otherwise, they would have looked ridiculous since I'm so short.

Under everything, I wore padded shapewear that made sure to smooth out the dips and bumps of the burn scars. It was kind of cheating, but it wasn't like anybody would ever see my hip and thigh. Nobody but Dr. Rose when I flew to Iowa City once a year. She assured me that the nerve connectivity was improving.

To hell with that noise. It had been ten years. I was Dr. Rose's protégé. She wasn't seeing me objectively anymore; she was wish-doctoring. But she was one of the two people I loved in this life and enjoyed their hugs. I would never stop my visits.

I heard the knock on the door when I was still dithering on which top to wear. My hair was pretty, and my toenails were painted. I pulled out the purple sweater that kind of matched my blue eyes and slipped it on. I looked in the mirror and grinned.

Boobs.

Not much. But some.

Hopefully, Renzo wouldn't notice my limp this way.

He knocked again.

I rushed to the front door, checked the peephole to make sure it was him, then unlocked it and opened it halfway.

He was smiling. He was almost always smiling, unless I was in pain. Then he hadn't been smiling. He held up a bottle of wine and a pink box. I didn't recognize it. It wasn't from Down Home or Pearl's.

"Where's that from?"

"Let me in and I'll tell you."

I backed up and opened the door wider. He walked in. He was still careful not to get too close, and I sighed in relief. He had touched me the last time he was here, but he was careful with me tonight. I appreciated it. It was almost like he understood I needed to warm up to him all over again.

He walked over to the bar that separated the kitchen from the dining and living rooms, then set down the wine and mystery box.

"I smell something good." He turned, the delight in his eyes was clear. It made me happy. "And I have to say, you look beautiful tonight. Usually, you look pretty as all get-out, but tonight, Cariña, you take my breath away."

I could feel myself blushing. Gah, when would I be able to have him compliment me without looking like a Red Delicious apple?

"I made the chicken parmigiana and cheesy garlic bread with a Caesar salad. I put the dressing to the side, because I didn't know how much you'd like on your salad."

He tilted his head. "How do you get your groceries?"

"Roger's grocery store delivers to me at least once a week, sometimes twice a week if I get a wild hair and really want to cook a lot. That's usually when Little Grandma is coming for a visit."

"So, you *do* have visitors. I wondered."

"Just her. Well, and her daughter and granddaughter and great-granddaughters, but that's because she doesn't drive anymore. She's kind of pi— upset about that."

Renzo laughed. "You can say pissed. Trust me, I

have heard and said a heck of a lot worse than that," he grinned.

I grimaced. "But you just said heck, so you don't really swear."

"I'm pretty sure I was swearing when you were in so much pain. But you're right, I'm trying to curtail my swearing. My wallet can't handle the cost."

Now I was confused. "I don't get it."

"Hasn't Little Grandma told you about Bella Clark? She's Trenda and Simon's daughter."

"Trenda is one of the Avery sisters, right?"

Renzo nodded.

"She was before my time," I explained. "But I went to school with Chloe, Zoe, and Piper. They weren't in my grade, but I knew them. They were nice. But Piper seemed sad."

"I haven't met Piper, but I've met some of the others. Did you know Evie or Drake? Those two are something else. Evie is a pistol, just like her niece."

"But you were talking about your wallet."

"Yeah, here's the deal. Bella collects money from anyone who swears in front of her. Drake has an account with her. I'm pretty sure between him and Aiden, they've paid for her first year of college."

"How old is she and who's Aiden?"

"She's eight, and Aiden is Evie Avery's husband. Or should I say Evie O'Malley."

Renzo was smiling down at me.

How did he get so close and I hadn't even noticed?

He smelled good. Like spice and juniper.

"So, are you going to feed me?"

His low, growly voice made me tingle. What was going on? I took a big step sideways and only got a little bit away from him.

He's so big.

Renzo stepped backward and gave me a comforting look. "I didn't mean to get too close, Cariña."

"No. No. It's okay. It's all fine." I sounded out of breath. Like when I tried to run under the canopy of blossoms that the apple, pear, and peach trees made.

"You're right, it is." He reached out and stroked his hand from my shoulder down to my hand, where he tangled our fingers together. "It's fine, baby. Everything is good, isn't it?"

I couldn't stop trembling, but I wasn't scared. Not exactly. I don't know what I was. I realized I was holding onto his hand for dear life.

"Millie?" he asked quietly.

I didn't know what he was asking. I was too scared to speak, so I nodded.

He lifted our clasped hands and brought them up to his face. He looked deep into my eyes, then turned my hand, exposing my wrist. Then he kissed me. Right there, on my pulse point. His gaze never leaving mine. It was the most intimate thing I had ever experienced.

I whimpered.

Somehow, Renzo knew I wasn't upset or scared. His lips moved softly until he had my hand cradled in his, then he kissed the palm of my hand and I felt like I was melting, but at the same time I felt like I was coming to life.

He raised his other hand up to my face and it hovered over my cheek. I winced. He dropped his hand back to his side. I was sure he was going to be mad, but instead he lifted his head, his lips no longer caressing my palm. He smiled at me, then brought my hand up so that I was cupping *his* jaw.

Renzo closed his eyes. It was as if he was savoring my touch.

That can't be right.

But then I didn't care, as I felt the heat of his skin beneath my palm and reveled in the feel of the rough bristles of his unshaven face as they abraded my skin. I went farther up until I was tracing the curve of his ear, then pushing my fingers into his short, dark curls. They should have made him look feminine, but instead they highlighted his masculinity.

I traced my way back down, slowly. Taking my time to test the soft beauty of his lashes, and watch them flutter, then I followed the line of his straight nose. My fingers hesitated over his lips.

Dare I?

They were well-defined, but it was his lower lip that drew me in. It was the part that lifted up and smiled, and I'd felt it more as he'd kissed my hand. I couldn't help myself a minute more. As lightly as I could, I tried to be like a butterfly. I traced my finger over his bottom lip.

Did I feel him tremble?

Really? Is it really true?

But I definitely saw his eyelids flutter again.

"Millie," he whispered against my finger.

Everything I'd ever believed told me to pull back, but I didn't. Then he did the most outrageous thing. He kissed my finger, and my stomach clenched and goosebumps flared all over my body. My scalp even tingled. I watched as his mouth opened and he lightly licked the tip of my finger.

I didn't wince. Instead, I melted, and found myself leaning against his body for support. Renzo clasped me to him, in the lightest of hugs, one of his hands resting on my lower back, and one supporting me between my shoulder blades. He didn't try to pull me tighter; he just held me enough so that I could stand. I hadn't felt this safe since my parents had died.

"More?" His whisper was barely a breath of sound.

I nodded, but he didn't see me.

"Yes," I whispered.

My eyes widened as I watched him open his mouth and surround my finger between his warm lips. It wasn't a whimper that left me this time, it was a moan. He sucked my finger deeper and I felt his tongue lave against the tip. I felt that caress all over. From my toes to the end of each strand of hair, but then it settled between my legs, to my very core. Heat blossomed, and

I thought I might come apart just because of this small caress.

Who is this man and what magic does he wield?

His hand on my upper back moved upwards and was soon sifting through my long hair. Again and again, his fingers tangled in my hair, softly pulling, adding to the sensation of him sucking and licking my finger. I pressed closer to his body.

So many sensations were gliding over my skin, *under* my skin, until I felt the sensations sparking through my very veins. As I tingled with warmth, I realized I was feeling desire for this man, and I wanted so much more from him. I tugged at my finger, forcing him to release me. He opened his eyes. They sparkled like black diamonds.

"Too much?" he asked.

"Not enough."

I pushed both of my hands up and wrapped my arms around his neck.

"Kiss me, Renzo."

His gaze searched mine. "Are you sure, Millie?"

I nodded.

He tugged at my hair, arching my head back even further, and slanted it to the left, then he smiled. "You're in charge. Anytime you want to stop, just pull away, or pull my hair, okay? Do you understand?"

I nodded.

"No, sweetheart, tell me you understand."

I rolled my eyes. "I understand."

He didn't even chuckle. His gaze rested on my lips and he lowered his head. Then he brushed his lips against mine, as soft as a butterfly, but that wasn't what I wanted. I wanted more.

I pushed up hard and smashed my lips against his, grinding my teeth against the back of my lips. I mewed with pain.

Renzo gently pulled me back and gave a soft chuckle.

"Impatient?"

"I thought so, but that hurt," I admitted.

"Why don't you let me take the lead? Let's start with training wheels, then I promise to take them off, okay?"

"That sounds wonderful," I smiled.

"How about we get more comfortable?"

I tried to push away from him. "I'm too heavy. I shouldn't be leaning on you like this."

Renzo let out a long laugh. "You're too tiny to ever be a burden. No, I'm talking about sitting on the sofa. Can I carry you there?"

I squinted at him. "I'm more than capable of walking."

"Yeah, but I enjoy carrying you."

I rolled my eyes...again. "Fine," I huffed out.

I held out my arms so he could lift me up, and Renzo laughed harder. Then he swung me up into his arms, bridal style. In mere seconds, I was sitting sideways across his lap, my butt nestled against his lap.

There was no way I couldn't be aware of his erection. Were all men's erections like Renzo's? It felt like I could feel his heartbeat.

I squirmed, trying to get into a better position. Trying to sit on his thigh, not on his lap.

"You're killing me, Millie. Stay still."

I stopped moving and stayed still like a statue.

"Now you need to relax," he whispered with a smile.

"Stay still or relax? Which is it, Drakos?" I snapped at him.

He laughed again.

Did everything make him laugh?

Chapter Nine

This was either my best idea ever or my worst idea ever.

I looked down at flashing violet eyes. I was glad she'd been snapping at me, because she'd otherwise be a lot more nervous than she was right now. I was ninety-nine percent sure she'd never been in a man's lap before, and definitely not in one where the guy had a raging hard-on!

"You haven't answered me," she grumbled.

"Relaxed. You should definitely relax."

"Well, it isn't easy." She wiggled again, and I bit back a groan.

"Cariña, I'm begging you, stop moving."

She frowned at me. "I'm trying to get comfortable. You're the one who told me to relax."

So much sass.

I wrapped one arm around her shoulders and pulled her close to my chest, the other around her hip to stop her from squirming. As soon as I did, she turned to stone. It was as if I was holding a statue. Millie had even stopped breathing. I moved my hand from her shoulders and worked to tip her chin up so I could see her eyes.

Nothing.

It was like she wasn't even there.

"Millie?"

That's when I noticed a slight sheen of perspiration on her face. I traced her cheek and forehead with the back of my fingers. She felt clammy.

"Millie?"

Again, nothing.

"Millie," I said louder as I jostled her. "Millie, talk to me. Come back to me."

Nothing.

That's when I realized she'd closed up as soon as I'd touched her hip.

Her injured hip.

Her scarred hip.

It'd been fine when she'd been in the middle of muscle spasms. Hell, Frankenstein's monster could have massaged her leg and she wouldn't have cared. But right now? Yeah, it was bad.

I slid my hand upward until it rested in the middle of her back. Slowly, life came back to her eyes, but unfortunately, it was shame.

"No, Millie. You're fine. Everything's perfect," I crooned.

Her eyes glassed over, but no tears fell. I doubted she ever let herself cry.

At least I didn't have to worry about my raging hard on any longer. I traced circles in the middle of her back until I felt her relax. Millie shuddered.

"Renzo?"

"That's me," I teased.

"I panicked, didn't I?"

"Seemed like."

She shoved her face into my chest and mumbled something I couldn't hear.

"What?"

She said something I couldn't hear again.

"Cariña, you're going to have to stop talking to my shirt if you want me to be able to hear you."

She looked up at me.

"You never told me what cariña means."

"It means sweetheart, in Spanish."

"Oh," she nodded. "I kind of like it."

"I'm glad. Now, what were you saying to my shirt?"

"I was apologizing for being a fool."

"You aren't a fool. Did you panic because I touched your scarred hip?"

Her eyes widened. "You know?"

"Irv told me you survived the fire your parents died in. He mentioned you'd been in the burn unit for quite a while. I figured out pretty quickly that your leg must have been injured when I saw you limp. It was confirmed when I saw you cramp up. What I don't understand is why you don't want me to touch you."

She struggled to get out of my lap. I considered keeping her where she was. Proving to her that I would not let her go because of some silly scarring, but I didn't want to take away her autonomy. I helped her sit beside me, then turned so that we were facing one another.

For a long time, she just stared at me. Finally, she lowered her eyelashes. "Maybe we should just kiss again."

"Oh, baby, we're definitely going to kiss again." I tucked a strand of her long hair behind her ear. "We might even go further. I have to tell you, in that top, I haven't stopped thinking about how pretty your breasts look. I keep wondering what they would look like with just my hands holding them."

She gasped.

Her blush is a delight.

She leaned forward and I leaned back. "But before we kiss, can we talk for just a moment? Three minutes, tops."

She sat back and pushed out her bottom lip into an adorable pout. Yep, given a chance, this woman could wrap me around her little finger. "I suppose," she grumbled.

"Millie, I have scars too. Not burn scars, but scars. They're not pretty. But my two sisters from Africa both have scars. It took years for mom to help them heal the scars on their inside. Those were the worst."

Millie shook her head, her hair flying.

"How bad? Be real, Renzo, how bad are their scars, really? Is their flesh mottled and pockmarked? Does their skin look discolored and gnarled? Because that's what it looks like almost up to my waist, down to my knee. Yeah, that's something I want to show off. That's something I want someone to touch or see."

I sighed. How could this beautiful woman not see herself? Could she only define herself by some scars on her body?

"Millie, after we had dinner together, do you know what I did?"

She was panting. I know her tirade had taken a lot out of her, but now wasn't the time for me to back down.

"Do you, Millie?"

"No. What, Renzo?" She was sarcastic as hell.

"I went online and pulled up people with burn scars. I looked at every single image I could find. I zoomed in so I could see what they looked like. Then I also zoomed in on so many people who were smiling as they showed off their bodies. I clicked on their pictures and read their stories. A lot of them were older than you, but do you know what I found?"

She just stared at me, her eyes flat.

"They weren't embarrassed by their bodies. They were comfortable in their own skin."

"Well, goodie for them," she practically yelled. "Aren't they just perfect?"

She shoved me so hard that I rocked back. She tried getting up off the sofa but fell back down. That didn't stop her. She pushed against the back cushion with one hand, while using her other hand to push on the cushion she was sitting on, and shoved up. She swayed when she got to her feet, but it was obvious that she didn't care as she glared down at me.

"Get out, Renzo." She ground out the words like her mouth was filled with gravel.

"Millie, I didn't mean to upset you," I soothed. "I just wanted you to know that nothing I saw bothered me in the slightest. Anything you had to show me wouldn't matter one bit."

She grabbed my shirt sleeve and yanked. "I want you out of my house. Now!"

Ah, God. I could see the shimmer of tears in her eyes.

"Please, Millie, you have to know I would never do or say anything to hurt you. You're special to me. In my eyes, you're beautiful."

"Get. Out. Of. My. House."

She was barely keeping it together. I was worried that she would topple over. I got up and put my hands on her shoulders, making sure she was stable. She tried to wrench away, but I couldn't let her.

I just couldn't.

"I'll get out, sweetheart, but on one condition."

"What?"

The first tear was ready to fall. I watched as it clung to her eyelash, just waiting for me to leave.

"Sit down. Just sit down for me, Millie. Then I'll leave. Okay?"

She wavered. "Then you promise to leave?"

"I absolutely do. I promise."

"Okay."

I helped her to sit down.

"Do you need anything before I leave? A glass of water? A pain pill?"

She was staring down at her hands, where they were twisting together on her lap. "I just need you to leave."

"Okay, Cariña, I'm leaving now."

Even when I had the door open, and then shutting it behind me, she didn't look up. Instead, I just saw her shoulders slumped in defeat.

It killed knowing I was the one who'd done that to her.

I'd tried as hard as I could to put Renzo out of my mind after shoving him out the door, but it was six days later, and I was still thinking about him, mooning over him, obsessing over him. It wasn't good. It needed to stop.

I got out of the shower and dried off. I used all of

my best products today. I wanted to feel good when Little Grandma and all of her 'kin' came over. After I was done brushing my teeth and putting on my face cream, I grabbed the burn scar ointment that didn't do crap, but I promised Dr. Rose that I would use. Last year, she told me I should sit down and close my eyes and slowly rub it in with love. Whatever the hell that meant.

You know what she meant.

I shook my head, trying to rid myself of that pesky, reasonable voice in my head.

Heading to my bedroom, I lifted my duvet and lay down on my pretty lavender sheets. Then I closed my eyes and started to softly rub the cream into my scars. I pictured the girl that I'd watched on the internet the day after Renzo left. She was fourteen, the same age I'd been when I was caught in the fire. When my parents died.

The difference was, she'd been burned as a baby. Just like Renzo said, she was smiling in the video. She was wearing a swimsuit, even though one of her legs was spindly from the burns. It didn't seem to matter to her.

I pretended I was rubbing the cream on her. Somehow that morphed into me rubbing the cream on my younger self. Almost like I was my mom, soothing my hurt and lavishing love, hope, and beauty on my teenage leg and hip.

You're beautiful to me.

It was Renzo's voice in my head. His voice and words had been in my head a lot.

Millie, you take my breath away.

But how could he say that? He hadn't seen me. He hadn't seen the real me. He hadn't seen my scars.

Sweetheart, he does see you. He sees the real you.

Now it was my mom's voice in my head.

I stopped rubbing the cream into my hip.

"This is stupid."

I pushed up off the bed and glared at the tube of medicine. I needed to be pragmatic. This talking to myself was getting me nowhere, and neither was thinking about Renzo all the time. Of course, him calling me twice a day was not helping to get him off my mind. Not that I answered.

But I listened to every single one of his voicemails.

I couldn't help myself.

First, there was that seductive Spanish accent.

Then there were those beguiling words that tempted me to believe in him.

And then there was all of his emotion.

Dammit, he sounded like he really cared.

I needed to get myself together. I needed to put all thoughts of Renzo aside. It was time to focus on the here and now.

I glanced over at my phone on the nightstand—just to check the time, not to check to see if Renzo had texted or called. Little Grandma and her family were going to be here in less than an hour, I needed to get it together. I rushed to the closet and grabbed the outfit I'd planned to wear. I pulled on my underwear, then stepped into the white-denim cropped pants with the hem folded up. I put on the white blouse with cherry blossoms. I even bought some red and silver jangly bracelets to go with it. The girl on the website wore her hair up in a high ponytail, so that's what I did. I felt cute. Now I just needed to get my butt into the kitchen and make sure brunch was ready.

By the time I heard the buzzer at the gate, I had the food ready. I never knew who would be with Little Grandma so I always made sure to have enough. Today was brunch day and I had something special for them that I hoped would knock their socks off.

When I pressed the button to open the gate, I peeked outside and saw Little Grandma's sky-blue nineteen-sixty Oldsmobile coming up to my front steps. Thank God Little Grandma wasn't driving anymore. I remembered when I was little and she would come over and visit my mom and dad, she could barely see over the huge steering wheel.

I opened the door.

"Hey y'all! I brought a couple of people," Little Grandma yelled out the window from the backseat. I couldn't help but grin at her enthusiasm. She'd celebrated her hundred-and-first birthday four months ago. She'd tried real hard to talk me into going to her party, but it just wasn't possible. There were three other people in the car with her. Her daughter Patty was a go-getter at seventy-seven and Patty's daughter Lettie didn't let anything slow her down at fifty-two.

I bit my lip when I saw it was Theresa driving. She was nice and all, but I still didn't feel completely comfortable around her. She was Lettie's seventeen-year-old daughter. She reminded me of some of the girls I had to go to school with in Des Moines before I talked Aunt Marge and Uncle Phil into letting me do online courses.

She's a sweet girl, and you're not fifteen anymore. Suck it up.

"I wanted to bring Theresa's cousins, but they're out with their daddy today. He sure does have his hands full with those three." Patty helped her mom out of the car. I knew about those Magill girls. Little Grandma called them high-spirited.

"Come inside. I hope you're hungry."

"Lord yes," Patty said as she patted her stomach.

"You're always hungry," Little Grandma said to her daughter. "You're tasting too much of the food you're cooking."

"The customers like the food, don't they?" Patty lifted her eyebrow as she slowly guided her mother up the porch steps.

"Yes, they do," her mother admitted.

"Then it's a good thing I'm doing taste tests."

"I gave you my recipes. You don't need to do taste tests if you follow them," Little Grandma grumbled. She held out her arms to me and I gave her fragile body a soft hug, but she was having none of that. She gripped me hard, then whispered in my ear. "Love you, Sweet Girl."

"Love you more."

She let go and I stood up and found Patty grinning at me.

"So, what treat do you have for us today?" Lettie asked as I ushered them into my house. I crossed my fingers that they would like the eggs as much as I did. Yesterday, I had thrown out three batches before I had gotten them right.

"Why don't y'all have a seat, and I'll just put some food out for you to munch on before I get the eggs benedict out to you."

"Honey, you don't have to go to that much trouble," Patty said as I put the platter of deviled eggs on the table. Everyone but Theresa put one on their plate. I knew they looked different from the norm, but I was pretty sure they were going to like them.

I tried to hide my grin when I saw Patty sniff hers. Theresa just smiled politely and took a sip of her orange juice. Lettie pulled the little piece of bacon out of hers and nibbled on it. Leave it to Little Grandma. She took a big bite of hers, then moaned as she started chewing.

After she was done with her bite, she looked at me with wide eyes. "Darlin', what is this sinful delight?"

"Do you like it?"

"I don't like it. I love it."

I giggled as Patty took a bite and her eyes lit up too, and Theresa took one of the eggs off the plate.

"Sit. Sit. Don't bother with the eggs benedict, let's just eat these for a while. Tell me how you made these."

"Do you have more?" Patty asked as she reached for another. "What's the recipe?"

I sat down next to the lady I adored and reached for one of the half-filled eggs and put it onto a plate. "Actually, it's pretty easy. It's the normal deviled egg recipe. The yoke, mayo, paprika, salt and pepper mixed together, then add in some cooked breakfast sausage. Not too much. I used my food processor to mix it all together, then I used my pastry bag to fill the egg white. After that I cooked and crumbled a pancake, sprinkled that on top with some maple syrup, and garnished it with a quarter of a piece of bacon."

I glanced over at Patty. She was devouring her third egg while Theresa was nibbling on her first and smiling.

"This is really good, Millie," Lettie said as she wiped her mouth with one of the cloth napkins I had set out. "I know you provide us with fruit for the restaurant, but you need to start providing us with recipes."

"What she needs to do is come and cook for us. Patty isn't getting any younger," Little Grandma said.

"Mama, if you can work the hostess stand, I can work the griddle."

We all laughed.

"Everyone is right, Mizz Millie, these are really

good. Could you teach me how to make them? I have to bring something to Gabe's house next Sunday for their family brunch."

My insides melted. "Of course, I can, honey. You stop by anytime."

Little Grandma grabbed my hand and squeezed it then gave me an approving smile. Maybe I was getting better.

Another hour passed, and I found myself on the loveseat. It was just Little Grandma and myself. The others were in the kitchen getting everything cleaned up before leaving.

"Now tell me what's been going on with you," Little Grandma demanded in that way of hers.

"I got this big corporation to give our alliance one of the biggest donations we ever received."

She patted my hand. "Don't try to pull one over on me. I raised four boys and three girls. Something else is going on with you. Now tell me."

Her blue eyes might be a little watery, but I swear she could read me like a book. "There's a man," I started.

She cackled. "Tell me more. What's his name? Do I know him? What does he look like?"

I tried to back away, but she grabbed my wrist. "You're not going anywhere until you tell me everything."

"It's not like you're thinking."

"You don't know what I'm thinking. So tell me."

"His name is Renzo Drakos—"

"I know him. He helped Trenda and Simon a while back. Renzo's a good man."

I bit my lip. "When Irv was sick, he came over to help clear debris after the storm. Then he came back a couple of times and I made him cookies and dinner."

"And...?"

"I really, really like him. But I shouldn't."

She patted my hand again. "Why not, Millie?"

"You know." I lowered my head and looked at her hand on mine. "My scars."

"Does he like you?"

I nodded. I looked over at the kitchen. The others were still occupied. I leaned in and whispered. "He kind of kissed me."

"Explain that to me, sweet girl."

"He kissed the palm of my hand. Then he carried me to the sofa." I nodded to the couch across the room. "I know he was going to kiss me, and I wanted him to, but I froze up."

"Why did you freeze up?" she asked gently.

"Because he touched my hip."

"Your scarred hip?"

I nodded.

"Did that bother him?"

I shook my head. "He said he looked up burn scars on the internet, and they don't bother him. He said he read burn survivor's stories and oftentimes they were living good lives and smiling."

"Oh." She said that one word with buckets of sympathy.

"Yeah. You understand. I said goody for them, and kicked his condescending ass out of my house."

"Was he really condescending or was he trying to put your mind at ease?"

I didn't answer her. I didn't want to think of him being nice and empathetic. It was easier seeing him as an ass, then I wouldn't have to deal with him. Except I didn't. I really thought he was wonderful and I wanted him to come back and kiss me.

"Millie?"

"I looked up some of the same pictures and stories he must have seen. He was right, they were smiling. Their stories were uplifting."

Little Grandma traced her fingers along my cheek. "Did they make you feel better?"

"A little bit."

"Then that's what's important."

I loved her smile. I loved her touch.

"And your young man?" she asked.

"I don't know. I have to think."

"You do what you need to do, sweet girl. You call me anytime, you hear?"

I nodded. "I hear."

Chapter Ten

She still wasn't answering my calls or calling me back. It had been ten days. On Saturday, it would be two weeks, and that was when I was just going to show up. I was sick of this. I wasn't angry.

Okay, I was angry.

But not really.

I was frustrated.

And hurt.

God, I hated feeling like that. It had been years since I'd felt so abandoned.

Abandoned?

Where in the hell had that word come from? Millie hadn't abandoned me. We'd spent maybe twenty or twenty-five hours together total, and a lot of those hours had been on the phone. How could a woman who I barely knew have possibly abandoned me?

Cut the horseshit, Drakos!

I shook my head and got out of my truck to visit Wylie Plumbing Supply again. Junior Hanson better be there this time, or I was going to kick his motherfucking ass. I went in the back door; I didn't want to deal with the showroom.

I nodded to Baily. She was another one of Wylie Senior's grandkids.

"He's not here," she said before I could even ask my question. "But Jenny said you could go on back."

I nodded and weaved my way past Baily and the file cabinets and headed down the hall. Junior's door was open, but he wasn't there with his eyes stuck to his computer monitor. I had a bet with Harvey that Junior spent all day just surfing porn sites, but I hadn't been able to prove it yet. Harvey's bet was that he was just reading articles on hunting and fishing. I kept telling him that Junior couldn't read, so I had to be right. One day I would get proof, and I'd win my hundred dollars.

I tapped on Jenny's doorjamb so she wouldn't be surprised when I walked into her office. Her eyes were glued to her monitor, but I had no doubt she was doing work.

"So how bad is it?" I asked.

She looked up at me, her face pale.

"Real bad." She waved at me to sit down on one of the threadbare chairs in front of her desk. That was about all her tiny office could handle.

"Hold on while I print these reports out for you."

"Jenny, it's going to be okay. I'm just going to go with another contractor for the school build. It's not the end of the world."

"I wish it were that simple." She blew her bangs away from her face. She had that whole nineteen-fifties pin-up girl look going on, with a Bettie Page haircut. Right down to the cat's-eye glasses. I wondered how many times Junior had hit on her.

She pulled papers off the printer and handed them to me. The first page was titled, *Report for Sadowski Construction prepared by Jenny Brooks on Behalf of Wylie Plumbing*.

I scratched the back of my neck. "Isn't this kind of official?"

"It needs to be. I emailed both Senior and Junior last night to say that I would be presenting this to you. I left them voicemails as well. Like normal, they ignored me. I couldn't, in good conscience, not tell you my findings."

I frowned and started reading through the pages. At first, I thought she'd made a mistake, then I started getting concerned. When I got to the part where she showed that the substandard material had been used for all our jobs as soon as Junior took over the company, I was furious.

"How did you find this out, Jenny?"

"I couldn't understand how Junior could possibly

post better quarterly results than his daddy ever did, since he took over. His men hate him, and he doesn't know shit about business. So, I started digging."

"That's when you figured out he was sourcing low grade product?"

Jenny nodded. "He also started an account in Nashville with a large printing company. He'd been personally signing off on the receipts, and when I called over to the printer and asked for proofs of the artwork, that's when I found out he was having boxes made to mimic the higher-grade suppliers."

"The fucker was then switching the low-grade stuff into the high-grade boxes, then when it showed up at our job sites, we'd be none the wiser," I spit out.

Jenny nodded. "I'm so sorry, Renzo.

"You realize we're going to have to go in and replace the plumbing on all of those jobs, right?"

She nodded again.

"Where the fuck is Junior?"

"He said he was taking a vacation. He wouldn't tell any of us here where he was going, but he's kind of dumb."

"But he fooled all of us, so not so dumb," I bit out.

"Dumb enough to use the company credit card so I knew everyplace he's used it. He was staying at the MGM Grand in Las Vegas at a suite, but he checked out almost immediately after I sent out my report to him. Then he pulled out a cashier's check for forty grand. So, I guess he's smart again."

"Of course. Look, I've got to take this to Harvey. We need to determine what our liability is. How many more contractors do you have to talk to?"

"None."

"So, it was just us, huh?"

She nodded. "You're our biggest client. You know that."

I nodded.

"Jenny, don't talk to anyone about it yet. I don't want Junior or Wylie Senior to come at you. Let Harvey and me talk, then we'll talk to Wylie Senior. I don't want you in the crosshairs."

Her chin jutted out. "I can handle it."

Great, another stubborn woman.

"Jenny, I have no doubt that you can handle it. None at all. After all, you are Beckett Brooks' daughter." She and I both grinned. "However, I would just like all of your ducks in a row before you do. Do you trust me?"

"Fine. Whatever."

"Thanks. And thanks for doing the right thing."

"For that, Renzo, you will never have to thank me. That's always my path."

"Well, thank you anyway. Not everyone takes that path."

～

On my way to Harvey's house, I called Millie again, expecting her voicemail. I was stunned when she actually answered.

"Hello, Renzo."

I took a moment to savor the sound of her voice.

"Hi, Millie. I'd ask you why you decided to pick up, but I have a policy to never look a gift horse in the mouth."

She giggled. I savored that as well.

"I'm glad you picked up. I didn't want to show up unannounced."

"How come I'm not surprised that was going to be your next play?" she teased.

This time I chuckled. "Maybe because you've gotten to know me?"

"Maybe a little bit. Were you planning on bringing chocolates?"

"I only bring chocolates if I know there will be food waiting for me."

"There's always food at my house."

Was I imagining it, or did her voice sound a little sexier?

"Okay, I have to ask. Why did you decide to answer the phone this time?"

She sighed. This I didn't savor. As a matter of fact, I didn't like it. I didn't like the thought of her having to gather her courage to talk to me.

"For the record, you weren't the only one who

suggested I research other burn victims. My friend Dr. Rose has been telling me to do this for years."

I waited.

"So, I did."

I waited some more. When I was met by silence, I prodded. "What did you find?"

"It was like you said. The scars were bad. A lot of them were worse than mine, but most of the people had come to grips with their scarring. They weren't hidden away in their houses like I was."

I hated what I heard in her voice. It was self-recrimination.

"Hey, none of that. You were watching and listening to people who had come out the other side. We don't know what it took for them to get there."

"But some of them were young children. They were so well-adjusted," she protested.

"You didn't have your parents who could have helped you through this. Instead, you had your aunt and uncle. From what you told me, they weren't the best people to help a young girl navigate such a rough time."

"I told you about Aunt Marge and Uncle Phil?"

"It was the night you said there were only real-life crime dramas on TV, and I was supposed to entertain you. We stayed on the phone for three hours, remember that?"

"Oh yeah," she breathed. "You told me about having

to go out to Hollywood and oust your sister's boyfriend out of her condo and then had to take his place on the red carpet. You sure sounded pissed about it."

"Beating him up wasn't a problem. It was more of a problem having to dress up and having my picture taken."

Millie giggled again.

What I wouldn't give to actually see her smile and giggle and maybe, just maybe, out-and-out laugh.

"So, when can I come over?" I pressed.

She sighed. "Not today. I have company coming over."

"Little Grandma?"

"Actually, it's Lisa Reynolds, and she's bringing Bella Clark."

"I know Bella, but who's Lisa?"

"She runs the auto shop in town. She's been over here a couple of times. She's a little bit like you."

I frowned. "What do you mean?"

"Pushy." I could hear the smile in her voice.

I paused. "Do you like her?"

"Actually, I like her a lot. She's been coming over here for the last six weeks. It's been fun."

"And Bella?"

"I don't know. This will be the first time she's bringing her over. I hope she'll like me."

I could hear the trepidation in her voice. "Just swear in front of her, then she'll like you."

"I don't understand."

"Then you'll owe her money. Once you pay the little minx, she'll love you."

Millie laughed again.

Damn, I wanted to see that in person.

"Cariña, I've got to go. I need to go visit with Harvey."

"Okay."

Chapter Eleven

JUNE, JASPER CREEK

Ever since he said he had to talk to Harvey, he hadn't called me. I didn't understand what I had done wrong. I thought about calling him, but I wasn't brave enough. The only good thing going on was that Lisa and Little Grandma knew I was sad, so they stepped up their visits. I had to admit that it was hard to be sad when I was around little Bella Clark.

I meandered out to my lavender field and basked in the soft summer sunlight. Then I took deep breaths of the heavenly smells as I checked the new growth. The scent calmed me.

"You're doing well," I smiled as I knelt down and caressed my babies.

I broke off a sprig and rubbed it between my palms, praying that the scent would last throughout the day. I looked up and saw two clouds drift toward one another. One of them looked like it was reaching out to the other. I continued to watch until I saw it envelop the smaller cloud.

I wiped away a tear.

Getting up, I wandered over to my orchard. The peach trees were heavy with fruit. It would soon be time to start the harvest, but not quite yet. Irv and I had talked, and the trick was to let them get ripe and sweet, but not too ripe. Irv was thinking of July for harvest.

I plucked a peach from the tree, took a bite, and groaned.

"So good."

I continued to eat my prize as I walked back to my house. Maybe I could be brave. Maybe it was time to call Renzo after all.

When I got inside, I washed my hands and put on some mascara.

"Foolish girl."

But I wanted to look nice when I called him. Even if he couldn't see me, it would give me confidence, and maybe he'd hear it in my voice. I picked up my mobile phone from the charger and pressed his number. I wanted to cry when it immediately went to voicemail. Had he seen my name and pressed decline, or was his phone off?

I couldn't bring myself to leave a message, so I hung up.

I called Lisa.

"Hi, Millie. You read my mind. I was thinking of you."

I gave a half-hearted smile. "You were?"

"Yeah. I'm not going to be able to bring Bella over. She has a playdate, so it'll be just you and me on Saturday."

"That sounds wonderful. Maybe we can binge watch some shows with good-looking men," I suggested. Anything to get my mind off Renzo.

"That's not a bad idea. I need to refocus my brain," Lisa admitted.

"Is this about Roan?" I asked.

Lisa huffed out a breath. "Maybe."

"Care to talk about it?"

"Just have cookie dough ready when I come over."

"You've got it."

She said goodbye, and just with that brief phone call I felt better. It was nice having women friends who were going through some of the same things as me. With that thought in mind, I was able to head over to my desk and get started on work.

Three hours later I pushed back from my desk and pulled my hair back from my neck. I was back where I started the day, in an unsettled and almost cranky mood. The usual donors were not returning my calls, just like Renzo.

I needed to get a new perspective on things. I powered off my computer and shut off the power strip that my monitor and computer were connected to, then snagged my cell phone. I got up, stretched, grabbed my tote bag, and headed to the mudroom. I put on my thick boots, then went outside.

I aimed straight for the peach trees. Even now, the smell of peaches about knocked me over. I took deep breaths with every step I took. I never could decide, was it the smell of peach blossoms I liked the best, or was it the smell of peaches? Today I decided it was peaches. Definitely peaches.

There were three rows of peach trees, twenty-three trees each row. When they were in bloom, it was as if I was walking through a cathedral of blossoms. Now, I felt like I was surrounded by the bounty of life. Sometimes it felt like Mom and Dad were walking with me, because the ash from our burning house had floated into the orchard's soil, and now they were creating life and sustenance.

By the time I got to the end of the first row, I had half my tote bag full of perfect peaches for cobblers and pies. I looked longingly over at the blackberry brambles that were growing wild next to the pond. It was a hundred yards away. I knew it for a fact, because I knew how far the pond was from the last peach tree. Trying to pick the blackberries was a stupid idea; I was already limping. My hip was beginning to ache and my thigh was downright hurting. But I'd found a great new recipe for a peach and blackberry cake. I'd thought of a couple little tweaks that could really up the pizazz level, and I wanted to try it out and have Little Grandma come over for a tasting. If they liked it, maybe she'd serve it at her restaurant.

I looked at the brambles again and made up my mind. I would not let my injuries get the best of me. I was doing my stretches and yoga religiously. I could do this!

I stalked over to the last peach tree in the row and slowly lowered myself against it. I stretched both my legs out and grabbed one of my peaches and took a big bite. I didn't care that the peach juice was dribbling down my chin onto my tank top. Nobody was going to see. That first bite must be what ambrosia tasted like. Surely, the Greek gods couldn't have wanted anything better. I grinned.

I took my time doing some stretches and massaging my thigh. By the time I was finished with my peach, I was feeling better. Not great, but better.

"Time for blackberries."

I was singing a different tune when I got to the blackberry brambles. Now my hip was hurting, and my thigh felt like it was on fire.

"Suck it up, Millie Jane and eat a berry."

It was good advice.

I started picking the succulent, plump berries, and for every four I placed on top of the peaches, one went into my mouth. I looked up and saw a cornucopia of even plumper berries just out of reach.

Maybe if I stood on my tip toes?

"Ahhhh!"

My scream seemed to go on forever and ever as my damaged leg collapsed under me and I hit the ground.

I couldn't move. I couldn't breathe. Tears of frustration hit the back of my eyes. Shit, this was worse than it had been when Renzo had been with me. So much worse.

What's that sound?

I realized it was me whimpering. I needed to stop.

I wiped at the tears that streaked down my cheeks. I hated this. First, I was a shut-in and then I couldn't handle picking berries?

Looking around me, I saw the peaches had rolled around like balls in a pinball machine; they were everywhere, and I swear to God, most of the berries were underneath me. I looked like a purple mess.

I rolled over and gritted my teeth against the pain, but it was the only way I was going to get up. Once I was on my stomach, I pushed upwards and tried to get onto my knees, but my right leg quivered and gave out while my left leg stayed in place. That was a victory. I looked around for something I could grab onto to help me get into a standing position.

Anything.

The only thing that was even remotely close was

the blackberry bushes, and sure as a bear shits in the woods, I would end up falling into them.

Or you could call someone for help.

I bit my lip.

My leg spasmed.

My laugh sounded like a wet sob. I hated the idea of anyone finding me in this vulnerable position.

"Dammit! Dammit! Dammit!"

I crawled as best I could over to my phone but didn't make it before my leg screamed in pain and I dropped to the grass and bit back a wail of agony.

I managed to reach the phone with my fingertips and pull it to me. By then I was dripping with sweat.

Irv. I was going to call him first.

Please let him answer.

My bottom lip started to tremble when it went to voicemail.

I listened to Irv's thick Tennessee accent. It was usually soothing, but not this time.

"Hey. Gone fishing. Try back later."

I wiped away more tears.

I didn't want to call 9-1-1. I didn't. There was only one other person in town who I could call, not that she could come and drag me back to my house, but she was wise. She would think of something.

It was lunchtime. Little Grandma would be answering the phone for the Down Home Café. I pressed in that number.

"Down Home. We don't take reservations."

My snort of laughter resulted in tears and snot. "Little Grandma? It's me."

"Millie. You don't sound right, girl. What's ailing you?"

I sucked in a deep breath. I wasn't a victim anymore. I was *not* going to cry like a baby, I was stronger than that.

"I'm in a bit of a pickle." I was proud at how level my voice sounded.

But she must have heard something in my voice. "What's wrong? What do you need? Is it your leg? Are you hurt? Do you need help? Answer me."

How a woman who was over one-hundred years of age could sound like a drill sergeant was beyond me.

"I'm fine," I said, offering up my go-to phrase. Then winced. "Not really," I amended as fire streaked up my leg, then up my side until even my ribs burned.

"Baby girl, talk to me. Do I need to call an ambulance?"

"No!" I shouted. Then, "No," I repeated in a calmer voice. "No ambulance. I'm at the orchard, and I overdid—" The last word ended in a high squeak as another lightning strike of pain shot up my thigh. Dropping the phone, I gripped my thigh with both hands, trying desperately to stop the spasms that were bouncing against every nerve in my body.

"Millie! Millie! Talk to me!"

If I could have, I would have. All I could do was

pant and whimper through the pain. I heard Little Grandma talking to someone. It was a man.

"Christ!" The man shouted.

"Don't take the Lord's name in vain. Now get moving."

"Millie, can you hear me?"

"Millie. Talk to me."

Red. All I could see was red. It was like I was in the fire again; the pain was back. The flames were eating my flesh.

"Millie, talk—"

Black.

Blessed black.

I lowered my forkful of chicken pot pie when I heard Little Grandma mention Millie's name. I dropped my fork and pushed up from my table. I wound my way past the other tables filled with lunch diners and went to stand next to the hostess station where the white-haired lady sat on her specially made chair.

"Baby girl, talk to me. Do I need to call an ambulance?"

Little Grandma practically growled the question into the phone. I approved.

"Where is she?" I demanded to know.

What was I doing yelling at an old woman?

"Calm down, Renzo. You getting angry isn't helping Millie."

"Where is she?" I asked again. This time, I was under control. "What's wrong?"

She didn't answer me. She was listening to whatever Millie was saying. I so wanted to grab the phone out of her hand. Then she turned to me.

"She's in her orchard. She said she overdid, but she was in pain. I could tell."

"Well, call 9-1-1."

"Millie! Millie! Talk to me!"

I was done. "I'm going over there." I didn't wait for Little Grandma to say anything more. "I'll pay for my meal tonight," I promised as I walked out the door. I practically ran down the sidewalk to where my truck was parked and got in. My truck was heading east out of town in less than five minutes, and I was at Millie's place in another ten. I skidded to a stop in front of her barn, dirt flying. Even when I had been on the hillside, I couldn't see any sign of Millie, but with the trees heavy with fruit, I wouldn't.

I fished my phone out of my back pocket and called Millie's number. It rang five times, then went to voicemail. That meant she and Little Grandma probably weren't connected anymore, otherwise it would have gone straight to voicemail.

"Shit."

After I hung up without leaving a message, I called Down Home. "Down Home, we don't—"

"It's Renzo. Why are you answering your phone? Weren't you on the phone with Millie?" I demanded to know.

"Yes, but it was silent for over ten minutes, so I hung up."

I wanted to roar at her. She should have kept the line open.

"Shouldn't I have?" she asked tentatively. It was the first time I had ever heard Little Grandma's voice quaver.

"No. Don't worry about it." I stalked over to the orchard.

"Are you there yet?"

"I'm here. It won't take long for me to find her," I lied. "I've got to go."

"You better be calling me as soon as you find her. You hear?"

"I hear."

"Find her fast," she said softly.

"I will, ma'am."

I hung up. I needed to be searching. The trees were planted eleven across, going east to west and twenty to twenty-five deep going north to south. It only made sense to search north to south. I started at a jog toward the peach trees that were closest to her house. They were heavy with peaches, and if it weren't for how Irv kept the grass cut around the rows, I wouldn't be able to see through to the next row.

"Millie!" I shouted her name over and over again as

I carefully looked and slowly jogged until I reached the south end of the peach orchard. As soon as I got out from under the shade of the trees, the bright sun hit my face and I had trouble even seeing the farm's pond off in the distance. That was the source of water for the orchard and the lavender that Millie was starting to grow.

I didn't see any sign of her, so I started up the next row, just to be sure I hadn't missed her. She was a tiny little thing.

"Millie," I shouted. "Call out. I'm here to help."

I stopped to listen, but still nothing.

It took me over an hour to go through the orchard.

Nothing.

"Fuck!"

Chapter Twelve

I got out my cell phone.

I needed help.

Fast.

"Hey, Renzo. How are you doing?" Simon asked as he answered his phone.

"Not good. I'm over at Millie Randolph's place. She called into Little Grandma at Down Home that she was injured." I looked at my watch. "An hour-and-twenty-five-minutes ago. She said she was in her orchard, then she stopped talking. I just searched her orchard. She's not here. I need to track her. I'm a fair hand at it, but two people are better than one."

"Got it. I'll be right there. I'll call when I get there."

"Appreciate it."

I was positive she wasn't in the orchard, but where did she go from there? I stood at the spot where I had started and looked at the first column of trees. There were peach trees, Macintosh apples, Pink Ladies, Granny Smith apples and pear trees. Some trees were blossoming. Would she have been picking flowers?

If she had been, then she would have brought them back to her house, and then she would have told Little Grandma that she was at her house. I'd already called the Down Home Café and confirmed with the woman that Millie had definitely said the orchard. So, since she wasn't there, she had to be somewhere close, or the orchard was her starting off point.

"Fuck! Fuck! Fuck!"

I could feel my heart beating faster, and all I wanted to do was run around the orchard again and again, yelling her name until she answered.

Calm, Drakos.

I tried to think what my brother Jase would do. I knew he and his team were on a mission. He'd already sent the family a group text that he'd be out of touch for a while, and that we should look in on Bonnie and the kids. If he hadn't sent that text, I would have been calling him for advice. It was the reason I called Simon; he used to be a SEAL like my brother.

I looked down the row of trees again.

"Dumbass! You're a fucking dumbass!" I shouted as I ran to my truck. Seriously, Jase would kick my ass if he were here.

I needed to look at each tree around the perimeter of the orchard and see if there was any kind of sign that she had left the orchard and which way she went. I jumped into my truck bed and opened up my toolbox, grabbing my heavy-duty flashlight. It might be two o'clock in the afternoon, but the shade of the trees made it too dark to look for clues.

I ran back to the first peach tree and started my search. I was on the fifteenth peach tree going north when Simon called out. I stopped what I was doing and stood up straight. I looked down the line of trees and saw Simon looking my way. There was another man beside him. They looked to be about the same size, but I could tell Simon by his silver hair.

"We're here."

"Who's we?" I yelled as they ran toward me.

"My partner, Roan Thatcher. He's a good tracker. What have we got?"

"I've been through the orchard pretty damn thoroughly. Right now I'm checking each tree on the perimeter to see if I can find any indication of where she might have wandered off."

Both Roan and Simon nodded. "That sounds good," Roan said.

"I'm taking the east side, south to north," I told them.

"We'll take east to west, and south to north on the west side. You should meet up with us on the north side of the orchard."

"Sounds good," I replied. "Take flashlights. It's dark under the trees."

"Understood."

I stepped back under the peach tree where I had left off. It wasn't until I had rounded the corner and was on the third tree that I found something. It was a peach pit with some of the flesh still on it. When I picked it up, it was still wet. Millie must have just eaten the peach. When I looked closer, I could see where she had sat down against the tree. I called Simon's cell phone.

"I found where she rested," I said before he could say anything.

"That's good. Are you along the north side?"

"Yep."

"We'll be right there."

I shoved my phone into my back pocket and looked for signs of where she might have gone. There was grass all around the tree, and other than the depression where she'd sat, I couldn't discern a damn thing.

Roan got to me first. "Whatcha got?"

"This peach pit is still wet. She must have eaten the peach recently. Do you see the imprint of where she sat?"

He nodded. "She started walking here." He pointed away from the trees. "Does she have a limp?"

"Yes. You can tell that?" I looked down at where he was pointing, but I really didn't see anything.

"Do you see the depression in the grass here?" Roan asked me, and Simon who just arrived.

Roan pointed to something in the grass that was about four yards from where she had been sitting. "You can see where she was walking, and she was definitely putting more weight on her left foot."

After he pointed it out, I saw the depression in the grass, but I sure as hell couldn't discern that one foot was leaving a deeper indentation than the other. This guy was good. I looked up. "She's headed toward the pond."

"We need to follow her tracks. That pond looks big, and we might miss her if we don't exactly trace her steps."

"That's fine," I agreed. "For now."

Simon rolled his eyes.

"I've never been a soldier, I don't take orders well."

"Sailor," Simon corrected.

"Marine," Roan said at the same time. He continued to concentrate on the brush in front of him. The meadow grass was high and was peppered with wildflowers. Now that I knew what to look for, it was easier to see Millie's steps. When we had gone fifty feet, I stopped and looked up to see where she was headed.

"She's going to the blackberry bushes," I announced.

"Are you sure?" Simon asked.

"Positive."

"I'm going to keep tracking in case she veers off," Roan said. "You two head toward the blackberry bushes."

Simon and I started running. I was watching the ground, making sure that I didn't hit a gopher hole.

When I got to where the blackberries started, I began to yell her name.

"Millie!"

"Millie, answer me! Millie!"

That's when I saw a peach. Then another.

There she is.

I skidded to my knees so I could cradle her in my arms.

"Simon," I shouted. "I found her."

"Millie. Cariña. Baby, wake up." I pressed my fingers to her neck and checked her pulse. It was rapid, but steady.

Then I saw it. Even under her jeans I could see the muscle of her thigh jumping. Millie started to groan.

I heard Simon behind me call for Roan.

"Snakebite?" Simon asked.

"I'm pretty sure she passed out from nerve pain. Somebody needs to call Doc Evans and tell him what's going on. I'll carry her home."

"What do you mean, nerve pain?" Roan asked as he leaned over and looked at Millie.

"She was badly burned in a fire when she was fourteen. Hip and thigh. I've seen her cramp up, and then seize up from the nerve pain."

"Fuck," Simon said.

"In that case, let's hope she stays passed out," Roan said.

Then, as if she heard his words, Millie began to groan, then she opened her eyes. I looked on helplessly as she bit her bottom lip and tears leaked out of her eyes and dripped down her temples.

"Hurts," she gasped out.

"I know, baby. We're going to get you help."

"I called the doc. He said we should get her to the hospital," Simon said.

"Nooooo," she wailed.

My heart just about broke.

"Call him back. Tell him to get his happy ass over here," I growled.

Simon gave me a considering look then made the call.

I picked up Millie who cried out. I tried not to jostle her as I double-timed it to her house, but I couldn't help it. Her whimpers were killing me. The last time I felt so bad was when Malik, Jase, and I had rescued Angelica from those sick fucks at her orphanage.

"Hold on, Millie. We're almost there," I lied.

She moaned, then she passed out, her head dropping against my chest.

"Wet heat. Massage. Pain pills."

"Understood."

The last voice was Renzo's. He sounded upset. It was almost like he was mad.

"It would be better if we took her to a hospital."

"No, she hates hospitals. I'll stay with her. You can come and check on her tomorrow."

Renzo's going to stay with me?

Why did I feel so funny? It felt like I was floating on top of a fluffy white cloud. It felt like it was embracing me.

"Millie." I felt my shoulder being softly shaken. "Millie, Cariña, I need you to wake up. Just for a little while."

I drifted down from my cloud and came to earth, but I found myself just as comfortable. I was in my bed with Renzo sitting beside me. His fingers were trailing along my cheek.

"Let me see your pretty violet eyes."

"Blue. They're blue."

"I beg to differ." His smile was beautiful. "Since you're arguing with me, does that mean you're awake?"

"I'm not arguing with you," I argued.

"And so, it continues," he smiled and continued to caress my cheek.

I frowned. "Why did you wake me up if you're just going to pester me? And why don't I hurt? How did I get here?"

"Can you sit up? Doc Evans wanted to make sure you got plenty of fluids. Then when you were up for it, he wanted me to feed you."

I rubbed my eyes, trying to come to grips with what was happening around me. Somehow Renzo was here in my bedroom.

"What sounds good to eat?"

I rolled my eyes. "Talk about déjà vu. Aren't you sick of this? Sick of me? I mean after all, you basically stopped talking to me, so I got the picture."

I saw him wince.

"That wasn't on you, that was on me. Now let me help you sit up, and I'll get you some water."

"You don't have to stay here. I feel fine. I can get my own damned water." I threw back the covers and gasped. I grabbed them back up as fast as I could. My gaze zeroed in on Renzo.

He acted like nothing had happened. But that wasn't true. I was wearing just my pajama top and a pair of panties, and there was a warm wet towel over my scarred leg and hip, covered by plastic. I recognized the compress. The moist heat was needed to help loosen my overtaxed muscles so that they would relax.

"Who did this? Who undressed me? Who dressed me? Who put on the compress?"

"Lettie Magill came over with Doc Evans. She was the one who undressed you and put you in your pajamas. Doc Evans showed me how to do the compresses before he left."

I was horrified. There was no other word that could describe my feelings. "How long have you been here?" I choked out the question.

"I've been here almost since you called the Down Home Diner. That was fourteen hours ago."

"So...So..."

"Yes, Millie. I've seen your scars. I've applied the compresses onto your hip and leg. They didn't bother me. They didn't disgust me, like you were worried they would. They're scars, Cariña. Nothing more. Nothing less."

I kept looking at him, and he stared back.

"I believe you," I whispered.

"That's good because I wouldn't lie about this. This is too important."

I wanted to ask him why, but I was scared of what his answer would be.

"I think I'm ready for that water now."

He bent over and brushed his lips against my forehead. "I'll be right back."

Chapter Thirteen

Millie didn't last much longer after I got some of Down Home's chicken pot pie into her. Despite all the sleep she'd had, once she had two pain pills, she was out like a light. I couldn't say the same thing for me. There was just too much on my mind, and damn near all of it centered around the woman in the bedroom across the hall.

I'd had to chuckle when I found out that Millie had a guest bedroom. I'd teased her about it before she fell asleep. She told me that her mother would have been appalled if she hadn't had a guest room always made up and ready for someone. I just shook my head and smiled, then wished her sweet dreams.

I should have wished myself sweet dreams. I got up out of bed and headed for the living room. I sat down in Millie's desk chair and looked at the time on my phone. It was still fairly early, so I made my call.

"Hey, Renzo," Jase answered. "How are you doing? Any more stories about Drake Avery?"

"No, but Simon Clark sure helped me out today."

"Really? What did he do?"

"He helped me look for a woman who was in distress. He and his partner were able to track her down on her farm."

"That sounds like Commander Clark. Is she okay?"

"Yeah, she's asleep now. The doc looked her over. She needs to take it easy, but she'll be right as rain in a couple of days."

"That's good. I hope you're not calling to weasel out of being my best man."

"No way," I assured my brother. "Would it work?" I asked hopefully.

"Nope."

I laughed. "Didn't think so."

"Are you calling for any particular reason?"

"Just need to talk something out."

"Shoot." Renzo could hear the affection in his brother's voice.

"I'm in deep with this woman. I really care for her. But she's been isolated most of her life. If I take this one step further, it has to be for the long haul."

"So don't."

"Huh?"

"Renzo, is this Millie?"

"Yeah."

"Thought so."

I'd talked about her with Jase the last time I'd been in Virginia.

"How do you feel about her?" Jase asked.

"I've never met anyone like her before in my life. At first, because of the way she lives her life, I thought I would just feel sympathy for her. That's not it at all. I feel protective. I feel like I want to fight her battles for her."

I looked down at my boots.

"And?" Jase prompted.

"It's bigger than that. I feel happier when I'm around her. It's like it is when I'm with our family, only better." I shoved my fingers through my hair. "I can't explain it."

"Shit, talk about isolated. You've been living in the field too long, Renzo. At least I knew what I wanted, and I knew what was happening when I first saw Bonnie."

"You think she's my Bonnie?"

"Sure as shit sounds like it."

"Jase, I can't make a mistake about this. I have to be sure. Mom told me to never play games of the heart, and it would rip me to pieces if I hurt Millie's heart."

"The last time we talked about her you were thinking you were just going to up and leave. Is that what you're thinking is going to happen now?"

"No. Absolutely not."

Renzo heard Jase's growl of frustration. "So, what is your problem?"

"I have to be ready to commit to her. Mind, body, heart, and soul."

"Haven't you been listening to yourself? You're halfway, if not all the way, there."

I sat up in the chair. "Huh."

"Like I said, you haven't been around people and relationships enough when you've been globetrotting to know what is right in front of your face." Jase chuckled.

"You don't have to sound like a know-it-all."

"Sure, I do, cause I *do* know it all."

This time it was my turn to laugh. "You're an asshole."

"Ah, but you love me."

"Sometimes," and with that I hung up.

When I went back to bed I slept like a baby.

I jerked awake and was out of bed before I knew what was happening. The screams were horrifying.

Millie. It was Millie.

I raced to her room.

She was tangled in her sheets, and she let out another long wail of pure anguish.

When I got to her, her face was a mask of pain.

I was afraid to touch her, I didn't want to make things worse.

"Millie. Cariña. Wake up."

Another scream of anguish, and I couldn't help myself. I pulled her into my arms. "Millie, please. You're safe, baby. You're safe. I've got you."

She squirmed and flailed. Her shrieks and wails were now down to sobs, which were somehow worse.

"Baby, wake up. I'm begging you."

"Where are they? You've got to get them. Please get them."

Her nails sank into my chest and her eyes opened.

"Save them. Please save my mom and dad," she sobbed. "You've got to save them."

Her sobs turned to whimpers, and I wanted to reach into the past and save her parents.

Save Millie.

"Please, Renzo. Save them," she begged. "Please."

She stopped fighting and her body went limp, but her eyes stayed locked with mine. Tears streaked down her face. The duvet comforter and compresses were long gone, and her sleep shirt was rucked up almost to her breasts. Her lacy white panties glowed underneath the moonlight.

Her whimper changed. I could tell she was no longer back in time. Now she was here with me, and she began to push me away while reaching for her lavender sheet.

"Stop," I whispered.

"Please don't look," she pleaded.

I trailed my fingers from the top of her knee on her injured leg, up her scarred thigh, and rested them on top of her white panties. "This is what I was staring at, baby. Under the moonlight the white of your panties almost glows in the dark. How could any man look at anything else when he's holding you in his arms?"

She tore her gaze from mine and looked down at where my fingers rested. Her expression changed. There was disbelief, and I stroked my fingers over her panty-covered hip bone. Again, then again. She looked back up at me. She must have read what I was thinking because her look changed to one of wonder.

"But my scars—"

"Don't matter. I told you, you're beautiful to me."

"But I can't be."

I pulled her closer. Now that I wasn't scared out of my mind that Millie was being attacked, my body had come to attention. I found everything about Millie intensely desirable, and my dick was leading the charge. I decided it was time to show her just how irresistible I found her.

I stretched out my legs and pulled Millie closer, careful to keep my hand on her pretty panties. I knew a part of her was uncomfortable with this, since she had scarring on her hip, but fuck it. My hand loved where it was, and I intended to keep my hand happy.

"Renzo?"

I moved her closer.

I heard her swift intake of air. "Renzo?" she asked again.

I pulled her even closer until her butt was firmly nestled against my erection.

"What are you doing?" she asked after a long moment.

"Proving to you just how beautiful and desirable I find you."

I let my words sink in, not minding her silence. Then, my little minx did a soft shimmy and my dick got even harder. Thank God I wasn't wearing jeans, otherwise there would be train tracks running up and down my penis.

I spread the fingers of my hand so that it covered not only the side of her panties, but so that it was touching her scarred flesh. Millie jumped. Just a little. I kissed her temple.

"Have you figured out I enjoy touching you?"

"I'm thinking you have a thing for lace panties."

I choked out a laugh and squeezed her tight.

"My girl is feeling feisty."

Her body didn't relax against mine. It wilted.

"I think that's all the teasing you're going to get out of me tonight."

"Do you want to tell me about your dream?"

"You know what it was."

I moved my mouth to the shell of her ear. "Tell me about it."

I hated even thinking about that night, and I hadn't discussed what happened in almost ten years. I didn't know if it was even possible.

"Cariña, you're safe with me. Maybe if you talk about it, your nightmares will go away."

I arched my neck and looked up into his midnight eyes. "Do you think that's possible?"

"It's worth a try, baby."

Thinking about that night killed. It just killed. I'd tried to stuff it down into the littlest compartment in my brain, but sometimes it crawled out like some kind of spider. A spider with claws and a poisonous bite.

"Dad had cooked that night," I started. "He almost always cooked dinner, unless it was spaghetti or grilled cheese sandwiches. Mom could cook those."

I must have paused too long because Renzo asked me a question. "What did your dad cook that night?"

"Chicken stir-fry with snow peas. It was great. He knew just the right amount of spices to add to make it taste great. Dad could always get mom and I to eat our vegetables."

"Yeah, I didn't notice too many vegetables in your fridge," Renzo whispered as he tugged me closer.

"What happened after that?"

"Mom asked me what homework I had to do, and I kind of lied and told her about a math assignment that I'd already finished. I didn't tell her about my English essay. We'd been playing this big Scrabble marathon that week and I wanted to see if I could beat Dad. Mom was kicking both of our butts, so there was no way I could beat her. But I really wanted to finish and beat Dad."

"They sound cool."

"They were. It was us against the world. We were a team. I could tell how much they loved each other, but they never made me feel excluded."

Renzo didn't say anything, he just kissed the top of my head.

I huffed out a laugh. "You know, I forgot about our Scrabble marathons. Part of the reason Dad always lost is cause he would make up words and Mom would always challenge him. She caught him every time." I smiled at the memory.

"I bet you're good with words with all the grants and proposals you have to write up," he whispered into my hair.

"I do okay," I admitted. "I take after my mom that way. She was a college English professor. Dad was a tow truck driver. He had his own business. He had four trucks and five people working for him..."

Oh my God.

"I don't know what happened to them. I never asked. Who paid them? What happened after dad died?" I twisted around to look at Renzo. "What happened to them? How do I find out?"

"Easy, Cariña. I'm sure they were taken care of.

Your dad had to have had an office manager who took care of everything. It's fine, baby."

I blew out a deep breath and felt tears coming.

"There's so many things that I didn't think of. That I don't know what happened, you know?"

"You were only fourteen. You were in the hospital for months. You weren't expected to take care of anything but getting better."

I took a deep breath. He was right.

His cheek rubbed against mine. "After Scrabble, then what happened?"

I thought back. Remembering. "It was ten o'clock, and it was bedtime. It was then that I confessed I had an essay to write. Mom was pissed, but Dad calmed her down. He said I had to be in bed by midnight. I knew that meant he would set his alarm to come check on me. I wheeled my way into one o'clock. It was due the next day, and I was going to need the full three hours. Dad laughed and kissed me goodnight. Mom ended up hugging me too, even though she mumbled something about me needing to have better study habits. I remember Dad winking at me. I didn't laugh, cause then we'd both be in trouble with Mom."

"I really like your parents, Millie."

"They were the best," I whispered. "I miss them so much, Renzo."

He hugged me even tighter, and I turned and nuzzled his neck. He smelled so good. Tangy. Like lime.

"Can you tell me what happened next, baby?" he asked softly.

"I'd gone upstairs with them and got into my pajamas, then I came back down to do my essay. I curled up on the couch in the living room. I can't remember when, but I went into the coat closet and got Dad's leather jacket and put it on because I was cold. It was really big and was like a warm blanket. That's probably what put me to sleep."

I remembered the feel of the corduroy couch, and my favorite velvet throw pillows. I remember the paper was supposed to be on my favorite book.

Flowers for Algernon.

"My coughing woke me up. It was so bad that I ended up rolling off the couch. The fire department said that probably saved my life."

"There was so much smoke, and I couldn't breathe. I couldn't see, and I didn't know what was going on. Nothing made sense. Nothing. I didn't figure out it was a fire until I heard the roar."

I was so lost in the past that I didn't realize I was covering my ears to try to block out the monster's roars.

"I looked behind me, into the dining room and I saw streamers of red and orange sucking up the table... the Scrabble board. Then they started towards me. They started twisting, turning, and reaching for me."

I couldn't breathe.

"Breathe, Millie. Take a breath."

I felt something stroking my throat, helping me suck down air.

"Something fell onto the couch. I couldn't see what it was, but it was crackling. I had to get away. I had to. I tried to get up and run, but I was coughing too bad, and I didn't know where to run. I tried to figure out where the back door was."

"I yelled out for Mom and Dad, cause I knew they would be worried for me, but I couldn't hear my screams over the roar, crackle, and spits of the fire. I crawled as fast as I could, then I finally touched the back wall of the house. I was close to the door. I tried to yell for Mom and Dad again, but my voice wouldn't work."

I sucked in a deep breath. Then another. It tasted smoky.

"I reached up for the door handle, but Dad's coat was in the way, then I had to open it with the coat over my hand. As soon as I opened it, I heard an explosion. The fire grabbed me. I screamed for Mom. I screamed for Dad. Then I screamed for someone to kill me as the pain burst through me. I couldn't get up. I couldn't crawl. I could only roll away from the house. That was another good thing according to the doctors."

I lay there, panting, with Renzo stroking my hair, my shoulders, and my back.

He kept saying something but I couldn't understand. I was too exhausted.

I don't know how long I lay in his arms.

A minute?

Forever?

"I think about them... my mom and dad... every time I go into the orchard," I whispered.

"You do?"

"The house was burned to the ground with them in it. Nothing but ash was left. Most of it drifted over the trees. I like thinking that when I'm in the orchard, they're there with me."

He tightened his hold on me again.

"They're watching over you, Millie."

Chapter Fourteen

She was staring at me again. It was Wednesday morning. I'd carried her from the blackberry bushes on Sunday. Considering how willing she was to kick me out of her house back in May, it shouldn't have been too tough to kick me out now, but she hadn't.

I'm getting to her.

"We are not going to watch soccer again," she griped as she tried to grab the remote from me.

"It's not soccer. It's fútbol."

"This is America, bub. It's soccer. And another thing; when did I start getting this cable channel?"

"I put it on my credit card." I grinned. I held the remote over my head. She had two choices, she could get off the couch and get it, or she could lean over me and try to get it. I was hoping she would try for number two.

"And how come you have extra clothes over here? How did that happen?"

"Simon brought them. He was worried about you too, so he brought me clothes so I could watch over you."

"Simon? Bella's father?"

"Yeah."

"Why would he be worried about me?"

I looked at her, then I realized we hadn't really discussed much about her rescue on Sunday. "Simon, Roan, and I were the ones who found you on Sunday."

"Roan? Lisa's Roan?"

"Yep, Roan Thatcher. All three of us were worried about you, so that meant that Simon's wife Trenda was worried about you, and so was Lisa. Hell, everyone has been. Little Grandma, Lisa, Trenda, and Bella all want to come over and make sure you're doing okay."

She looked both shocked and horrified. "But why?"

"Because they care," I said softly. I put the remote on the coffee table, and put my arm around her.

"But not all together, right?"

"No, baby, not all together."

She gave out a relieved sigh.

"Millie, have you thought about going out with me? Maybe going to Little Grandma's diner? We could do it before they open up, or after they've closed. It would just be her family, you, and me. What do you think?"

This time there was no shock in the look she gave me, just horror. "I can't do that, Renzo. Do you know how big it is that I've let you and Lisa come and visit me this year? For years, it's only been Little Grandma and her family."

"What about your check-ups? Haven't you had to go in for additional surgeries?"

She bent her head. "You saw the grafts?" she asked softly.

I kissed her forehead. "Yes."

"Aunt Marge would give me a sedative before I went to the hospital. I'm weak, Renzo. I'm weak."

I couldn't help it. I laughed.

Her head shot up and through a sheen of tears she scowled at me. "Why are you laughing at me?" she demanded to know.

"Is this the same ballbuster who demanded millions from good ole Chuck at Luxton?"

"That is not the same thing at all," she spit out. "That's my job. What's more, I don't have to leave my house, now do I?" she challenged as she scrambled out of my grasp and off the couch. I smothered my smile as she slammed her fists onto her hips and glared down at me.

"Are you still laughing at me?" She leaned over and poked a finger in my chest.

"Maybe."

"Well stop. This isn't a laughing matter."

I tugged her back down onto the couch. "Calm

down, Cariña. I didn't mean to start a fight. I just was making a suggestion."

"It was a stupid suggestion," she mumbled.

"All right," I agreed.

"Almost as stupid as calling soccer football."

"Blasphemy." I pulled her onto my lap and aimed my fingers for her ribs. She shrieked with laughter as I continued to tickle her. "Admit it, you love soccer."

"I...I...I..." she kept laughing, and I kept tickling.

"Admit it."

She squirmed away. "I might love how their silky shorts show off their butts and legs."

I roared with laughter.

Was it only four months ago that this woman could barely bear touching me when she handed me the keys to the cherry pickers?

"Come here, Cariña. You deserve a punishment for that."

Her eyes twinkled. "I do not. You deserve a punishment for eating me out of house and home and adding new channels to my cable bill."

I tugged at her hands and she allowed herself to fall against my chest. Yeah, my Millie was all up for any kind of punishment I was willing to dish out. We'd shared two kisses since Sunday, but it was time for more. Maybe even a lot more.

～

"Can you give me a better suggestion than watching fútbol?" Renzo asked with his sexy Spanish accent. Every time he watched a soccer game I imagined him wearing those silky shorts that would show off his butt and legs. God knew why, considering the fact that he got up every morning just wearing sweatpants and I had his muscled chest to contend with.

He's driving me crazy!

Then there were those two kisses he'd given me. They confused the hell out of me. Where did I stand with this man?

"Did you hear my question, Millie?"

"You know I'm not going to watch soccer with you." I gave him an exasperated look.

He mirrored my look. "That wasn't what I asked. I asked if you had a better suggestion than watching fútbol."

It was at that second that I realized I was practically laying across his chest. That was another thing that had been going on. Every evening he would somehow arrange it so that we were snuggled up together on the couch, watching some kind of mindless television, that we would ignore so we could talk.

"We could talk," I suggested.

"We've done a lot of talking. Got another idea?"

"There's still some chocolate chip mint ice cream in the freezer. Let me up, I know you won't pass that up," I smirked.

He didn't let me go. "Wrong."

I frowned up at him. "What do you mean, wrong?"

"I want something sweeter."

I watched as his eyes lowered and he looked down at my mouth. He bent his head toward me, and I pushed at his shoulders. "Wait."

"What?"

"I don't want this."

He looked up at me.

"Millie—?"

"I don't want to kiss you again, without knowing where I stand with you. Before you rescued me, you'd cut off contact for almost a month. That hurt, Renzo. It hurt a lot. I need to understand why."

He shut his eyes, but his hold on me tightened.

"You're right, baby. I need to explain."

I didn't like how he said that. I hadn't wanted to ask, because I didn't want to know what his answer was going to be. But one thing I had learned after all my hospital stays and surgeries, it was better to just get things over with.

Renzo adjusted how we were sitting so that I was on his lap and now he was looking down at me. God, he was beautiful. I especially liked it that he hadn't shaved for two or three days. He was the definition of masculinity.

He took a deep breath, then let it out.

"Just tell me," I pleaded.

He nodded.

"There's this thing going on with work. I've been

trying to track down someone and bring him back to Jasper Creek. Harvey and I need some answers."

"That's a bullshit answer." I hissed.

"No. It isn't. I've really been tracking this guy. But I definitely used that time to get my head on straight about the two of us."

I wanted to touch him so badly. But even more, I wanted him to touch me. Stroke my hair. Caress my cheek. Kiss my lips. Anything. Anything that would take away the sting about what he was going to say next.

Please say he discovered something good about the two of us.

Renzo reached up and stroked my hair. He nuzzled my neck with his scruffy cheek, then made his way over to my lips. I sighed as his lips settled over mine. Just a whisper of a kiss that played a perfect note. A musical note that started a hundred glorious melodies. He lifted his head then looked down at me, his heart in his eyes.

"My head is on straight, Millie. I love you."

I bit my lip. He was giving me my dream. Not just a prince who has seen my scars and loves me, but my Prince Renzo. But this was so not what I was expecting. This was impossible. He had it wrong and it was my job to set things right.

"I love you too, honey. You're my best friend. I don't want to ever lose you."

His eyebrows crashed together.

"Millie, you're not listening to me. I'm in love with you."

I tried to get out of his hold, but he made it impossible. "Let me go," I begged. But he wouldn't let go of me.

"No."

"You're not in love with me," I protested. "That's not possible."

"Really think it is, Millie," he said sarcastically.

Ooops, there went Prince Renzo.

"You love me as a friend."

"I'm in love with you. I want to start a family with you. I don't want to hear anymore bullshit about your scars."

I struggled against him, and this time he let me go. I scrambled to the opposite end of the sofa. "I'm not talking about my scars. I'm talking about the fact that you're thinking about tying yourself to someone who, except for yearly doctor's appointments, hasn't left her house in five years." I coughed out a bitter laugh. "Yeah, I'm a winner."

"Yeah. You are. Now get back here."

Renzo scooted over to where I was and put his hands on either side of my face. "You listen to me, Millie Jane Randolph. I don't give a shit if we live in this house for the next sixty years. And by the way, it's absolute bullshit that you haven't left your house in the last five years. I'm pretty sure I had to carry your pretty ass in from the blackberry brambles just the other day. So don't give me this bullshit about not going outside."

I tugged at his hands, but he wasn't letting loose. "You know what I'm talking about," I wailed.

"Sure I do. I also know that who you were four months ago, and who you are now are two dramatically different people."

"Renzo, if you think—"

"Hold up there, Millie. Don't go putting words in my mouth. I just told you that if we're living in this house, on this land for the next sixty years, I'm fine with that. And I am. As long as you are. I'm just pointing out that you've changed a lot, and you might find out you'll change some more. But baby, it doesn't fucking matter to me. Not one fucking bit. Because I love you exactly as you are. Right now. You prickly little porcupine!"

"Did you just call me a prickly porcupine?" I practically shouted at him.

"Yes. If the prickle fits."

I looked at him. Stunned. Sixty years?

"You are an idiot, Renzo Drakos."

"No I'm not. I'm a man who has had time to think, and knows what he wants."

"Renzo, go talk to your family. They'll tell you how wrong this is."

He laughed. "I have talked to my family. They think you're wonderful."

"They can't. This is impossible." I shook my head again.

"It's not impossible, and you love me more than just as a friend," he smirked. "Admit it." His right hand dropped from my cheek and reached for my ribs.

"Stop! No! No tickling."

His fingers started to brush against my ribs. Just a feather touch. More of a threat, not a real tickle. But it was enough for me to say what I desperately wanted to say.

"I admit it. I'm in love with you too!"

He wrapped his arm around my waist and pulled me close. "You are a romantic fool, Millie Jane."

I felt my bottom lip begin to wobble.

I loved him. I was *in* love with him.

He loved me. He was *in* love with me.

How was this even possible?

"It's possible because we deserve happiness in our lives," Renzo said as he bent forward and touched his lips to mine.

Chapter Fifteen

I felt peace settle deep in my heart. Millie didn't know it yet, but she was going to marry me. She was going to marry me, Irv was going to give her away, and she would walk toward me from underneath the canopy of peach and apple blossoms in her orchard, and my entire family, including Grandma Maureen, would be watching on.

Her breath caught as I brushed my lips against hers for a third time. The fourth time I didn't brush her lips with mine, I settled against her sweetness and coaxed her to open for me. She did...with a whimper of need.

Millie wrapped her arms around my neck and held on for dear life and I gloried in the feeling. I wanted her to need me, I wanted to be her person.

I slid my tongue along the seam of her lips and relished her immediate response. She invited me in for a delicate dance of tongues. My cock twitched when I heard her innocent mewl of need as she twisted closer to me. I desperately needed to get her out of the soft blue sweater she'd been wearing all day. Twice now she'd worn leggings instead of jeans, and this time she'd worn a damn sweater that had covered her heart-shaped ass. It was a crime against humanity.

What's more, I wanted to see if she wore a lacy bra or a plain bra. I was hoping it was lacy like those lacy panties I'd seen on Sunday night.

Millie nipped my bottom lip, and all thoughts of her sweater or ass rocketed out of my consciousness, all I was aware of was the writhing, beautiful woman who was in my arms, catapulting me to a level of need I had never experienced before.

I don't know when she'd moved her arms, but I felt her nails biting into my chest through my Cristal fútbol club jersey. She wasn't clawing me; it was as if she were a kitten, kneading her way into my chest, into my heart, and it was working.

She broke away from my lips to look into my eyes. Her lips were swollen and glistening in the yellow lamplight.

When had I turned off the TV?

"Tonight is more than kisses, right?"

I nodded.

"You promise?"

This time as I brushed back the hair that had fallen out of her ponytail, I went further, and pulled out the band that was holding her mane and delighted in the lush fall of her hair as it danced around her shoulders and back.

"Yes, Cariña. I promise."

"I love it when you call me that. It makes me feel special."

"You are special. You're the woman I love."

Her eyelids fluttered shut.

I tilted her chin up.

"Look at me, Millie." Slowly, her violet eyes opened wide. "You might not believe it tonight, or tomorrow. But I'll be here, and I'll keep saying it and showing it and proving it until my truth is stamped onto your heart."

I saw a world of heat swirl in her eyes.

"Do you love me?" I asked.

"Yes," she finally whispered.

"Baby, your truth makes me soar."

I got up from the couch and picked her up.

"Renzo?" I heard trepidation in her voice. Millie might have said she wanted to go further, but I knew this was a big step. I was going to take it slow.

"It's all good. In fact, it's wonderful," I whispered as I walked down the hall to her bedroom. I took a deep breath and it smelled wonderful. Lavender, peaches, and cookies.

It smelled like her.

It smelled like home.

I placed her onto the bed so her head was lying

against the pillows, her dark hair fanned out against the lavender sheets.

"You're gorgeous. You know that, right?"

"To you, maybe," she answered softly.

"It's true, I see your beauty, but one day soon, you'll see it too, and you'll share it with the world."

Again, her eyes filled with hope. Then I pulled my fútbol jersey over my head and tossed it to the floor. I grinned when I saw the gleam of lust in her eyes.

"I think you like what you see," I teased.

"You know I do. You've caught me staring often enough."

"Now, don't you think it's my turn to stare?"

She slowly nodded, then pushed herself into a sitting position. She tugged at the hem of her sweater.

"Let me help." I took over and pulled it over her head then tossed it on the floor, not caring where it landed.

Lace. Peach-colored lace. The lace was so sheer that I clearly saw the raspberry color of her aroused nipples. It took me a long time to stop staring, and when I looked back up at her face, she had a dreamy look in her eyes.

"I like lace," I murmured. I gently pushed her back down against the pillows, then settled my lips against hers. For long moments we savored one another with languid, lush kisses. She broke our kiss, and I looked down at her flushed face. That was when I felt her.

Millie's small hands trembled as they touched the bare skin of my chest.

I groaned.

"You like this."

"Baby, I love this."

She got bolder, pressing the tips of her fingers into my pecs, sliding her hands all over until she passed over my nipples and I groaned. Her head shot up to look at me.

"Renzo?"

"Yeah, I like that too."

"Really?"

"I'll prove it to you."

I moved my hands and cupped her breasts. Millie closed her eyes and shuddered. When I used my thumb to tease her nipples, she moaned.

"Do you like this?" I asked.

"Baby, I love this," she said, throwing my words back at me.

If I wasn't so turned on, I would have laughed at her bit of sass, but she kept running her fingers over my nipples, and now I was the one shuddering.

"Cariña, I need you to stop now."

"But why?"

"We've got other things to do."

This time when she trembled, I realized it was like when she was coming out of her nightmare, there was a little bit of fear.

"It's going to be all right. I promise."

She buried her face against my chest. "I know."

I wrapped my fingers around her jaw and tilted her head up.

Those lips. Positively sinful.

I went in for another long, luscious kiss. I couldn't stop myself. Soon we were chest to chest, her lace-covered nipples scraping against my chest. I unhooked her bra and she sighed as she shrugged out of it.

I trailed kisses down her jaw, her neck, her sternum until I had her gasping for air as I sucked one delectable nub into my mouth.

"Renzo," she whispered. Nothing more, just my name. Her legs were restless as her desire ramped up. I traced my way down her stomach until I met the top of her leggings. Millie grabbed my hand and pushed it under her clothes, under her panties.

She stopped guiding me as soon as my hand found the wet seam of her sex. She yanked her hand back and held onto my wrist. She wasn't pulling me away; it was as if she needed to hold onto something. Anything. That was when I realized her legs had stopped their restless movements. Everything had stopped.

"Breathe, baby. Breathe."

She took in a deep gulp of air, and that was my signal to explore deeper. I parted the lips of her sex, and was rewarded with a beguiling bit of flesh that was eager for my touch. I brushed over her clit.

She stopped breathing again.

"Take a breath."

She did.

I kissed my way up from her breast so that I could look in her eyes. Continuing my soft strokes over her sensitive flesh.

"Please let me taste you," I begged as I searched her face.

She knew what I meant. I caught her clit between two of my fingers and gently squeezed.

"Oh, God. This is too good."

"It's only going to get better, Millie." I brushed my thumb over her captive flesh and squeezed just a little more. She bucked up.

"Renzo! It's too good."

I grinned.

"It's not even close. Let me undress you. Let me spread your legs and put my mouth on your pretty pink pussy. Let me taste and savor you."

She was panting.

I kept her dancing on a knife's edge. There was no way I was going to let her come until my mouth was on her pussy. She needed to know her scars didn't matter one damn bit.

She moved her hand off my wrist and off my shoulder. Then she was pushing down her leggings.

"Easy, Cariña, I've got you." I brushed her hands away and stripped off her leggings and panties and stared at the bounty in front of me. Before she could worry, I put my hands on her calves and started sliding them upwards in a slow caress.

I was telling her the truth, the skin on her left side was just as beautiful as the skin on the right. In fact it was more so. In these scars, I could see her spirit. It showed me the story of her strength and resiliency.

"You're so strong, Millie. You're the strongest person I know."

I peppered kisses over her knotted flesh.

"Renzo, no."

"Yes." I was careful with her. I didn't know if caressing her with my unshaven cheek would hurt, so I touched her reverently with my fingers and continued to lavish kisses on the rough patches of her skin. Ever higher, past her tempting curls, until I was gently licking her hip, then kissing and worshiping.

"Your scars aren't ugly, my love. They're beautiful. They show me your strength, your power, and your courage. I am in awe of you."

She began to tremble again, and then I heard her crying.

"Millie, no."

I glided up and looked at her. There might have been tears, but her smile was wide and bright.

"Is that truly what you see?"

"Absolutely."

She clasped my cheeks and drew me down for a sweet and salty kiss.

"Thank you, Renzo."

Her tears had stopped.

"You have nothing to thank me for. I'm telling you

another truth." I swept my hand down her body and found her legs parted. I slid down, eager to continue. I needed to pleasure her, to taste her.

I draped her legs over my shoulders. "Does this hurt?" I didn't want to be putting her scarred leg in an awkward position.

She shook her head, dark hair floating across her breasts.

She looked like a pagan goddess.

I'm not going to survive.

Her pretty pussy was flushed, and her clit was peeking out. I could see all of her sweet arousal glistening there, and she smelled so good. Even here I swore I smelled peaches.

I parted her nether lips and then, finally, took a leisurely lick along her folds, tasting heaven. Millie let out a sharp gasp, but I wasn't worried. Both of her legs had gone taut; this wasn't pain, it was pleasure. I took another long lick, then another.

She started to make the sexiest little mewling sounds, then I felt her fingers in my hair, pulling, then pushing. She could pull all she wanted, there was no way I was going to stop enjoying my treat.

When Millie was writhing and mewling, I took her clit into my mouth and sucked. Hard.

"Renzo," she wailed.

It wasn't enough. I needed to take her higher. I slowly pushed one finger into her tight, hot depths, and twisted. She yelled my name again as her pelvis bucked up, and her hands pushed my head down.

I continued to tease her with my tongue and finger, prolonging her orgasm as long as I could. Finally, she dropped back down onto the mattress and her hands slid out of my hair.

I kissed my way back up her body until I could look her in the eye. They were gleaming.

"Just one more thing," she whispered.

"Anything."

"Get naked."

Chapter Sixteen

I'd lied when I said I was fine with my legs on his shoulders. I'd been sure it was going to hurt, but right now, I wasn't just pain free, I felt like I could fly.

Orgasms beat pain pills all to hell!

Renzo came back into the room and dropped condoms onto my nightstand, then he stepped out of his sweatpants.

Good God.

He was amazing. He looked better than any of the naked men I had seen online. His cock practically vibrated as it pointed at me.

I reached out, then snatched my hand back. What was I thinking? I had no idea what I was doing. I hadn't watched porn online. I'd read romance books. But they really didn't provide a step-by-step manual of what to do. I definitely should have watched a porn film. But ick!

Renzo was watching me carefully. "I think I should have kept my boxers on," he said ruefully.

"Well, I was going to have to get used to your penis eventually."

I slapped my hand over my mouth.

Was that me talking?

Was this me about to have sex with the most beautiful man I'd ever met?

I brushed my sweaty hands over my thighs and jerked. I'd forgotten that my left thigh had scars.

Holy hell! How could I forget?

Renzo pushed back the covers and crawled into bed beside me.

"Are you going to turn out the light?"

"Nope, wasn't planning on it," he answered. "Need to see to put on the condom."

I frowned at him. "Is that true?"

"Nope."

He rolled over, so that his forearms were on either side of my head, and his legs pushed between mine.

"Isn't this going kind of fast?"

"Nope."

Damn, he had a nice smile. Kind of mischievous.

He lowered his chest so that his chest hair brushed against my tight nipples. So good, so damned good.

He bent and nuzzled my neck, then whispered in my ear. "I'm not going to do a damn thing until you're ready. I promise."

Muscles I hadn't even realized I'd been holding tight, relaxed. Renzo peppered kisses along my jaw, then down my neck until he reached my right nipple. He blew on it, and then blew again.

"Don't tease. Suck it," I begged.

He did. He licked and stroked and sucked until I was mindless, then he moved to my other nipple. My head was thrashing back and forth against the pillows.

"Your fingers," I panted.

I didn't have to ask twice.

Renzo moved his big hand down the front of my body, until it was sifting through my curls and his fingers were gathering up my wet arousal, then he inserted two fingers inside of me. I arched up.

"Okay?" he asked softly.

"So much more than okay," I sighed.

Again with the wicked smile before he once again bent down to suck on my nipple, and torture my pussy with his knowing caresses. When his thumb circled my clit and pressed hard, I saw stars. I was lost in space, and I didn't come back to earth until Renzo was kneeling above me like some kind of pagan god. He was holding the base of his swollen cock.

"Are you ready, Cariña?"

I was born for this man.

"Yes," I sighed.

He moved my legs so that they were bent at the knees on either side of his hips. I understood why when he grasped my hips and drew me toward him. As soon as the tip of his cock was nestled against my pussy, he stopped pulling me forward. Instead, he started to slowly push his way into my body. Joining us together.

I closed my eyes. I wanted to watch him. See that lovely look of concentration on his face, but I couldn't. The carnal sensations that were whipping through me were mind-blowing. Such a feeling of fullness. Then he pushed deeper and it stung.

He stopped.

I pushed up, but his hands kept me in place. "My way, baby." It sounded like he had a mouth full of gravel. I looked up at him. I saw the sheen of perspiration on his shoulders and forehead. I pushed up again, and he growled. "No."

I wasn't afraid of him. "Now!" I demanded.

He pushed in fast, ripping through my virgin flesh. I bit the inside of my cheek, stopping any kind of cry that might come out of my mouth.

Renzo moved fast, he was kissing my throat, my jaw, my cheek, whispering words of Spanish that I didn't understand, but his meaning was clear. He was offering comfort.

"I'm fine, you foolish man," I whispered back. My good leg wrapped around his waist, my scarred leg squeezed against his hip, holding him close. "Renzo, the pain is gone, show me the beauty."

His beautiful black eyes looked into mine and he

smiled. He started with slow, easy strokes that were like the beginning of a song. He studied me the entire time as he used his body like a bow across a violin, eliciting music that could only be felt.

Higher and higher he took me until I flew past the clouds and burst into sparkles of light, and I heard Renzo shout my name as he followed.

I woke up from a dead sleep, my eyes wide open. Millie was in my arms, her breathing was soft and even. In sleep, I realized just how tense she normally was. The only way I could describe her now was serene. She snuggled closer as I tried to loosen myself from her grip.

"Renzo?" she whispered.

"Water, baby. I'll be right back."

"'kay." She rolled over and buried her nose in my pillow and was asleep before I even left the bed.

When I got to the hall, I stood still and listened. It wasn't possible for a tree or bush to have brushed against her house because she had everything cut back twenty feet. She'd done it so a fire couldn't spread to her house. Everything about her house was fireproof, from the metal roof to the faux, cement siding. There was a sprinkler system installed throughout the house, and four fire extinguishers within easy reach.

When I didn't hear anything, I quietly padded to the living room.

Nothing.

I kept searching.

Then I heard it.

A scraping against her kitchen door.

Someone was trying to break in. Not that it was possible with the deadbolt.

Shit, why hadn't I had Simon pack my gun?

I raced to the security panel near the front door that operated the gate and slammed the button for the flood lights. I peered out the front window and didn't see a vehicle. Then I raced back to the kitchen. There was a window over her sink that allowed me to see out to her lavender fields and back porch. Millie's fence extended all around her house, with a back gate that opened to her lavender field. It was possible the intruder came from the back road past the pond.

I didn't see anyone jumping the fence. But I could swear I saw someone running through the lavender field. I went back to Millie's bedroom and quietly grabbed my cell phone. This time when I left the room, I closed the door.

I knew it called for rain tomorrow and I didn't want it to wash away the tracks, so I called the sheriff's department. I hoped Duncan wouldn't be working, he was an idiot. If he was, I was going to call Rivers on his cell. I hated to do that to the sheriff, but taking middle of the night calls was part of the job.

When I got through to the sheriff's office, dispatch was going to put me through to Duncan. I asked if there was anybody else available, and they said no. I hung up and dialed Nash River's cell. He answered on the second ring. For the middle of the night, he sounded somewhat awake. Not bad.

"Rivers," he answered.

"Sheriff, this is Renzo Drakos. I'm over here at the Randolph farm. Somebody just tried to break in. He ran off through the back field toward whatever the name of that little road is past the pond."

"Doesn't have a name. It's Lancaster's Private Road. Call into the sheriff's office, they'll send someone out to get some plaster casts before tomorrow's rain and fingerprints. They'll check anything else out."

"Duncan's the only one on duty," I told him.

I heard a muffled "Fuck."

"Give me an hour. Gotta get to the office and get a couple of extra supplies that aren't in my truck," Nash sighed.

"Why haven't you gotten rid of him? Besides being an idiot, he's a pain in your ass."

"He's the mayor's nephew. Election's next year. I've got my fingers crossed. Loretta King is planning on running against the old fart. If she wins, Duncan is out on his ass."

I chuckled. Small town politics.

"Hanging up now. I'll see you in an hour," Nash said.

I went over to the coffee maker and started a pot.

I woke up when Renzo slid into bed. The sun was coming up and I realized I'd had one of the best nights' sleeps of my life. He pulled me into his arms and kissed me.

"Good morning, beautiful," he whispered.

"Good morning, handsome."

"What would you like for breakfast?"

I stretched and considered his question. "I don't have anything frozen for breakfast, so how are you going to manage?"

His hand brushed against my ribs and I giggled.

"Smartass, I have been cooking for myself for years. And I see you have my same penchant for bacon, so we're good. How about waffles, eggs, and bacon?"

"Uhm, you can have all that. How about I have a waffle?"

"Sounds good. I cut up your strawberries, so you can have it with strawberries and whip cream."

"You cut up my strawberries? All of my dreams have come true."

He caressed my cheek. "I thought all of your dreams came true last night." I could tell he enjoyed seeing me blush.

"Get up and come into the kitchen with me."

I frowned. "How about you give me twenty, and then I'll meet you. I like to shower in the mornings. That and a cup of coffee get me moving."

He tangled his fingers in my hair and pulled me in for a long kiss. "I think I know something else that can wake you up," he murmured.

"Honey, that just puts me in la-la land. I can't function, let alone get dressed. Let's save that until after breakfast."

I watched as he frowned.

"What?"

"We'll talk after breakfast."

"No, tell me now."

He slipped out of bed and held out his hand. "Shower, then strawberry waffles, then talk."

My gut clenched. "Are you leaving again?" I hated the wobble in my voice.

"No, Cariña. I promise. I told you, I'm here. I'm sticking."

I put my hand in his and let him pull me out of bed. Then he kissed the inside of my wrist. I felt myself melt. There was something about that kiss, that was so sensual, so intimate, so Renzo. I swayed against him.

"None of that. Get your fine ass into the shower, then get out into the kitchen. How do you take your coffee?"

"Half cream, half coffee and plenty of sugar."

"My God, woman. Have you had your blood tested

for diabetes? High cholesterol? How do you get to the doctor?"

I pursed my lips. "Doc Evans comes here. I'm healthy as a horse." I never really liked his visits, but Dr. Rose insisted.

He brushed his nose against mine. "Well, good. Now get a move on."

Chapter Seventeen

"What do you mean, someone tried to break into my house?"

She was having trouble breathing. I could tell she was on her way to a panic attack, but she was doing her best to fight it off.

"Easy, baby." I stroked my fingers down her throat. "Take deep, slow breaths for me. Can you do that?"

She nodded.

We were sitting on her couch and I had my arm around her. "Sheriff Rivers was impressed by your locks. He said that any burglar would have a hell of a time getting in."

"But why me?" she gasped.

"Nash thought it was because you're out of town and isolated."

"But wouldn't my fence be a deterrent? When I

had it put in, the contractor said nobody else had anything like it in Jasper Creek."

"Actually, Nash thought that it might have made you more of a target. Somebody might think you have more to steal."

Tears shimmered in her eyes. "But I don't. I don't even have any cash. I do all of my purchasing through on-line banking. All any burglar could get would be a TV and computer. That's all I have of value."

She pressed closer to me, and I loved it. Having her come to me for reassurance was everything I could have hoped for.

"I have another theory; I think somebody was after me."

"Why would somebody be after you?"

"I told you that I was out tracking someone. Well, it's Junior Wylie. He's been running his daddy's plumbing supply business for the last few years. He's pulled some shady shit, and I need some information from him."

"What did he do?"

"He gave Harvey sub-standard plumbing material that he imported in from China and foisted it off as the high-grade material Harvey paid for. Harvey and I are going to have to retrofit all the jobs that have sub-standard material. Unfortunately, we don't know what jobs those were. Harvey is praying it wasn't the apartment complex he built. We need to find out from Junior.

He's the guy I was tracking when you and I weren't talking."

Millie frowned. "I remember Junior. He was a senior when I was a freshman. He was not the sharpest tool in the shed. He was a big guy so he was on the football team, but some of the girls I hung out with were dating football players, so I know that even his teammates made fun of him."

"Yeah, that's how he struck me, too. Harvey's pissed as hell that it is Junior who pulled something like this over on him."

"Isn't there anyone else who knows what he sold?"

"They had a guy working at their company who was older than dirt doing their shipping and receiving. He'd enter anything Junior or Senior told him to into their system. I only found out about all of this because Jenny Brooks, their new office manager, put it all together and informed me."

"Can't she tell you which jobs?"

"Nope."

"How is it you didn't notice the crap plumbing supplies?" Millie asked.

"It was before my time. It was Harvey's old GC, Red Simpson, who took receipt. Junior packaged the shit material in forged boxes. So that's the deal. I've been trying to track him down, but he's in the wind. People around town know that I've been here, so I think Junior might have come here."

"What do you think he was planning on doing?"

I rubbed the back of my neck and picked up my iced tea from the coffee table and took a sip. "I hope he was just planning on trying to talk his way out of things. But I also think the dumbass is desperate, so I don't know what he's planning."

"Well, that's stupid. He can't have planned to hurt you. He must realize that Jenny and Harvey know, too."

"It's like you said, Millie. He's not the sharpest tool in the shed."

When Renzo went to talk to Roan and Simon, I decided it was time to get my house in order. Laundry had been piling up, and the stove needed a thorough scrubbing. That's what happened when you let a man cook.

My hip was giving me trouble, but not enough to take a pain pill. I just needed ibuprofen. I wanted to have everything clean well before Renzo was due back so I had time to shower again and put on another cute outfit. I'd been living in my sweats and pajamas for the last few days, and I really wanted to show off.

As I walked down the hall toward the laundry room I caught a look at myself in the mirror. My hair was a mess and there was grease on my cheek from the stove cleaning adventure. But besides that, I looked different. I stopped to try to figure out what it was.

I laughed when I realized I was going to brush back some of my flyaway hair with my rubber gloves.

"Good one, Randolph."

I moved in closer. It was almost like I was wearing make-up, and I didn't mean kitchen grease. I tilted my head and leaned in, then laughed again. There it was. Whisker burn.

Holy hell, I have whisker burn!

I threw my hand up in the air.

Me, Millie Randolph had whisker burn from the sexiest man alive. I turned my face and looked some more. Finally, I realized it was my eyes. They looked brighter. More alive. I was totally, irrevocably in love with the sexiest man alive. And he wasn't bothered by my scars.

"He says I'm strong."

I heaved in a deep breath that was almost a sob.

"Stop it! There's no crying on laundry day."

He said I was strong and beautiful. He kissed my scars.

I smiled before a tear could fall. I had laundry and primping to do. Maybe I could make up a batch of snickerdoodle cookies.

Harvey's office was in the county municipal building. He was on the second floor and had four offices, a reception area, and a conference room. It was over-the-top for the size of his business, but that was Harvey.

Roan, Simon, Harvey, and I met in the conference room. Rhoda had gone out and gotten pastries. Because of me, she knew to get things like oat bran muffins and slices and zucchini bread. Harvey liked Bavarian cream donuts. She called it right when she went heavy on the healthy side when Roan and Simon were our visitors.

After Harvey finished his first donut and had snagged his second, he turned to me. "This is your meeting, so start."

"Did you get a chance to read Jenny's report that I sent you?"

Both men nodded.

"Seems kind of slick for Junior to have come up with."

"It does, don't it?" Harvey said as he reached for his coffee cup. "That's what I told Renzo. Junior is a few sandwiches short of a picnic, if you get my drift."

We all nodded.

"Course, he fooled Red. I guess that shouldn't be that big of a surprise. Red missed a lot of things. That's why I fired the man."

"So what do you want us to do?" Simon asked.

"Junior can't be found," I explained. "Not only do we want him prosecuted, we need to find out which projects did he sell Harvey the shitty material."

"Exactly. I'm going to lose my shirt having to

retrofit my projects with the right stuff. I don't want to do every project, just the ones he fucked me over on. I need answers." Harvey hit the mahogany conference table with his fist.

"This is what I know. Four weeks ago he was at the MGM Grand in Vegas. At that point he was using the company credit card. He stopped using any credit card that Jenny Brooks has access to. Plus, he pulled forty grand out of the company's payroll account the day after Jenny sent out a report outlining what she would be presenting to me."

"Is this that report?" Simon asked as he pointed to the report sitting in front of him.

I nodded.

"She emailed it to him?"

"Yeah. She sent it to both Junior and Senior. When I've talked to Wylie Senior, he's not saying anything. No apologies, no comment on where his son is. Nothing."

"Why haven't you brought in the police?" Roan asked.

"We're afraid we won't get the answers we need," Harvey answered. "He might be charged and out on bail for God knows how long before they pull him into court. I wanted Renzo to lean on him. I heard rumors about how Renzo beat up his sister's boyfriend. That's what I needed to have happen."

"What?" I turned to Harvey. "How in the hell did you hear about that?"

"Evie Avery, or O'Malley, or whatever her name is. She mentioned it to my wife. Apparently your brother was bragging about it. Anyway, I figured if you'd do that for your sister, you could do it for our company," he said hopefully.

Simon chuckled. "You beat up your sister's boyfriend?"

"He was a douche and he was threatening to go to the tabloids with some lies about Angelica. She's an actress. He needed an attitude adjustment," I explained.

"You did the right thing," Roan said.

"Anyway, we need to hire you two right now. We think that Junior's back in town. We think he tried to break into Millie Randolph's house last night."

"God, he is stupid," Simon said. "You got a gun?" he asked me.

"I'll pick it up from the cabin this afternoon."

"I've got a SCAR. That'll protect you. I've got one for everybody in the house."

Of course he did.

"Your wife and Tina both have assault rifles?" Roan asked.

"Yep. My wife only uses hers when I take her out for target practice, but Tina keeps hers under her bed. Just like the brochure says, it's great for home defense."

Roan caught my eye and I knew what he was thinking. Harvey had done a hard sale on him to marry Tina. Same as me. The broad was scary, and now knowing she kept an assault rifle under her bed just made her scarier.

"Harvey. I'm all about personal safety, but don't you think a handgun might be wiser?" Simon asked.

"Hell no. Somebody comes into my little girl's bedroom, I want her to have the firepower to take him out." He pulled the plate of pastries to him to see what was left. He picked a chocolate donut and pushed the plate back into the middle of the table.

"Thanks, Harvey, I'm going to decline on the SCAR. I'm good with the gun I've got."

"Okay. But if you change your mind, just let me know."

"In the meantime, I'm going to stay close to Millie."

Simon gave me a slow smile. Yeah, he was one to be giving me looks; I remember how it went with him and Trenda. He had been staying real close with her too when things were looking kind of hairy.

Chapter Eighteen

Waking up with Renzo in my bed had to be the best thing in the world. Now I understood why Lisa was smiling all the time. I'd made breakfast this morning. Boy did he eat a lot. But he probably weighed twice as much as I did, and his was a physical job, so it made sense that he would need a lot more fuel.

Except for the fact that we still didn't know who might have tried to break into my house, and now I had a gun—which was locked up at least—life was perfect. Heck, Renzo had even picked blackberries for me a couple of days ago so I could try making the peach and blackberry cake. I had him pick a lot because I usually screwed up my first two attempts of whatever I made.

Lisa and Bella were coming over this afternoon so I'd given myself enough time to make the cake three times. I was right, the first one was a mess. It came out cakelike, but the blackberries had exploded in the cake. I figured out they were too ripe and juicy. I used smaller blackberries and dunked them in cornstarch the second time around. When I opened the oven, I was confronted with a perfect cake.

Yay me!

The iced tea was cold, and so was the lemonade for Miss Bella. I also had some homemade peach ice cream to go with the cake. Hopefully this would be a hit. I grabbed a bowl of ice cream and headed to my computer. Today was grant day. It wasn't nearly as much fun as donation day, but it definitely needed to be done.

I was halfway through my bowl of ice cream before I decided which two grants to apply for that would work well for the Burn Alliance. The first one wanted our financial metrics, our tax form and disclosure policies, key accountability metrics and measurable impact and results. I had all of that, so this one was going to be easy, but the second one was a little tougher. They wanted our adaptability story. That was going to take some research. Well, that's why I got paid the big bucks.

I giggled. Yep, a salary of zero was certainly the big bucks.

I was lost in work when the fence sensor went off. When I looked at the clock on my computer I realized three hours had gone by. How in the world had that happened?

I got up and peeked out the front window and saw Lisa's baby blue Dodge Charger. Bella spotted me because she was waving wildly from the front seat. I waved back as I pushed the button to open the gate.

I was hungry, so I couldn't wait to see what Lisa had picked up for lunch. I opened the door and invited them in. I was surprised to see a bag that said Pearl's on it. I was just conditioned to think Down Home when it came to takeout food here in Jasper Creek.

"I see that look, Millie. Trust me, you'll like it. I got you a Rueben," Lisa said as she went to the dining room table and plopped down the bag.

"I got a grilled cheese with ketchup," Bella said excitedly.

"You mean ketchup for your French fries?" I clarified.

"No, for my grilled cheese. You dip it in the ketchup, and then it's like you're dipping it into tomato soup. It's really good. Wanna try it with your sandwich?"

I shrugged. "Sure."

"Feeling adventurous these days, huh?" Lisa said as she pulled out the sandwiches, napkins, utensils, and ketchup packs.

"I've decided that adventurous has its advantages." I tried to sound prim, but my laughter blew it all to hell.

"I hear you, sister," Lisa grinned.

"What are you laughing about?" Bella asked us as

she opened the wrapper around her grilled cheese sandwich.

"We're agreeing it's good to take chances," Lisa told her.

"I'm getting dishes and drinks." I headed to the kitchen.

"I'll come help."

We soon had the food prepped and the drinks poured and were eating lunch.

"I'm liking the ketchup, Cariña." I smiled at Bella.

"That's what Mr. Renzo calls me! Do you know Mr. Renzo?"

"Yes, tell us," Lisa prompted as she grinned. "How well do you know Mr. Renzo?"

"I know him really well," I answered. "He comes over and visits me."

"I didn't think you liked people coming over. That's what my mama told me. She said you were shy."

I heaved out a sigh. "I guess that's one way to put it. I had to spend a lot of time in the hospital when I was younger. A lot of doctors and nurses were always around me. I never got any privacy. It made me not like people. Then when I had to go back to school, the kids made fun of me because I was the new girl and I limped, so I really didn't like people."

"I wouldn't have made fun of you, I would have been your friend."

I looked at her troubled little face, and I grabbed

her hand. "I know you would have. You are the best kid I've ever met."

"That was mean of the other kids to make fun of you for limping. They were bullies."

"Yes they were. But between the hospitals and the kids at school I shut down more and more."

"What about your mom and dad? Didn't they help you?"

Boy, she sure knew how to go to the heart of the matter. "My mom and dad died."

Bella looked at me with such sad eyes, and her bottom lip trembled. "When you were a little kid?"

"Yeah. They died when I had to go to the hospital."

She shot up from her chair and rushed around the table to hug my waist. "I'm so sorry," she wailed into my chest. "I didn't know."

"Of course you didn't, sweetheart."

Her expressive eyes were filled with tears. "So you were sad and scared, right?"

"I was."

"Did you have aunts and uncles like me?"

"I had an aunt and uncle, but they came from far away and I hardly knew them. They took me away from Jasper Creek so that made me even sadder. But I'm much happier now. I have friends like you, Bella. And Lisa. And Renzo. And Little Grandma."

"And my mama wants to be your friend, but she didn't think that you wanted her to come over."

I looked down at her precious face. "Yes, I would love to meet your mama sometime."

"Mr. Renzo loves my mama's lasagna. You should come with him when she makes it."

I shot Lisa a helpless glance. She toasted me with her glass of sweet tea.

"I'll think about it." I brushed a kiss against her forehead. "Are you ready for dessert?"

"Did you make us something?" Her brown eyes gleamed greedily.

"I made blackberry peach cake with homemade peach ice cream."

Her eyes got even wider and she turned her head slowly to look at Lisa. "Did you hear that?" she practically screamed. "She made homemade ice cream! I didn't know you could do that." She turned back to me. "Can we make Captain Crunch ice cream?"

"I suppose, but you'll have to ask your mother first."

"Maybe we could make it for dessert when she makes lasagna. That would be epic!"

Lisa and I burst out laughing.

"We've found him," Simon said after I answered my cell phone.

The lump in my stomach that had been churning

since the night someone had tried to break into Millie's house, started to dissipate.

"Where is he?"

"He really is an idiot. He's been living in his aunt's shed. Seriously, we could have just followed the ding-dong and ho-ho wrappers instead of doing any real sleuthing."

I chuckled.

"Can you do me another favor?"

"What?"

"Harvey and I have this bet going on. Junior is always in front of his work computer when we go in to see him. Harvey thinks he's reading Outdoor Life, I say he's surfing porn. Anyway, you can let us know who's right."

"Oh, you win on that one. We checked his work and home computer. Nothing but porn. Another thing of interest is that he has downloaded every picture of Tina Sadowski that there is."

"Tina?"

"Yep."

"Hmm."

"So you don't know what that's about?" Simon asked me.

"Not a damn clue. Where's Junior now?"

"I've got him at our second office. We have a cabin further out than the one that I'm renting to you. Nice and quiet. A perfect place for people to stop and contemplate life."

I chuckled. "Give me the coordinates. After I talk to Harvey, I'll be there."

Simon gave me the coordinates and I promised to see him in a couple of hours.

I was standing in Harvey's study when he called out for his daughter. I'd worried that they weren't going to be doing well after Harvey had to lay down the law about her would-be fiancé. It turned out that she was doing fine.

Simon and Roan did a background check at Harvey's request and found that Tina's boyfriend had three failed businesses behind him, his car was about ready to be repossessed, and his house was in foreclosure. Not a stellar candidate for a future son-in-law as far as Harvey was concerned. But Tina didn't seem to care.

However, she did care when he explained that Roy's extensive collection of Japanese sex dolls were also going to be auctioned off. He explained that some of them had been purchased for more than ten thousand dollars. At that point Tina was more than happy to scrape him off.

"You wanted to see me?" Tina said as she sauntered into her father's study. She gave me quite the onceover, then licked her lips. Seriously, Harvey should have just let her marry Roy.

"Yeah, Renzo and I were wondering why Wylie Junior might have a bunch of your pictures downloaded onto his computer."

"Ewww. Junior? That oaf? I can't stand him. He followed me around for three months after Jessica's wedding. I couldn't pry him loose to save my life. I swear he took stalker classes."

"Why didn't you tell me?" Harvey asked.

"Because I knew you would go ballistic. I had Cousin Forrest take care of it."

"What did he do?"

"Well, that's the thing, Daddy. I'm not really sure. But now, every time Junior sees me in the store or on the sidewalk, he turns around and walks the other way."

"I always did like Amalie's boy. Got to give him a good bottle of bourbon for that."

"Is that all you needed me for?"

"Yeah, that was it."

"Good, I have a date tonight. I need to go get prettied up."

Harvey frowned. "Who is he? Do I know him?"

"He's one of the Beaumonts from Knoxville. You and Mama know them from the country club."

"Is he the bad son, or one of the two good ones?"

"It's all a matter of perspective," she laughed. She looked over at me and winked. "Good seeing you, Renzo." She tried to sway out of the study, but she just didn't have Millie's behind to do it right. I turned back to Harvey.

"She's going to be the death of me. I swear it."

"So do you want to go with me while I talk to Junior?" I asked him.

"Nah, just get me the information I need. Really mess him up."

I rubbed the back of my neck. *This is the whole reason I don't want to be Harvey's employee. He doesn't think straight.* A partner? Yes. An employee? No.

"Harvey, I'm not going to beat the shit out of some guy tied to a chair. This isn't like some episode of the Sopranos. I just plan to scare the shit out of him, so he gives me all the info we need before he lawyers up."

"I don't care how you go about it, just find out the truth."

"I will."

Before I walked out the door, I turned back. "By the way, you owe me a hundred bucks."

"For what?"

"Simon checked. All of Junior's screen time at work was spent on porn sites."

"Yeah, a minute after I made the bet, I knew it was a bad one." He pulled out his overstuffed money clip and peeled off a hundred-dollar bill for me. I really needed to introduce Harvey to Bella. She would be attending an Ivy League school, for sure.

Chapter Nineteen

I'd given Renzo one of the gate openers, just like I'd provided one to Irv, so they could both let themselves in and out. So when I heard the gate opening, I knew it was him. Plus the fact that he'd called five minutes ago to tell me he'd be here in five minutes.

I was too tired to get up off the couch. First there had been the grants, then there had been lunch with Lisa and Bella, and then there had been an impromptu training session with two new grant writers. After that I had desperately needed time in the lavender field and the orchard. I pretended that I was determining when things needed to be harvested, even though I already knew the answers. Actually, just touching the flowers in the field and picking a peach here and there provided me with serenity and balance. I hadn't been using my land for that lately.

I giggled as I heard Renzo opening the door. I

hadn't been walking my land for comfort because I hadn't needed to.

"Hi, Beautiful," he greeted me with that smoldering Spanish accent.

Lately I'd been comforted with Renzo's love and affection.

"Hi, Renzo." I smiled at him.

"Did I hear you giggling?" he asked as he tossed his keys on the table by the fence and floodlight switches.

"Yes. You did. I was thinking about how I don't need to go meditate in the orchard as much as I used to now that I have you here to help me relax."

"Is that so?"

I stood up and held out my arms. He circumvented the coffee table, pulled me close, and kissed me. Soon my head was spinning and I was ready to head to the bedroom. Then I heard Renzo's stomach growl. I pulled back.

"Have you eaten?"

"Not since lunch."

"It's nine o'clock," I admonished. "Let me get you some food."

"Sit down, honey. I'll fix myself a sandwich. Go back to watching TV or whatever you were doing."

"It'll take just a few minutes to boil some water and get the ravioli going. I've got some good marinara sauce that I can heat up to go with it. But I don't have any salad fixings."

"Really? Nothing vegetable-like in your refrigerator? Shocking," he teased.

I grabbed his hand and pulled him toward the island. I sat him down and soon had a plate of ravioli in front of him. "Now tell me what you don't want to say."

He finished his bite, then put down his fork. "Am I really that easy to read?"

"Ah-ha. So I'm right!" I turned to pull out the peach ice cream from the fridge. I didn't want him to see the look of concern on my face. I'd really been hoping my guess would be wrong.

"Cariña, turn around and look at me."

"Gotta get the dessert ready." I got down the bowls, and got the spoons out of the drawer. Then I brought the ice cream to the island. "This is homemade," I told him.

"Really? I don't think I've ever had homemade ice cream before."

"Hold on, there's cake to go with it." I kept my eyes down as I turned to get the cake. I knew whatever he had to say I wasn't going to like. "Do you want your cake in the bowl, or a separate plate?"

"The bowl is fine, Millie."

I brought what was left of the cake over to the island.

He dished out the ice cream as I served up the cake. He didn't say anything as we had our first bites of the treat. He was seated on the stool. I stayed on the kitchen side, leaning against the counter. It was the most comfortable position for me right now. As I ate the dessert, I found mine didn't taste nearly as good as it had when I was eating it earlier with Lisa and Bella. I put down my spoon.

"Okay, spill it."

"We got Junior. I had a nice long talk with him today. We got all the information we needed to know which projects we have to retrofit."

I stood up taller. "Well, that's good news."

"Yeah, it is," he sighed. "The bad news is, he insists that he didn't try to break into your house."

"So, he lied."

"That's what I think, but Simon's not so sure. There were no recent fingerprints but yours and mine on the kitchen door, and his foot size was the same size as Juniors. The sheriff is going to need to get a warrant to check to see if he can find boots at his house that match."

"Well, if you're sure, what's bothering you?" I asked.

"Two things. One, your alarm system isn't going to be installed until next week. I hate that, but according to Simon and Roan, Ace Alarm Systems is the best. I'll call Fred tomorrow and see if they can fit you in any earlier."

"Why the rush?"

"I need to go back home to Springfield for a couple of days."

"Why? What's wrong? Is it your grandmother?" I knew that she hadn't been feeling well.

"Yeah. She developed an infection while she was in the hospital getting her hip replaced. Mom's trying to say everything is fine, but Elani sent a group text saying we should all come out for a visit. What I'd really like is for you to come with me."

My stomach lurched, and I thought I might throw up my ice cream. Never had my agoraphobia felt so much like a disability before. I rushed around the island and threw my arms around Renzo. "Honey. Are you all right?"

"I'm doing okay. Jase got one of his SEAL friends to hack into the hospital records. It sounds like Gram is responding pretty well to this third batch of antibiotics, but she's really worn down since it's taken so long to find the right ones. I really think she'll bounce back, but all of us just want to be there to lift her spirits."

"How many of you are planning on being there?"

"I'm not sure yet. Jase is still out of the country."

"But you just said he had his friend find out your grandmother's records."

Renzo gave me a half smile. "Jase has a lot of friends. Personally, I think we're going to end up renting out the nearby La Quinta."

He hugged me tighter. "Renzo, I would do anything to be able to go with you," I mumbled into his shirt.

"I know, baby. I know." He tipped up my chin. "I'm only going to be gone two days at the most."

"Don't cut your visit down because of me. When was the last time you were all together?"

"There was Sandy's wedding. That was last summer. Then about six months ago I saw Jase, Malik, and Angelica in Virginia. That's where I met Bonnie and the kids."

"You deserve some time with your family. Take a week, Renzo. You're still not fully committed to Harvey. Take the time."

"Millie, I'm committed to you."

I looked him in the eye. "We're never going to work out if I'm an anchor hanging around your neck. You'll come to resent me. You've got to promise me you'll take your time."

I watched as he struggled with what I'd said. Then he gave a decisive nod.

"Four days."

"A week," I countered.

"Three days." He countered my counter.

"Honey, I negotiate for a living. If you step foot on my doorstep in less than a week, I'm going to call the cops for harassment."

"You wouldn't."

I squinted at him. "Wanna try me?"

He studied my face. "Five days, my final offer."

"Good enough. Now take me to bed."

Chapter Twenty

"They're going to discharge Gram tomorrow," Renzo told me over the phone. "The guys and I already have the modifications done on her house to handle a wheelchair. She shouldn't need it for long, but Gram has also been talking about knee replacement surgery, so it's best to get ahead of this."

"You're already done? How did you get it done so fast?" I asked.

"Daw and Narong already had men started on it when Gram first went into the hospital. Luckily, the plans were sound so I didn't have to beat the shit out of them for not coming to me."

"Are you always so nice when dealing with your brothers?" I giggled.

"That *is* me being nice. You should have heard them when I told them I was planning on buying some real estate without talking to them. They called me all kinds of fool."

"When was this?"

"A while back. Trust me, if we aren't giving one another shit, then we wouldn't know we loved one another."

I laughed hard.

"I'll try to call you tomorrow," Renzo said, "but Sunday is pretty jam-packed. If you don't hear from me, just know that I love you, okay?"

"I do, honey."

"I'll be back on Tuesday."

"I can't wait to see you. I love you."

"I love you too." he replied.

We hung up and then I went back to my desk. It might be a Saturday, but there was always work to be done. I needed to check up on the Luxton donation. We'd gotten partial payment, and now I wanted to track what we'd done with it, and how we were going to communicate it back to Chuck and his team.

"Where's Lisa?"

I whirled around in my office chair and saw a man I didn't recognize. He was holding a dagger in his hand. His hair was greasy and he had a scraggly beard. He was standing right in front of me.

How had he gotten into my house?

"Who are you?" I squeaked out the question.

"Where's Lisa? It's almost lunch time. This is when she comes over."

"Who are you?" I asked again.

In a flash one of his hands were gripping the left armrest of my chair and he had the dagger pointed under my chin. "Where the fuck is Lisa, you dumb bitch?"

"She's not here," I whispered. "Please don't hurt me."

He pressed the knife closer to my chin, but he didn't break the skin. "I know she's not here. I asked you where the fuck she was."

I gasped in a deep breath. Then I tried to take in another, but it wasn't there. I couldn't breathe. There was no air.

"Don't fucking mess with me. Don't play games. Tell me where Lisa is."

My mouth was open like a goldfish, sucking in and out, but there was no air. I shook my head. I knew the knife was going to cut my throat. I was going to die. This crazy man, who was in my home, was going to kill me.

"Fuck!"

I looked at his face. Spots were blinking in front of him. It was getting darker and darker.

It was so good seeing Mom and Dad. How many times had I sat with them at this kitchen table and told them exactly what was going on in my life and had their full attention? Too many times to count.

It wasn't until I was in my late twenties that I realized how amazing that was, considering the fact they had sixteen other kids in their lives. That was what was so remarkable about Christos and Sharon Drakos. They made each and every one of us feel like we were special. Like we were the center of their universe. I could only pray that I would be half as good of a parent as they were.

"She sounds remarkable," Dad said, as he twirled his bottle of beer.

"She is. The problem is, she doesn't see it. I think if she did, she might be able to leave her house." I picked at the label on my beer.

"I don't know, Honey. Have you done research on agoraphobia?"

"Really, Sharon?" my dad looked at my mom with a raised eyebrow. She blushed.

"Sorry, Renzo. I forgot who I was talking to. Of course you've done your research."

"Yeah, it's not genetic or biological, so that's good," I said. "From what I've read, her case is trauma-related that turned into psychological issues and were exacerbated by her environment in the hospital, then school and all that time living with her aunt and uncle who had the emotional capacity of ice cubes."

"Okay, so you know the cause," my dad said. "What's the cure?"

I grinned. "Like I said, she needs to see herself for who she really is. She has great self-esteem when it comes to her job. Hell, she's a ballbuster."

My mother laughed. I knew she'd like hearing that.

"They say cognitive-behavioral therapy is the best way to go. It would help her to identify and challenge negative thought patterns and confront her fears through exposure. To tell you the truth, she's doing that almost every day. Her scars were big ones. I could see the wonder in her eyes when she realized they really *weren't* the end of the world."

"You helped her see that, didn't you?" Mom asked as she covered my hand.

"A little bit," I admitted.

"I'm proud of you," she whispered.

"There's nothing to be proud of, Mom. You're the one who taught me to not notice that kind of shit, and I also watched you with Zuri and Nia. I just took a page out of your book."

"Renzo's right," my dad said.

"I call bullshit, but whatever." She took the beer out of my dad's hand and took a sip, then handed it back to him as she blushed.

"Now back to her agoraphobia. Are you prepared to marry someone who is housebound for the rest of her life?" Dad asked me.

"Absolutely," I answered. "But she isn't totally housebound. She has her farm. She feels comfortable on her land. Dad, if I thought the best thing for her was to stay just as she was, I would happily live with her there, for the rest of my life. Hell, no matter what, I want the wedding to be in her orchard. But here's the thing, I don't think she's happy living her life just on the farm. I think she wants a bigger life."

"Are you going to try to get her some online counseling?" Mom asked.

"That's where I plan to start," I said. "And, I know that there are a couple of more people in her life who have been pushing for her to come out into the light so to speak." I laughed. "I don't expect anything any time soon. But eventually my girl will get there."

"Like I said." Mom smiled. "She sounds remarkable."

I woke up on my couch. My hands hurt, and I tried to rub my wrists. It was when I tried to move them and I couldn't, that I remembered what had happened.

I tried to sit up, but my feet were tied together the same way my wrists were tied. My hip was on fire.

"So, you're awake. Maybe now you can tell me where Lisa is."

"Who are you?"

"The last time we played that little game, you passed out and I almost slit your throat on accident.

Are you sure you want to play again? Tell me where Lisa is."

"I don't know. She told me she couldn't make it for lunch until Monday."

"Fuck!" He jumped up out of my sofa's matching armchair and threw the knife across the room. It flipped over and over and over, until it stuck into my pearl-gray paint. "What do you mean she won't be here today? She's always over here on Saturday."

"She didn't tell me why she couldn't make it," I whispered.

"It's probably because of that Roan Thatcher guy." He plopped back down into the armchair. "Call her. Make her come over now."

"I told you, she said she was busy."

There was no way I was going to have Lisa come over to my house and be ambushed by this whack job. I needed to start talking to him. Find out how he knew Lisa. See if I could talk some sense in him.

"And I'm telling you, you need to call her."

"It'll probably just go to voicemail."

He looked around the living room, then his eyes rested on my desk in the corner. I knew the instant he spotted my cell phone. He stormed over to it, then marched over to me, grabbed my arm, and pulled me into a sitting position.

"Call her!" he demanded.

"I can't. My hands are tied."

"Do voice command."

"My phone doesn't work that way, I haven't set it up," I lied.

He stalked over to the wall where his knife was, pulled it out of the drywall, and came back to me. I cringed backward, figuring he was going to push it against my throat again. When he grabbed my hands, I didn't know what to think.

With one slice, the twine around my wrists fell away.

"Now call her."

I tried to think of what I could say to her to let her know I was in trouble. To let her know that if she came over to my house, it would be a trap. I pressed her number.

"Hi, this is Lisa. I'm sorry I wasn't able to take your call. If you leave a message, I'll be sure to get right back to you."

He yanked the phone out of my hands and threw it against the armchair he had been sitting in. I watched how it bounced off the back, then fell to the floor. Hopefully it didn't break. I was going to need that phone if I wanted to get out of this.

The man began to pace back and forth. He muttered Lisa's name over and over again. I heard him mention a tattoo many times, and then the name Lonny. The only good thing about his pacing is that he forgot to tie up my hands again. I didn't want to make any movements that might have him notice me.

Instead, I slowly lay back down on the sofa and carefully pulled my knees up into the fetal position.

The twine that was binding my ankles was cutting off my circulation. I needed to get it off. Not just to stop the pain, I also knew I needed to get loose so I could get to my phone. When was this idiot going to get tired?

I worked on the knots at my ankles for hours. All I seemed to accomplish was making my fingers and ankles bleed, but I wasn't giving up. At dusk he stopped pacing. He looked out the big window that looked over the orchard then spun to look at me.

"I'm hungry."

I didn't respond.

"You need to feed me."

I didn't have to do jack shit.

I didn't respond to him.

"Are you listening to me, bitch? You need to feed me." He came over and crouched in front of me. He sniffed. Then grabbed my arm and sniffed my fingers. "Copper. Why are your fingers bleeding?"

He pulled me up straight so I wasn't in the fetal position any longer. He saw my ankles were bleeding and laughed.

"You trying to escape, bitch? Didn't do you any good, did it? I used to sail. I know how to tie knots."

"My feet hurt," I whined.

"I'll cut your bindings so you can cook us something to eat. How does that sound? Then you can call Lisa again. You do anything funny, and you'll regret it."

I could accomplish a lot with a gas stove and free arms and legs.

"What would you like to eat?" I asked sweetly.

Chapter Twenty-One

I'd tried to lure him into the kitchen and pour the pot of boiling water on him, but he never came into it no matter what I did. I'd even pretended to slip and fall, but he just told me to get up, and still hadn't come to help me. So here I was looking at my plate of food, listening to him slurp up his spaghetti.

"This is really good. You're a great cook," the man with no name enthused. "Why aren't you eating?"

I needed to keep up a cooperative appearance. If I could just get my phone and hit the SOS code, then the cops would come. If he realized I'd done it, he knew I didn't know his name. Maybe he wouldn't kill me. But if nothing else, he wouldn't be able to hurt Lisa when she came on Monday, or God forbid Bella if she came with her.

"Aren't you going to eat?"

"I'm not hungry."

"You should eat," he said.

I picked up my fork and stabbed at a meatball, then cut off a small bite and slowly chewed.

"Who was that guy who was hanging around? I followed him to the airport, so I saw him leave. Did he get sick of you? Did you bore him?"

I twirled some pasta around my fork and put it into my mouth.

BAM!

He hit his fist against the table.

"Answer me. Did he get sick of you?"

I swallowed the spaghetti and took a sip of water.

"I guess so."

"I thought so. You're nothing like Lisa. She's perfect. She is so kind. So brave. So outgoing. She helps everyone. She's just lost her way because of Thatcher."

"How do you know Lisa?"

"We were destined to be together. I was her muse."

Ick. It was like he got a doctorate in whack job.

"You must have meant a lot to her."

"I did. I mean, I do. She loves me." He pulled his dagger out of its scabbard. "Do you see this? She designed it for me. Isn't it beautiful? See this jewel? It's the same color as Lisa's eyes."

"It's beautiful," I said politely.

"She's beautiful."

I watched him get lost in thought.

"I need to go to the bathroom." It was true, but I

needed to make a move. I needed to do something to get out of this situation.

He looked at me. "Oh."

He looked down at his plate. "Uhm. Right."

He looked up at me. "Sure."

He stood up. Then he did something awful. He lifted up his shirt and pulled a gun out of the waistband of his jeans. "Head to the bathroom. I'll follow you. You have one minute. If you take any longer I'm coming in. Don't try something funny like hairspray or something like in the movies, cause I got this gun. Got it?"

I kept staring at the gun. I was shaking. I'd never had a gun pointed at me before.

"Got it?"

I just stood there.

"Bitch, do you got it!" he screamed in my face.

"Yes," I whispered. "I got it."

I got up out of my chair and held up my hands, then I turned and went down the hall. We had to pass by my phone that was on the floor. Now that I knew he had a gun, I had to be sneakier. But I had to save Lisa.

I took care of my business as fast as I could. I opened the door so he could see me washing my hands.

"Now it's my turn. Stay right where I can see you."

If I didn't want to grab my phone so bad, I would have asked to be tied up again. I looked down at the ground as I heard him take a whizz into my toilet. I hadn't heard him lift the toilet seat, so I was sure he'd made a mess.

"Come on, let's get you on the sofa. It's time for sleep."

It was now or never.

As he walked behind me, holding the gun, I pretended to trip right before we got to the chair. I fell on my phone and let out a harsh yelp as I landed on my scarred hip. Pain raced up my body, but I ignored it. I had to. I grabbed the cell and shoved it into the front pocket of my jeans. No-Name jerked me up, and it felt like he pulled my arm out of its socket.

"You're the clumsiest bitch I've ever met. Don't think because you're clumsy, that I'm not going to tie you up."

I looked over at the couch and saw the twine set out. It was the same twine I used in my garden; it was heavy-duty and it hurt.

He shoved me face first into the sofa, and the phone fell out of my pocket and clattered to the floor. I looked over my shoulder and I saw his face turn red with rage. I lunged for the phone. He took his gun and crashed it across my face. I was on the floor staring up at him, my face on fire when I saw his fist coming toward me. I turned my head and he hit my ear.

"You fucking bitch. You no-good fucking bitch. I trusted you!" He grabbed my hair and yanked me off the floor. I tried to look for the gun, but I couldn't see anything but his face swimming in front of mine.

"Are you listening to me?"

Again, he hit me, this time in my gut. Meatball coated my tongue. He hit me again and I felt bile dripping down my chin.

"Don't you ever try to fuck with me again. You got it?"

He swung me around by my hair and tossed me on the couch. He made quick work of tying my hands and feet. I wanted to ask him if that was the best he had. I wanted to ask him if he felt like a big man for beating up a woman who was half his size, but I held my tongue. I needed to save Lisa...and Bella.

"I'm sleeping on the couch, bitch. Not you."

He yanked me with my tied wrists and swung me to the floor. Once again, I hit my left side and agony blazed up my side. It was nothing compared to the night of the fire. He was nothing. He was no one. He thought he could deliver pain?

Bring it on!

He kicked me in my hip.

Everything went dark.

~

"He's going to forget the rings. You know he will. You should have picked me," Malik teased.

"Nah, the real problem is he'll get drunk and spill all your secrets during the best man toast. Bonnie will be asking for a divorce an hour after the wedding," Bruno grinned.

"I think the real reason Jase chose Renzo is he needed someone shorter than him so he'd look good in the pictures," Kato laughed.

I looked around the table at my brothers and shook my head. Damn, it was good to be with all of them again. I don't think all ten of us had been together since we'd become adults. Ronnie had been at the police academy for Mom and Dad's thirty-fifth wedding anniversary, and Bruno had been doing something for Homeland Security for Sandy's wedding.

"I'm still amazed that Jase sweet-talked someone into marrying him," Gustavo said. "She should have talked to our sisters first."

"Nah, I have enough to hold over their heads, they won't say a bad word about me." Jase puffed out his chest.

"What about you, Renzo? You've been awfully quiet. Angelica told me that you've been stateside for the last ten months. What's up with that?" Malik asked.

"It's a woman," Jase answered.

"I figured that," Malik rolled his eyes. "Only a woman was going to stop this rolling stone. Tell us about her."

"She's strong. She's one of the bravest women I know. Life has knocked her down, but she's come out fighting. She doesn't see it, but I do. And man, you should see her kick some corporate ass. If you need someone to raise money for your friends at *Doctors Without Borders*, Gustavo, she's your woman."

"Really?" I watched as my little brother, the doctor, sat up and took notice.

"She works for the National Burn Alliance, and she shamed this one company into giving her millions. It was a beautiful sight to behold."

"Are we meeting her at Jase and Bonnie's wedding?" Ronnie asked me.

I grimaced. "I don't think so. She owns a farm. She doesn't leave it. She's working on it. I figure given another year or two she'll be traveling all over the place, but right now she only feels comfortable in her space."

Gustavo frowned. "Agoraphobia?"

I nodded. "Like I said, life's knocked her down. She was badly burned in a fire when she was fourteen. Her parents were killed in that fire. Before that she didn't have any anxiety issues, but now she does."

I looked around the long table where we were all sitting. On every single face I saw similar expressions of compassion. Mom and Dad had done one hell of a job raising their kids.

"Can we visit?" Jase asked. "I know Amber and Lachlan would love visiting a farm. Does she have horses?"

"No animals, but she has apple, pear, and peach trees. Maybe the kids can pick fruit?"

"They'd get a kick out of that. I'd just have to have

a talk with them ahead of time so they don't think they can start having batting practice with the fruit."

Everyone chuckled.

"So, have we given the women enough shopping time?" Kato asked as he looked down at his watch.

"No," Malik shook his head. "Let's go get them while I can still afford next month's mortgage."

Chapter Twenty-Two

The sun was bright the next time I woke up, and it hurt my head. I took a mental inventory and realized everything hurt. My hands, my thigh, my head, my face, my ankles, but most especially my hip.

I heard snoring from down the hall. Apparently, No-Name decided to sleep in one of the bedrooms. When I looked outside again, I could see that the sun was high in the sky. If I had to guess, it was around eleven o'clock in the morning. Maybe even noon.

Everything hurt so bad that I had to fight back the tears. It was like I was back in the Nashville burn unit. There wasn't a chance in hell I was going to let No-Name know he had hurt me.

I rolled just a little, trying to take some of the weight off my hip, but I rolled onto my shoulder. The shoulder that had been dislocated.

"Shit," I yelled out.

I bit my lip to keep my mouth shut.

I stayed as still as I could and listened. There was silence. Dammit, had I awakened him?

I sucked down a deep breath of relief when he snorted and his snoring started up louder than before.

Thank God.

Now I needed to pee. But he was never going to untie me, and did I really want to use the same seat that he'd been whizzing on? I rolled again, and the room began to swim around me as the pain sent shockwaves through my brain.

I tried stretching out my thigh, but it made the nerve pain worse. I could hear myself whimpering.

Keep it together, Millie.

The room was getting darker.

Maybe it was for the best.

〜

"I'm hungry."

Huh? Renzo is hungry?

"You need to feed me."

"Inna minutz," I slurred.

"Not in a minute. Now!"

Renzo pushed his gun into my cheek and I howled with pain.

"Nooooo!"

"I untied you. Get up and fix something. You slept day and night. Now fix me something to eat."

That was when I remembered. "What's your name?"

"Jesus, not this shit again. Bitch, fix me something to eat."

I screamed when he yanked my arm and tried to get me to my feet. I wilted to the ground in front of him.

"What is wrong with you? Get on your feet and cook something."

"Can't." My voice sounded croaky. I hadn't had water in I don't know how long and I was thirsty.

I really couldn't. I'd been on the floor too long. My one arm was useless, and I would only be able to stand if I was leaning against something.

"I should just kill you now."

"Food in the freezer," I mumbled.

"What?"

"Chicken tortillas are in the freezer. Just microwave."

"I don't want some frozen food dinners," he whined.

"I made. Homemade. They're good. Made for Renzo."

He crouched down in front of me, his gun hanging loosely from his fingers. I wanted to lunge for it, but I didn't have the strength.

"It's breakfast time. I want breakfast."

"There are some biscuits I froze for Renzo in the freezer."

"Renzo? Is that the guy who abandoned you? The one who got sick of you?"

I forced back tears and nodded.

"I will never abandon Lisa. I'm her savior."

Oh yeah. Lisa. Must save Lisa.

"I have a bad hip injury. If you could get me a pain pill, I could make eggs if you like."

"Always with the excuses."

My gut churned. His words hit me like little missiles.

The nerve pain hit and I moaned.

"What a diva. Where are your pain pills?"

"My nightstand."

My cleaned-out nightstand with no romance books or sex toys.

He left me and came back with my bottle of pills. "The bottle says one to two, but you look pathetic. Take three."

"I can't. Only two. If I take three, I'll fall asleep and won't be able to fix you breakfast."

"Fine. Two." He poured some into his hand and handed me two. Then he swallowed the rest.

Maybe I would get lucky and he'd O.D.

"I need water," I told him.

"Chew them. Then get your ass to the kitchen. I need breakfast. Plus, I need to shower. I need to look good for Lisa. She'll be here in two hours."

I continued to sit on the floor after I had chewed and swallowed the two pills.

"I said get up!"

I pushed up, using the sofa as leverage. "Can you get me my cane? It's in the hall closet."

He didn't say anything, he just stalked over to the closet and pulled out my cane and handed it to me. Using the cane, I was able to make my way to the kitchen.

"I got out your waffle iron when I was looking around. I want a waffle."

I nodded, trying to push the hair out of my face so I could see what I was doing. I turned on the waffle iron, then pulled out the mix, eggs, and milk and then beat it all together. I soon had a waffle waiting for him.

"There, now that wasn't so hard, was it?"

I shook my head, letting my hair fall over my face so he couldn't see my hatred.

"Bring me syrup."

I turned and brought out some syrup to the dining room table.

"Now go sit against the wall. I'm going to tie you up while I enjoy my breakfast. Then I'm going to freshen up for when Lisa arrives."

This time he tied the bindings even tighter and tied my hands behind my back. I watched him finish his waffle, then head down the hallway. He was whistling "A.B.C". by the Jackson Five of all things. I watched him even dance a little. He was probably going to get urine on the toilet seat in my master bathroom too.

Asshole.

I looked around the room. I could see everything from where I was sitting. My computer, my front door, the stools that butt up against my kitchen island, and the hallway where No-Name had danced. But I didn't see a phone or anything that would help me untie myself.

Think!

I looked at the cabinet under the island. That was my storage for my lavender sachet making supplies. I wasn't to that point yet, but I'd gathered everything I needed, including a sharp knife to cut off the stems.

I heard the shower in my bathroom turn on. I didn't have much time. I heaved over onto my side and rolled over and over until I was in front of the stool that blocked the cabinet. I couldn't just knock it over because I planned to hide the knife. I pushed the stool out of the way, then used my fingernails to pry open the edge of the cabinet. It took at least four tries.

Fuck!

The knife was on the top shelf. Granted the shelves were low, but the top shelf was further than I could reach while I was on my side. I had to get up on my knees. I heard him whistling again. It was a different song. I didn't hear the shower running anymore. He still had to brush his teeth and shave, didn't he?

Please God, be on my side.

I backed up against the island wall and shoved up with my knees. I was now crouching. I inched over to the cabinet and felt along the shelf until I pricked myself with the knife. I was never so happy to get a cut in my life. I felt along it until I found the hilt, then grabbed it. I inched backward and closed the cabinet, then I turned around so that I could move the stool back in place.

He was still whistling. That was a good sign. Now if I could just figure out a way to roll back into place without stabbing myself to death, I would be home free. I duck waddled so that I was facing the island. Using my good shoulder, I nudged the stool back in place. I sighed in relief when it was done.

"Whatcha doing, Millie?" No-Name asked in a sing-song voice.

"Ahhh!"

I fell to the side, therefore I did not fall on the knife.

No-Name yanked me up by my hair so that my nose was almost touching his, my toes barely touching the carpet.

"You've been a very naughty girl."

We heard the distinctive sound of a large motor engine coming up in front of my house.

"Lisa's here!" His face went from monstrous rage to a bright toothpaste smile. He dragged me by my hair back to the wall where I had been. "You stay right there, and don't you move or say a thing. Otherwise, I will hurt you in ways you can't even begin to imagine."

"Millie we're here. We're here."

An excited little girl was at my door, and No-Name

answered it. He grabbed Bella by her arm and swung her inside. He raced over to me and dumped her beside me. His dagger pointed at both of us.

"I hope you have sweet tea," Lisa hollered from outside. "I have brisket sandwiches on fresh-baked bread." I could see her opening the door further. "Millie, I have lots of different desserts for you to choose from," Lisa continued. "Except you don't get the snickerdoodle cookie. Bella called dibs on that."

"What happens if I want the snickerdoodle cookie?" No Name asked.

Lisa spun around and looked at the three of us, then dropped the bags of food and her purse.

"What are you doing?" Lisa asked softly. "Why do you have a knife?"

"Lisa, it's not a knife. It's a dagger." No-Name smiled. "Look. I had it specially made. It has a green stone in the quillon."

Bella whimpered when he lifted the dagger up into the light.

"That's amazing," Lisa whispered.

I struggled to push away from the wall. I wanted to comfort Bella.

"What did you do to Millie?" Lisa all but yelled at No-Name.

"Don't look at me like that, Lisa. You know I'm not that type of man." He sounded hurt. "I would never hurt a woman in that way."

"Then why does she have bruises?"

They kept talking, but all my focus was on Bella who was crying.

"Millie, are you okay?" Lisa asked me.

"Water," I pushed out the word. "Please, water."

She turned to No-Name. "Have you even been giving her water?"

"Don't listen to her," he roared. He pounded across the floor and stopped right in front of Lisa. "You pay attention to *me*!"

Bella started crying harder.

"It's okay, Bella," I whispered. "Pay attention to me," I begged the little girl.

"I'm listening, Rod," I heard Lisa say.

"You better be. Because you sure weren't when I tried to get you to leave this town and come home to Elkton." He lifted the dagger over Lisa's head.

"He's got a knife," Bella whispered. "He's gonna kill Lisa."

"It's okay, baby." I promised her.

I heard Lisa asking Rod what his plan was.

"We're going to stay here awhile. We had a connection. I felt it. You felt it. You'll forget all about that Thatcher man. We'll go somewhere and make a life together."

"I can't do that. I need to take Bella home."

"I thought about that. You're going to call the brat's mother. You're going to say she wants to sleep over for a couple of days. It's going to be some kind of woman's night party."

"A girl's night?"

"That's right. Then we'll have time to get to know one another."

He was definitely a few fries short of a Happy Meal. But Lisa *really* needed to make that phone call. At this point, it was our only hope.

Lisa and I spent the next hours trying to placate crazy and comfort Bella. Rod insisted we weren't to make the call until later in the day. Things fell to shit when Rod thought Lisa had backtalked him and he pistol-whipped her.

Welcome to that unfortunate club.

Bella came unglued, but luckily between Lisa and me, we were able to glue her back together. Now she was out like a light, and it was time for Lisa to win an Academy Award.

"Make the call," Rod said as he shoved her phone at her. Lisa punched in Trenda's number.

"Hi, Trenda, it's me, Lisa."

Lisa paused while Trenda responded.

"Yeah, we're probably going to make another stop. Millie is itching to go to the mall."

Lisa paused again.

"Then maybe we're going to take in a movie. Millie's picked out a doozy. Then she wants the three of us to go out to dinner."

Lisa kept a bright smile on her face for Rod as she paused again.

"After that, she invited us to spend a couple of days

here to have a girl's night or two. Maybe do facials and stuff. Millie's going to show me how to do my make-up."

Lisa kept it up, smiling as if Trenda was excited, when I knew damn well that Trenda smelled a giant-sized rat.

"No, you and Simon don't need to come over here and drop off anything for Bella. We're going to buy her things to wear at the mall."

Then Lisa paused for the longest time. Probably because Trenda was trying to get Simon to come to the phone.

"Oh, you don't need to have Simon come over with Bella's teddy bear. And her uncles don't need to come over to say goodbye. She'll call them when we get back. Millie wants to spoil her because of all the times Bella has come over and kept her company."

Trenda must have said something short, because Lisa started talking again.

"Thanks, Trenda, I knew you'd understand. We're going to have a blast."

She hung up and looked at Rod. "Satisfied?"

"Yes. Now, let's get some ice on your face. You really shouldn't make me punish you."

This guy was.... Let me think. Yeah, Rod was one taco shy of a combination plate.

I should really write these down when we get out of this mess.

Chapter Twenty-Three

Bella hadn't heard the phone call. She was sleeping against me. Her body was hot, and her little baby snores sounded like purring.

God, please say that she's going to make it out of here alive.

She moved and snuggled closer against me, pushing against my scarred thigh. Pain shot up my side. For once I cherished the pain. It meant I was alive and I was giving comfort to this precious child.

I watched as Rod and Lisa went into the kitchen together. I had tuned the two of them out. Lisa was trying to sweet-talk him, keep him calm. It was the right thing to do, but it was making me sick to my stomach.

She came out of the kitchen and crouched down in front of me. "I've got yogurt and water," she whispered and gently shook Bella awake.

"What happened to your face?" she asked Lisa in a fierce little voice.

"I fell down," Lisa lied.

"I don't believe you. He hit you, didn't he?"

Lisa nodded. She put down the yogurts and the waters, then cut our wrist bindings.

"I'm scared," Bella whimpered.

"It's going to be fine. I promise," Lisa said as she held out a container of yogurt to Bella.

"I want water first," she said.

When we were done with our yogurt and water, Lisa tied our hands up again. They were looser, but it didn't matter. Bella started crying. Lisa and I were both trying to console her when we heard the sound of a truck pulling up. I knew it was a truck because of the big engine.

"What the fuck?" Rod said. He sounded angry. "I thought you told them not to come."

There was a knock on the door.

"Hey, Millie, it's me, Simon. Bella's dad."

"It's my daddy," Bella cried out. "It's my daddy!"

"Aw, fuck." Rod shook his head. He turned to Lisa and pointed his dagger at her.

"Get out there. Whatever you do, make him go away."

"He's going to want to see Bella. You can be damn sure of that," she hissed at him.

"I don't care. That's not going to happen. You get rid of him, or I'm going to slit the kid's throat."

Bella let out a high whimper. Lisa had tied my hands in front, so I put my arms over her head, and pulled her close. Rod stalked over to us and pointed his knife toward us. "You shut up. If you make any noise, I'm going to kill you, you got that?"

I turned my body so that Bella was hidden against the wall.

I heard Lisa talking. "This isn't going to work, Rod. You've got to let me untie her, and at least let her hug her dad. It's the only way he'll go away."

"She's a kid, she'll give it all away," Rod said.

"No, she won't. She's too smart for that."

"Millie? Lisa? Open the door." Simon knocked louder.

"Okay, do it." Rod said.

Rod yanked my hair, so I fell back on the floor. He bent over Bella and me until his nose was practically touching Bella's. "Do you see this knife? When you're out on the porch with Lisa, you hug your dad and make him go away, otherwise I will stick this dagger in Millie's eye. Do you understand me, little girl?"

Lisa ran over to Rod and shoved him away from Bella. "Scaring her won't help. She'll start crying and then she won't be able to fool her dad."

He looked at Lisa, then pushed his finger into her cheek and she gasped. "It's probably better that she answers the door anyway. You look like shit, and it will make him suspicious."

Simon knocked again.

Rod bent down and pulled Bella out of my arms, then he used his dagger to cut Bella out of her bindings. Lisa helped her to stand up.

"My feet don't work," she whispered to me and Lisa.

"You've got to try. I know you've been sitting too long. But lovebug, you've got to try," Lisa coaxed her desperately. Lisa walked with her really quick. When Bella's legs seemed to be working okay Lisa sent her toward the door.

As soon as Bella started to open the door my entire body shuddered with relief. At least Bella wouldn't die.

"Hi, Daddy," Bella said.

"Hi, Sweetheart," he replied.

Rod pulled me up by my hair.

Again.

Then pointed the dagger at my throat.

Lisa shoved at his arm holding the dagger and he teetered backward.

Rod righted himself and let go of me. Then he looked at Lisa. "Bitch!" His expression was maniacal. He lifted the dagger.

I heard the roar of an explosion.

Then another one.

Red. Bursts and streamers of red.

Like a fire, licking and dripping over me.

I fell to the ground and covered my head and started to roll.

Someone was screaming. "Get him off me! Get him off me! Get him off me!"

Then somebody touched me. I scuttled backward, trying to get away. Trying to get to the back door, but I couldn't find it. I couldn't see. I couldn't breathe.

I saw rivulets of red dripping down my arm. Fire. Fire was dripping on me.

"Millie."

The hands became firmer.

I hit my head on a wall. I needed to crawl to the door. I had to escape.

I tried going sideways.

"Millie, listen to me. You're safe."

"Fire," I sobbed.

"There's no fire. I'm Aiden O'Malley. I'm a medic. Let me help you."

My body felt like it was on fire. There was so much pain.

Wait. There was something else. Somebody else. I needed to remember. Not Mom and Dad.

"Bella?"

"She's safe," the man said.

"Lisa?"

"She's safe too."

I sighed.

The world faded away.

~

Sunday night had been a blast with my brothers, so I'd gotten up late on Monday. I called Millie but got her voicemail, then went with everyone over to Gram's. It was when Dad was manning the barbeque, and I was in the kitchen helping Mom peeling potatoes for her potato salad, that I realized I hadn't heard back from her. Not even a text.

I went to the front of the house and started walking. I passed Amadi who was smoking an e-cigarette and looking at his phone.

"Those things will kill you," I told him.

"We're all going to die anyway." He waved back at me.

I gave him a chin tilt and made a note to sic our sister Polly on him. Obviously, she didn't know about this, otherwise he wouldn't be smoking.

When I was in front of the Freeman's house, I called Millie again and got her voicemail again.

"Millie, I'm worried about you, Cariña. Can you please call me and let me know you're all right?"

I then texted her the same thing.

I remembered her out near the blackberry bushes. I should have called her yesterday.

Dammit!

I called Simon. I needed him to go check on her.

Another fucking voicemail!

I called Roan.

Another fucking voicemail!

Who in the hell in Jasper Creek was answering their phone?

I called Nash Rivers' cell phone.

The fucker went straight to voicemail and I sure as hell wasn't going to call the sheriff's department.

I called the Down Home Diner.

"Down Home. We don't take reservations."

"Where's Little Grandma? Why isn't she answering the phone?" I demanded to know.

"She's at the hospital."

That stopped me in my tracks. "Who's this? What's wrong with her? What hospital?"

"Who's this?" the woman asked.

"I'm Renzo Drakos. Who's this?" I asked again.

"Oh Renzo, hasn't somebody called you?"

An icy shiver ran down my back. A premonition. "Is this about Millie?"

"Yes. She's in Sevierville at the medical center."

"Why?" I could hardly speak.

"Honey, I don't know all the reasons. Nobody's called me back. Mama drove Little Grandma, and I'm holding down the fort. I just know that there was a shootout at her house a couple of hours ago—"

"A shootout!"

"She's not shot!" Lettie yelled over the phone. "I said that wrong. She's not been shot. She was held hostage for awhile is all. She's been injured. Somebody needs to call me."

I hung up the phone. Nobody was answering the

phone to give me answers. I wouldn't get answers from the hospital. I ran back to Gram's house as fast as I could, shouting for Jase and Bruno. One of them would be able to get me answers.

By the time I got to the front door, both of them were there.

"What?" Jase asked.

Bruno didn't repeat the question, he just waited for me to tell him.

"There was a shootout at Millie's today. According to one of the townfolk, she wasn't shot, but she's in the hospital in Sevierville. I need answers, and I need to get there ten minutes ago."

They looked at one another.

"I'll get him transport," Bruno said.

"I'll get you answers. Come with me," Jase turned around and went into the living room where Grandma Maureen had been holding court. "Gram, can we use one of the upstairs bedrooms? We need to make some calls."

"Of course you can. Is there anything I should worry about? Bonnie? The twins?"

"Nope, everything's fine," Jase assured Gram. He tilted his head at me, but I was already heading upstairs for the blue guestroom.

When he came in and closed the door, his phone was ringing. "Gideon? I need some help for my brother. The woman he loves was in the middle of a shootout during a hostage situation at her home today.

He's here with me in Springfield, and this happened in Jasper Creek, Tennessee. I'm sure Simon's all over it, but he's not picking up. Right?" He looked at me for verification, and I nodded.

"What's her full name?" Jase asked me.

"Millie Jane Randolph. This would have taken place at Randolph Farm sometime today. All I know is she's at a hospital in Sevierville, but not for a GSW."

Jase had his phone on speaker by that point so Gideon was listening.

"Give me five, maybe ten minutes and I'll let you know what's going on."

The door opened and Bruno came in. "There's a private plane heading for Mcghee Tyson Airport out of Springfield-Branson in thirty minutes. I put a call into air traffic control to make it an hour. You can make that flight."

"And the people on this private plane are going to let me on their plane why?" I asked.

"They're an up-and-coming country band. They are not going to let you go with them per se. They *will* let Angelica Drakos, Emmy Award-winning actress, catch a ride with them. You're her bodyguard, right?"

I shook my head in disbelief.

"You two are nuts. I never would have been cut out as a Navy SEAL or an agent for Homeland Security, would I?"

Jase laughed. "No, you wouldn't have been."

His phone rang. He put it on speaker.

"Can I assume I'm on speaker?" Gideon asked.

"Yes," Bruno, Jase and I said at the same time.

"Good. Millie Jane Randolph was admitted to LeConte Medical Center in Sevierville an hour and thirty-five minutes ago. Her vitals are stable, but she's in a great deal of pain. Her arm has been ripped out of its socket, she's been beaten and has severe nerve pain from her old burn scars. They're giving her IV pain meds and keeping her sedated. She doesn't need surgery, there is no permanent damage."

"What happened?" I demanded to know.

The bedroom door opened and Angelica came in. "Let's go, big brother. We need to make good time to the airport to make our flight, which shouldn't be a problem. I rented a GTO for this trip and I'm driving."

"What happened," I asked Gideon again.

"Give me your phone number, I'll text you a report."

I gave him my phone number and followed Angelica.

Chapter Twenty-Four

I took a deep breath, trying to orient myself before opening my eyes. I'd woken up a couple of times before, but those times had been brief and really fuzzy. Now my mind felt pretty clear and I felt rested. Just anxious. Not scared. Anxious.

The reason I wasn't scared was because of the man sitting in the chair beside my bed. I turned my head and opened my eyes so I could see him. It was the middle of the night, so there was only a low hum of electronics, and a faint light over my hospital bed. I heard a man and a woman talking outside my door. Not close by, but not far away, either.

I wondered how long I'd been here in the hospital. I took inventory of myself. I realized my arm was in some sort of contraption that had it pressed up against my chest so I couldn't move it. Immobilized, that was the word.

Yeah, from where that whack job had pulled my arm out of the socket.

I could see clearly out of both eyes, so that meant the swelling on my left eye had gone away. That meant I'd probably been unconscious for what? Three days? And all that time, I had Renzo beside me. Renzo talking to me. Renzo reassuring me that he would take me back to my home as soon as possible.

He obviously had been talking to me about a lot more than just taking me home. Somehow, I knew exactly what had gone down with Rod. How Roan, Simon, Drake, and Aiden had all come in loaded for bear. How Roan and Simon had killed Rod.

Hell, I even knew every aspect of how my new alarm system worked, and the fact that Bella wanted me to make her more peach ice cream. Yep, my man had been very talkative while I'd been sleeping. No wonder he was sprawled out in that chair next to me.

"Renzo?" I whispered.

If he didn't wake up, I'd just let him sleep. But if he did wake up, I was going to tell him to go home and sleep in a comfortable bed.

His deep brown eyes opened and he looked at me. He bent forward and coasted his fingers along the side of my jaw. I moved my hand so I could hold his, then I realized I had an IV stuck in it.

"Are you really awake this time, or are you messing with my mind again?" Renzo gently teased me.

"I'm not the 'messing with your mind' kind of gal. I don't believe in it."

"So, you're awake." He got up out of the chair and bent down and kissed my forehead, the tip of my nose, and then brushed the gentlest of kisses along my lips. He stopped too soon as far as I was concerned.

"Come back, honey. I'm not done with you," I complained.

"We have things to discuss."

"No. You've done enough talking. I'm surprised you don't have laryngitis with all the talking you've done."

"You heard that?"

"I must have. I even know that my alarm system will switch to a battery back-up during a power outage, and since it's on wi-fi, it will switch to cellular during the outage as well. Since I didn't know that before, I'm figuring you've been telling me this."

Renzo gave me a rueful grin. "Yeah, I did tell you that. Do you also remember me saying that as soon as you woke up, I was going to break you out of here? That I would do it in the dead of night with a blanket over your head so you didn't have to deal with anyone here at the hospital?"

I frowned. "I don't remember that part. But I do remember you being grumpy with two nice nurses."

"That's because there were two of them. Remember how you said you always felt like a piece of meat at the burn unit, and part of that was because so many people filled your room all at the same time. I told them that they could come in one at a time, or not at all."

"Renzo, honey, they're just doing their jobs."

Where had that come from? I'd never, ever, thought that way before about nurses.

I waited for the start of my panic attack. I was here in a hospital, talking about nurses coming in to poke and prod at me. Why wasn't I hyperventilating?

"Millie? What are you thinking? You went away for a minute."

"I'm waiting for my panic attack to start."

He gave me a curious look, then looked at the bed and lowered the rail. He carefully scooped me up and positioned me over to the side, then he climbed in. I noticed he didn't have his shoes on. It was a really tight fit until he then picked me back up and arranged it so I was nestled mostly on top of him.

I relaxed.

"So, you heard what I had to say, huh?"

I nodded.

"Now I want you to talk. I want you to tell me everything."

"I think you know everything. I'm assuming they kept me sedated until my nerve pain calmed down?"

He turned my chin so I was looking up at him. "No, not that stuff. About you being held hostage. I want to know everything."

"It wasn't bad," I lied.

"Millie." My name came out of his mouth as a warning grumble. "Tell me," he commanded.

"He didn't hurt me, hurt me. If that's what you're worried about." I said the last part with my face smashed into his shirt because I couldn't look at him without turning red.

"Okay. He didn't rape you. I get that. But he beat you pretty badly. He had you for two days. I want you to tell me everything that happened. I want you to release that poison and not let it fester. Can you do that for me?"

I tilted my head and looked at him. "Renzo, of course I'll tell you."

And I did.

~

I walked with Nash Rivers into Millie's house. The crime scene tape had been taken down.

"I know a cleaning company that can come in and make it seem brand new. I'll give you their card," Nash said.

"I'd appreciate it."

"God, Renzo. It guts me to think that Millie had to be traumatized yet again. Hasn't that woman been through enough in her life?"

I walked over to the kitchen island and pulled the stool away from where it stood in front of a cabinet.

"What are you doing?"

"I'm going to tell you a story. Millie wasn't a victim. She was a fucking fighter, Nash. My woman was fighting this motherfucker every chance she got. Even the day Lisa and Bella were due to come over, she was trying to get her hands on a weapon. And this was with her hands tied behind her back and her ankles tied together."

"What are you talking about?"

I opened the cabinet and showed him what she had done. He whistled. "Smart and gutsy."

"She constantly amazes me," I nodded in agreement.

"How is she with you? I know she's allowing you and a couple of others in her house now, do you think she'll backslide?"

I thought about her not having a panic attack in the hospital. "I'm not sure, Nash. Anything's possible."

"Are you going to stick with her?"

I frowned. It was a really personal question, and I didn't really know this man. Nash must have gotten my vibe because he grinned.

"I'm too old to have gone to school with Millie and too young to have gone to school with her parents. But I was born and raised here in Jasper Creek. Millie Randolph is one of my people. You're an outsider. I'm taking an interest. So I'll ask you again. Are you sticking?"

"What do you mean by taking an interest? Are you saying you're interested in Millie?"

"And if I said I was?"

"Then I'd tell you that you were barking up the wrong tree, because Millie is taken. I might not have a ring on her finger yet, but it's just because I haven't had the time to go shopping yet. There have been a few things that have kept me busy."

Nash grinned. "Good to know."

"How are things going with Junior?"

"It was like you thought. He's doing everything he can to work a plea deal with the DA. If someone needed information from him, they would have been real smart to have gotten that info before he was taken into police custody and demanded a lawyer."

"Hmm. If I'm ever in that situation, I'll remember to do that." I walked over to Millie's fridge to see if there was something to drink. "Wanna bottle of soda, water, or beer?" I asked Nash.

"Dr. Pepper if she has it."

I handed him one, then I took a beer and leaned against the kitchen island and looked at Nash. "How confident does Junior seem that he can work a deal?" I asked.

"Too damned confident to my liking," Nash said as he took a swig of his soda. "But he's using Stanley Rhoades as his lawyer. So of course, I found out that he's being his normal stupid self and doesn't really have shit."

"I'm not tracking," I told Nash.

"Stanley should have been disbarred years ago. He

drinks down at the Whispering Creek Tavern Monday through Saturday and talks far too much. Junior is thinking he can work a deal because he knows that Knoxville Plumbing has been selling to their contractors off the books so that they can avoid paying state sales tax."

"First." I held up my index finger. "Thanks for letting me know where to find a really good attorney. I'll just head on over to the Whispering Creek. Second. Is Junior out of his mind? Like that's a bargaining chip."

Nash snorted. "I know, right?"

"Does this drunk lawyer think he can work a deal with this?"

"Actually, Stanley might be a drunk, but he's a smart, greedy lawyer. So no, I doubt he thinks this will work. He's just stringing Junior along so he gets more billable hours."

"Couldn't happen to a nicer guy."

"Right?" Nash laughed.

We smiled at one another as we finished our drinks.

Chapter Twenty-Five

The boxes from Amazon were waiting on my doorstep when Renzo drove me home. I was so relieved.

"Did you order something?" he asked.

"Yeah. I'm hoping you'll take pity on me and be willing to do a little handyman work."

"Sure," he said as he opened my door and helped me out of his truck.

"I'm going to have to get some running boards," he muttered.

"What are those?"

"They're something you can step on to get in and out of the truck."

"I know what you're doing, Mr. Drakos. You're thinking if you get running boards you'll tempt me to go driving with you more often."

After he had me on solid ground, he put his arms around me. "We're taking baby steps Millie. I don't give a shit if that was the last trip you ever take off this piece of land. I'm with you for the long haul. But remember, you didn't have a panic attack at a hospital of all places. Therefore, I'm getting some running boards." He kissed the tip of my nose.

I shrugged. "Suit yourself."

We walked up the porch steps and he picked up the box and unlocked the door. When we got settled, he asked me what was in the boxes.

"Why don't you open them up?"

When he did, he laughed. "Millie, a cleaning crew has been through this entire house. Not just the living room where Rod died, but your kitchen, all bedrooms and bathrooms, every room of your house. They are professionals. Trust me, they charged like professionals. You do not need to replace the toilet seats."

"Yes, I do. And you better be showing me those receipts so I can reimburse you."

"No. I'm not letting you reimburse me."

"Look, if you want to talk about things like the long haul, then we might as well be up front about money. I own this farm and this house outright. There's no mortgage, no nothing. My aunt and uncle might not be all touchy-feely. But Uncle Phil is a big-time insurance executive and Aunt Marge is a financial planner. Uncle Phil made sure that both Mom and Dad and this property was insured to the fullest. So, I was covered when they died. Then Aunt Marge made sure that my money was managed well. And I mean, *well*."

"So that's why Irv gets most of the profits from the orchards, huh?"

"Yep. He does most of the work, so it's only fair. He won't take one hundred percent. Trust me, I've tried. But I'm giving him the most I can get him to take."

I walked over to him and put my one good arm around his neck. "So, give me the receipts, I'll pay for the cleaning. However, I will *not* pay for you installing new toilet seats."

He threw back his head and laughed.

"You've got it Cariña."

How could I be this tired after spending almost three days asleep, and then another two days just resting?

"Millie, it looks like you're done with this, right?"

I looked down at the plate in my lap. I'd only eaten one quarter of the grilled cheese sandwich and three spoonful's of tomato soup.

"I'm sorry I couldn't eat more, Renzo."

"I picked up some desserts from Down Home. Maybe I can tempt you with those. What do you think?"

He took the plate out of my hand and was looking

down at me with such a hopeful smile. I didn't want to disappoint him. "I think—" I couldn't stop my yawn.

"I think your yawn answers my question. Let's get you into bed."

"Seriously, I'm not that tired," I protested.

"You're lying. Let's get you settled. If you wake up in the middle of the night, you can have any one of the different treats that Little Grandma sent over. But in the meantime, I think you need to rest."

I shook my head. "I want a bath first. I feel grungy. The shower in the hospital hardly had any pressure at all."

Renzo put the plate down on the coffee table and sat down next to me. He picked up my good hand and brought it to his cheek. "Are you sure you're up for a bath? You look pretty beat."

"I'm sure. But are you sure they scrubbed the tub? I don't think he used it, but I just want to be safe."

"If you want a bath, I'll scrub the tub again before I let one of your dainty toes touch the water. How's that?"

"Have I told you lately how handsome you are?"

Renzo frowned. "Are you feeling woozy? Were two pain pills too many? Maybe you shouldn't take a bath."

I rubbed my thumb across his bottom lip. "No, I'm not woozy. It's just when you take care of me and are protective of me, it makes me feel wonderful inside. I haven't felt so safe since my parents died. That's why I said you were beautiful. Because you are. Inside and out."

"You deserve a long, leisurely kiss for what you just said," Renzo said as he backed his head away from my hand. "But what you're going to get is a bath with a bath bomb and then you're going to be carried to bed."

"By a beautiful man?"

I watched as Renzo blushed.

It was awesome.

"You are full of sass tonight, aren't you?"

I smiled. "Go start my bath, minion." I waved him away, and we both laughed. Soon I heard the water being run in the master bathroom. I leaned against the back of the sofa and tried to keep my eyes open.

"Baby, wake up. Your bath is ready," Renzo whispered as he crouched beside the sofa.

"That's good."

He bent and I knew he was going to carry me, but I wanted to walk. I needed to wake up a bit before getting undressed and soaking in the tub. I waved him away and got up from the couch. "See, I can walk," I smirked.

"Never doubted it," he replied.

"You so did doubt it, don't lie to me," I huffed out a giggle.

He followed me down the hallway, then on into the bathroom. I turned to him. "I can take it from here."

He raised an eyebrow. "You can?"

"Of course I can."

"Okay. Show me."

I reached down to start unbuttoning my jeans, but with only one hand it was impossible. I needed to get out of the shoulder strap. I looked it over, but couldn't seem to find where it hooked on, and I sure as hell couldn't remember how they put it on me at the hospital.

I turned to the mirror to check it out. It looked like there were some Velcro fastenings at the shoulder and the waist. I started with the shoulder. I yanked it loose and let out a cry as my arm lost its support.

"Now will you let me help, you stubborn woman?"

I nodded.

Renzo had me stripped in no time, as he showed me how to hold my injured arm. I felt uncomfortable being naked in the stark light of the bathroom, with him being fully clothed. Not only did I have the burn scars, now there were big splotches of bruising on my ribs, stomach, and hip. I turned away from him, trying to hide the ugly parts of my body.

"Millie, I thought we were past that," he whispered.

"It's not just my scars. It's everything," I whispered back. "And I'm the only one naked," I finally admitted.

"If you would invite me to take a bath with you, we can take care of the naked alone issue in one fell swoop."

His eyes were twinkling. I couldn't help but smile back. I looked over at the garden tub that had been installed in my bathroom. I remember thinking, when I first moved in, that it was big enough to have a pool party in. I looked back up at Renzo.

"Renzo, would you like to take a bath with me?" I made my tone as formal as possible.

He chuckled. "Why, yes, ma'am, I would love to partake in a bath with you."

"Then get naked."

He was stripped down in less than thirty seconds. He brushed another light kiss across my lips. "Now can I pick you up?"

"Why?"

"I've watched you favoring your leg and hip. I want to help you into the tub."

Was there anything the man didn't notice?

"Thanks, honey. I'd appreciate your help."

When he started putting me into the bathtub, I realized he had used one of my dragon bath bombs. They were my favorites. And they left me with glitter on my body. After he got me in the tub, he climbed in behind me. I managed not to giggle at the idea of him being all glittery at a construction site tomorrow.

Chapter Twenty-Six

It wasn't until I started using the loofah on Millie that I realized I was surrounded by sparkles in the water.

Fuck!

Not only was I going to end up smelling like strawberries and cream, but I was also going to be covered in glitter when I got out of the tub. Millie made a funny sound.

"Did you say something, Cariña?"

She shook her head.

She made another funny little sound. Almost like a whimper.

This time I recognized the sound for what it was. Suppressed laughter. "You knew I was going to be covered in glitter, didn't you?" I growled.

"Maybe."

I continued to wash her with the loofah and shook my head. It was good to see Millie smiling and laughing. Even if it was at my expense. After being held hostage, I was so impressed that she was doing so well.

Millie started to move in the bathtub, which would normally be just fine, but she was moving her injured arm.

"Millie, you need to leave it in place to let it heal. Just another few days, baby."

"I know. I know." She put her hand back up to rest under her chin. I finished washing her tummy with the loofah when I stopped.

"Millie, you don't use the loofah on your scars, do you?"

She shook her head. "Even that is too rough. I use my fingers."

"Gotcha." I poured some bath soap into my hand and slicked it over her hips and thighs. This time when she made a sound, it wasn't suppressed laughter. It was the kind of moan that I was intimately familiar with from our time together in her bed.

"Renzo, I don't feel grungy anymore. I'm ready for bed," she whispered. It almost sounded like she was slurring her words. Shit, she was too tired to eat, and now I was copping a feel with her in the tub. I was so out of line.

"Hold on, Cariña. Let me get out of the tub first, then I'll get you out. All of your clothes, linens, pillows, and towels have all been washed twice and put back away. The down comforters were dry-cleaned.

Again, that was part of the service. So, when I tuck you into bed, it will be on clean everything."

"So good. I hope you tipped them," she mumbled. I could barely hear her words as I stepped out of the tub and then picked her up and got her to her feet. She was woozy, so I put her good hand on my shoulder.

"Keep your hand there while I get us both dried off. You got it?"

She nodded.

I got us dried off in record time, then I picked her up and sat her butt down on the vanity. "Stay there. I'll be back with something for you to wear to bed."

I found a cherry blossom tank top with matching pajama shorts and went back in to find her slouched against the mirror with her eyes closed. I knew she wasn't asleep because she still had her hand resting on her shoulder to keep her arm supported.

"Millie. Let me help you get dressed, okay?"

Her eyes remained closed as she nodded. I got the shorts on her first. "Millie, I need your help with the tank top. Let me guide this hand, okay?"

She opened her eyes and slowly released her shoulder. I guided one hand through one sleeve of the tank, then another hand through the other, then pulled it down over her tummy. I propped her back up against the mirror, then picked up the brace and put it back on her.

"Renzo, not so tight."

"Okay." I loosened it a little. Then I picked her up

and put her to bed and crawled in beside her. It was going to be a long and uncomfortable night. I had never been so scared as when I'd found out Millie was in the hospital. Even when I found out her injuries weren't life-threatening, I still was scared. The idea that some man had been in her home for two days, terrorizing her and brutalizing her had been hell for me.

It wasn't until I climbed into that hospital bed two days ago and she told me what she had done, that I felt some relief. She'd never given in. She'd never lost faith. My Millie was a fighter. And I wanted to make love to her more than I wanted my next breath.

"Renzo?"

"Yeah, Cariña?"

"You're barely even holding me, what's the deal?"

"I am holding you," I disagreed. I had my arms settled around her, and her head was lying on my chest.

"Yes, but you usually hold on tighter. Our legs are usually tangled together. You usually have one of your hands on my ass..."

I tugged her closer. Tighter.

"Okay, you're right, this isn't like normal. But Millie, you're fragile right now," I said as I feathered my fingers down her back.

Hell, I'm fragile too, just thinking about what could have happened.

"The one thing I'm not is fragile. Didn't you hear

me in the hospital the other day? I kicked whack-job butt. Or I tried to."

"Yeah, baby, I heard. I've already been bragging about that to my entire family. Mom and Dad want to come out for a visit."

She lifted her head and stared down at me.

"You're kidding, right?"

"I'm not. But I told them that we'd talk about it after Jase and Bonnie's wedding."

She lowered her head back onto my chest. "Good."

I didn't tease her about coming to the wedding this time. I'd wait until she was back to her full fighting strength.

"I still want you to hold me—" She yawned. "Tighter."

I kissed the top of her head. "I will. Now go to sleep."

I woke up to butterfly kisses.

Renzo.

I tried to move my head to follow him, but I realized he was holding me in place. I was at his mercy. So many soft kisses on my mouth, until he finally relented and rested on my lips and I sighed.

I tasted his breath—mint and Renzo. He licked my bottom lip and I opened further. His taste was warm and comforting as his tongue slid sensuously against mine. This wasn't just passion, this felt like a gift. It was a feeling of safety, of love, of acceptance and homecoming. I tried to wrap my arms around his neck, and that was when I remembered I was in a brace. I broke away from his kiss and huffed with annoyance.

"What, Cariña?"

"This brace. It's in my way."

He looked down at me and laughed. "Millie, I saw all of your romance books in your nightstand. I took a picture of them, and I read a couple."

"You did what?" I squawked.

"I read some. It seems to me that we have a lot of things left to explore. One of those things I was planning on getting to was bondage," he whispered.

My heart stopped. It literally stopped. I knew which book he'd read.

Oh. My. God.

"Your brace is like training wheels for bondage. This is perfect, don't you think?"

I couldn't get out a word, so I nodded.

Renzo got out of bed and then pulled off all of the covers so that I was just lying on the top sheet, like some kind of sacrifice. It wasn't even light out yet.

"What time is it?"

"If you're asking questions like that, then I haven't captured your full attention. Let's see what I can do to remedy that."

He was right. How could I be wondering about the time when I had his body to adore? I loved his chest and shoulders, but I especially loved his hard abs. He didn't have a six-pack like on my book covers. Nope. Just one hard gut that looked like a man, along with that trail of hair that led down to something fantastic underneath his sweatpants.

"Millie?"

"Huh?"

"Okay, now you're paying *too* much attention to me, and not listening to what I'm saying."

"Sorry."

He sauntered around to the end of the bed, then put a knee on it. He looked huge as he made his way toward me. In one swift move he had my pajama shorts off.

"You slay me. The things I want to do to you," Renzo said as he stared down at me. He reached out and swirled his finger around my belly button. I arched up. Then both of his hands skimmed down each hip, then around so that he was on the inside of my thighs, parting my legs. "Are you with me, Millie?"

"Yes." The word was a low hiss.

He chuckled as he traced the outer lips of my sex. Warm waves of energy blasted through me. Thank God I was already lying down. I reached out with my one good hand and grabbed at him.

"Uh-uh. Put your hand back. You don't get to move your hands. That's part of our play tonight. You're my princess, and I'm the pirate who's captured you. Remember?"

Oh shit, he really, really, really had read that book.

I nodded.

He spread my knees outward, then lifted my feet so that they rested on his shoulders.

"Beautiful. You're so wet for me. I love that." He bent his head towards my core, then his tongue licked through my folds.

I tried to keep my eyes open, I wanted to watch him. But it was impossible. I felt him thrust two fingers inside me. He brushed his tongue around his fingers as they pushed in and out of my core. I felt myself spiraling upwards.

I opened my eyes and looked down at him.

"God, please touch my clit," I demanded.

Renzo chuckled. "First I want my honey."

I felt my sex pulse, and I knew that he got his wish as I felt myself get even wetter.

"Please, Renzo, I need..."

"I know what you need."

He twisted and spread his fingers, finding a spot inside me that send waves of sensations thundering through me, keeping me poised on the tip of a pin.

"Now, Renzo. Now!"

He took my swollen clit between his lips and sucked hard and I shot off into oblivion.

I opened the door to the smell of something heavenly. I wasn't quite sure what it was, but I couldn't wait to find out. Millie was a fantastic cook.

"Hi, Renzo," she called out from the kitchen. "Are the guys still giving you a hard time for being glittery?"

"Yep. It's been a week and they still are. Why didn't you tell me that that stuff hadn't all been washed off in the shower?"

"Because it was more fun watching you leave the house with glitter," she answered with a smile.

I went into the kitchen to steal a kiss and a cookie.

"What are you making?"

"It's a new recipe. Stuffed green peppers. I'm thinking with beef and cashews, that I can tolerate the peppers and therefore I will have eaten a vegetable."

I chuckled.

"I'm going to go wash up, then I'll come set the table."

"Sounds good."

I made it through the shower in record time and was back out to see Millie in less than fifteen minutes. She'd already set the table and had everything ready for us to eat.

"Cariña, I would have taken care of this, you could have waited."

"It wasn't a problem. Anyway, I wanted to talk to you about some things."

I picked up the beer she had put at my place setting and took a sip. "Okay, shoot."

"Eat first, then we'll talk."

"How about if I take a couple of bites and then we talk while we're eating?" I suggested.

She nodded.

I cut into the stuffed pepper and then took my first bite. It was a mouthful of flavor country. "This is great."

She gave me a funny look. "Yeah, it doesn't even taste like a vegetable."

I shook my head at her. "Baby, I'm so glad the doc tests your blood regularly; with the way you don't eat vegetables and pound sugar, I worry about you."

"It's nice of you to worry." She took another bite and smiled.

I was halfway through my meal before I asked her what she wanted to talk about.

"I think I'm ready," she said. "What do you think? Don't you think it's time? Do you think I can handle it?"

Does she know about the ring I have hidden in the gun safe?

"Well okay," I said slowly. If she wanted to get married now, we could swing it. I would have liked to have waited until after Jase's wedding.

"So, you agree. You think I'm ready, too?"

I frowned. "Cariña, I'm not sure I know what you're talking about."

"I'm talking about leaving the house. Leaving the farm."

I put down my fork and stared at her. I'd been so worried that after being held hostage, her agoraphobia would be worse, but then she didn't have the panic attack at the hospital, so that gave me hope. And now this.

"Millie, I'll back any play you want to make. I'm beside you or behind you, whatever you need, whenever you need it."

She picked up her water glass and her hand trembled, so she set it back down again.

"I'm scared," she whispered. "But I don't care if I am scared. I was scared the entire time that dick was in my house, and I handled things anyway. I can do this. I *want* to do this. I want to have a normal life."

"I want whatever you want, Millie. I'm here for you," I whispered.

She pushed her hand across the dining table toward me and I grabbed it.

"I don't want to just go to someone's house. What I really want to do is go to the same table that Mom, Dad and I always sat at, at Down Home, but I'm positive I'll have a meltdown with all of those people. But that's where I want to go."

I squeezed her hand and thought.

"I betcha Little Grandma would close down the diner for you to have meal at that table."

"No! I don't want her to lose business."

"How about if it was after the diner closes?"

"But then the staff would have to stay late. That's a lot to ask for."

I choked on my own saliva. "You're kidding, right? Little Grandma would shut down the diner for the entire week and pay her employees for that week if she thought you might possibly show up. She would do anything for you."

I watched her violet eyes consider what I'd said.

"I'm going to call her."

"I think that's a fantastic idea."

It took two weeks for Little Grandma to set things up. Not because she wasn't willing to close down the restaurant. Heck, the moment I called and told her my idea, she was ready to kick out all of the customers right then and there. Nope, it was trying to coordinate with everybody's schedules.

I wanted Lisa and Bella there for sure. I also wanted Simon, Roan, Drake Avery and Aiden O'Malley who had all helped in rescuing us. I wanted Little Grandma and her family and I had to have Renzo. The problem was that Drake and Aiden were both Navy SEALs who lived in California. We were just lucky that day that they were in town. They were away at work or on missions or something at the moment, so they couldn't come.

Then Simon was working on a case, and he couldn't come the next weekend, so we had to wait two weeks until we could get the people we wanted. We had Lisa and Roan coming. Simon, Bella and Trenda were all coming. Me and Renzo, then Little Grandma, her daughter, granddaughter, and great-granddaughter. It was going to take place an hour after closing on Sunday.

When it got to the point where we were fixing to leave my house, my palms were sweaty and my knees were weak.

"Are you okay, Cariña? We don't have to go."

Renzo had his arm around my shoulders as we looked out the front door toward his truck.

"Everybody is expecting me."

"Fuck 'em. You're the only one that matters." He turned me around so I was facing him. "They're your friends. They just want you to be happy. If you can't make it this time, they'll understand. If you arrange for this thirty more times and bail on them thirty times, they won't care. They love you."

"But—"

"No buts. It's the truth. Let's just go back on inside and watch some TV. I promise to not even watch fútbol."

I laughed, which is what he'd been going for. I shook out my hands and twisted my neck back and forth like some kind of prizefighter. "I can do this, Renzo. I've got this."

"Are you certain? Isn't there some reality show you wanted to watch?"

"You're the one who likes reality shows, so cut the crap. And yes, I'm sure. I want to go."

He caressed my cheek. "You amaze me, Cariña."

Renzo pulled open the door of Down Home. The door chime made me jump. I didn't look left or right as I walked inside. I kept my head down, forcing myself to take one step at a time.

"Welcome to Down Home Diner. We've got some great specials tonight."

I heard Little Grandma's voice from a long way away, but also really close. I swallowed. Then swallowed again. I looked up and saw her shining blue eyes.

"You made it, child. You made it."

She was sitting on her stool by the cash register, just the way she did when my parents and I used to come here.

It even smelled the same. There was definitely apple pie, but also cooking grease, and I was pretty sure I could smell brisket.

"You okay, sweetheart?" Little Grandma asked.

"Yes," I whispered. "What are the specials?"

"We have catfish with turnip greens. Chicken and dumplings. But what I would really recommend is our maple bacon grilled chicken. It comes with our hashbrown casserole and our breaded fried okra."

I giggled. "You know I can't eat all of that."

"So, you take some home and heat 'em up for tomorrow. It's all good."

I smiled. "It is all good, isn't it?"

She nodded.

Renzo took the menus from her and I turned up to look at him. "That's where we used to always sit." I pointed to a table that butted up against the window. "Lettie's already there."

"Well let's go sit down." He took my hand and then pulled out my chair for me so I could sit down.

After I was seated, I then noticed that Lisa and Roan were seated at the table to our left, and Trenda, Bella, and Simon were seated in front of us.

"Ms. Millie!" Bella cried out. She ran over to my table and plopped her elbows on it, then looked up at me. "Mama told me that this is an occasion. Is this your birthday?"

"It's more like my coming out party," I said.

"Do we get cake?"

"I'm sure we could get cake if we wanted it."

"Bella, why don't you come back here and sit down with us for a little while. You can visit with Ms. Millie after dinner. Okay?"

"Okay," the little girl said with a grin.

Like a streak, she was back with her parents.

I looked over at Roan and Lisa. Roan gave me a solemn nod, and Lisa gave me a wave. I waved back at her, then I turned my attention to Renzo.

"How are you doing, Cariña?"

"Good. Really good."

He smiled. "Millie, Lettie's coming our way to take our order."

I looked over and I saw her with her notepad. She was indeed heading our way.

"Hiya. What can I get you folks tonight?"

"Little Grandma suggested the maple bacon grilled chicken with hashbrown casserole and breaded fried okra."

Lettie laughed. "I bet she did. What would you like to drink, Millie?"

"Sweet tea?"

"Got it."

"What about you, Renzo?"

"Chicken and dumplings. I'll take the green beans and broccoli."

Lettie nodded as she wrote it down. "And to drink?"

"I'll have sweet tea as well."

"I'll have your drinks right out to you."

After she left, I blew out a stream of air. This was going pretty well. I mean, I wasn't ready to go out partying at a bar, but being someplace safe with friends? I could do this.

Renzo picked up my hand and kissed my inner wrist.

"You keep doing that, I'll melt right out of my chair and onto the floor."

"No, you won't. You have a spine of steel."

"You're just—" I stopped myself. I couldn't scoff at him. Not when he was looking at me like that. Renzo really meant that. He believed I was strong. He believed I had a spine of steel. And I was kind of believing it too. Did it take me having him as my mirror before I realized it, or was it there all along?

"Here are your drinks."

Lettie placed our teas in front of us.

I heard the sound of chairs scraping. I looked around and saw everybody standing, including Little Grandma. Even Patty had come out from the kitchen and she was standing. They were all holding glasses in the air. I looked back at Renzo to see if he could tell me what was going on. He was standing with his glass of tea raised as well.

"This toast is to Millie Jane," Little Grandma said. "I know your parents loved you beyond measure and were always proud of you, but today they are up in heaven applauding you, Millie darling. You have amazed them. Your strength and kindness have amazed us all."

"To Millie," Roan said.

"To Millie," everyone else said.

I did not cry.

I didn't cry through dinner.

I didn't cry through cake.

I didn't cry when I had to say good-bye to Little Grandma.

It wasn't until Renzo was deep inside of me that night, and he told me he loved me, that I cried my tears of joy.

Chapter Twenty-Eight

I shut the door of my Mini Cooper with my hip, then trotted up the stairs to my front door with my one little shopping bag. I needed to stop doing this. I went to the grocery store once a day, just because I could. First, it was just nice to know that I could go to the store and not freak out; instead I could sometimes say hello to a neighbor. Sometimes I even recognized somebody I went to school with. It was ridiculously fun.

Then second, it was one of the few drives I felt comfortable making. There were two stop signs and one red light. I only had to make two left turns on the whole trip, so it was really easy. Poor Renzo. He'd been so proud of me when I'd made it to Down Home six weeks ago, he didn't know that it was going to bite him in the ass. He came home every lunch hour and taught me how to drive so I could pass my driver's test in three weeks. Then I made him come car shopping with me, and he *hated* the car I decided to buy. I told him it was the Mini Cooper or a VW bug. And if it was the bug, I was going to put eyelashes on the headlights. After that, he saw the merits of the Mini Cooper.

I plopped the plastic bag with butter and sugar onto the kitchen island, then I grabbed my cell phone out of my purse. I knew I had Bluetooth in my car, but there was no way I was going to attempt to talk and drive. I was going to kill myself for sure if I tried to do that.

It was Trenda who had left me a message.

We've got the dresses. Get over here.

I bit my lower lip. It was only two o'clock. We would probably be done trying things on before dinner time. Trenda and Simon's house was farther than the grocery store, so I didn't want to navigate from their house back to my house in the dark. I called her back.

"They all came?" I asked.

"Yes. Plus, we didn't a little shopping too, so you have more of a selection."

"Who's we?"

"Lisa, of course."

"Sure," I agreed.

"Jenny Brooks. She works with Renzo, I think you've met her?"

"I have, she's great."

"Then some of my sisters."

I closed my eyes. "Just how much shopping did y'all do?"

"Just a little. It's mostly the clothes you bought off the internet that you had sent here."

"Okay, then. I just didn't want Renzo to see, in case I can't do this."

"Well, get your butt over here, Millie Jane."

I laughed. "I'll see you soon."

I hung up. I put the butter in the refrigerator and the sugar in the pantry. Then I pulled out a bunch of the pumpkin spice cookies that I'd baked out of the cookie jar and put them in a Tupperware bin so I could take them to Trenda's. I wondered what I was going to be dealing with.

"Mom and Dad are really chomping at the bit to come and meet Millie," Jase told me for the umpteenth time.

"I know, man, but they have their hands full. Sandy's moved back home, and they're babysitting Gustavo's kids while he and his wife are on that cruise. They don't have time for a visit."

"Sandy is babysitting Gus's kids. You know she wants at least five of her own. Grandma Maureen is doing great. Let the parents come and visit."

"It's too soon."

"Are you having second thoughts?"

"Fuck no! I was holding out the teeniest bit of hope that she would make it to your wedding, but it's not looking like that's in the cards. Don't get me wrong, she's doing a lot better. But I just don't see it happening."

"That was a big ask in such a short amount of time. The fact that it was even a possibility is amazing."

"I'm worried if Mom and Dad come before the wedding that she'll think I'm pressuring her. So no, I don't want them to come for a visit until next year. Could you talk to them? I just have too much on my plate. I've got to look for another job and I still want to be Millie's biggest cheerleader."

"What do you mean you need to look for another job?"

"That old coot I've been working for wants me to buy into his company for a half mil before he'll make me a partner. I could do it, but I refused. I'm going to double his business in the first three years, and he knows it. That's the reason he should make me a partner. The only other way that I can become a partner is to marry his daughter."

"Are you shitting me?"

"Not even a little."

Jase laughed. "Okay, so where are you going to work?"

"I just need another nine months to get my architectural license here in Tennessee. Then I'll decide if I want to hang out my own shingle or sell myself to the highest bidder."

"With your resumé it will be a really high bid."

I could hear the pride in my brother's voice and it made me happy.

"I've got your back, bro. I'll see you next month," Jase promised.

When I got to Trenda's house, it was like Macy's had exploded in her living room. I counted six women in the house and no sign of Bella. Of course, she could be hiding underneath a dress.

"Trenda, what have you done?" I asked. I tried to keep my voice normal, and not make it seem like I was panicking, but I was kind of panicking.

Lisa got up off the couch and rushed over to me. I took a step backward. Even though I loved Lisa, this was a lot.

A lot!

She gently took my hand in hers. "Trenda? Can Millie and I go hide out in your kitchen for a minute or two?"

"Sure."

Lisa guided me into the kitchen.

"Are you okay?" she asked me.

"No," I answered honestly. "I ordered five dresses online. There have to be at least thirty dresses out there. I only know you, Trenda, and Jenny. Who are the other three women?"

Lisa grabbed two glasses out of the cupboard and

got us water out of the fridge dispenser. "Here, take a sip and I'll give you the low-down."

I took a sip.

"Apparently, this is a thing the Avery sisters do. They dress one another. Maddie, who you'll meet, is epic at finding the right clothes for someone. She—"

"Has never seen me or met me," I interrupted Lisa.

"Yeah, but Trenda sent her a lot of pictures of you."

I tilted my head for her to continue.

"I'm the one who invited Jenny. We ran into each other at the mall in Knoxville. I told her I was looking for a dress for you to wear to Renzo's brother's wedding and I was heading to Macy's. She took me to this really cool retro shop. Oh my God, Millie. She has an eye for some of the cutest stuff. She can do the rockabilly style but really classy."

"Lisa, this just seems too overwhelming. I think I need to just take my five dresses and go home."

"Just give us ten minutes, okay?" she begged.

"I don't know. I'm not sure that I can."

"Sure you can. You handled Rod. You can handle some flipping dresses."

I choked out a laugh. "Okay."

When we went back out into the living room, there were only two dresses to be seen, and only Trenda and Jenny were there.

"Where is everybody?" I asked.

"I asked my sisters to go get some refreshments from the store. My cupboards are bare."

I scowled at her. "You told them to leave because I was having a panic attack."

"No. I told them we needed refreshments. I gave them money and everything. But the reason why I wanted them out of here was to give you a chance to regroup, because I was an idiot and ambushed you."

Jenny and Lisa laughed.

"You were kind of an idiot," Lisa said.

"Yes, Lisa, I've admitted that," Trenda scowled. Then she turned to me. "Do you really want to go to this wedding? Renzo has nine brothers and seven sisters. God knows how many nieces and nephews. You're going to be ambushed a hundred times worse than this."

"If I have Renzo beside me, and I know to expect it, yes, I'm positive I can handle it," I told her.

"Well okay then. Let's get you dolled up." She grinned.

"You know I only need one dress," I pointed out.

"Millie," Jenny smiled at me. "You're going to need more. There is the bachelorette party, the rehearsal dinner, the wedding, and then whatever festivities the day after the wedding. How long did Renzo say he was going to Springfield for?"

"A week," I whispered in horror.

"Yeah," Lisa nodded. "You need a lot of outfits. We

didn't just bring dresses, we brought picnic outfits, boating outfits, and cocktail dresses. You'll be covered."

I gulped. "I didn't know about all of this. I've never been to a wedding before," I admitted.

"Are you sure—"

I interrupted Trenda before she could go on. "Yes, I'm sure I want to go."

"Well, okay then, let's get this party started."

"Where's Bella?" I asked.

"I sent her over to a friend for a playdate. Trust me, this is tough work, this is not playing."

I gulped again. Nope, it didn't seem like playing at all.

Chapter Twenty-Nine

JASPER CREEK, OCTOBER

It rankled that Millie wasn't here. She knew I was going to leave for the airport in less than an hour and then I would be gone for a week. Yeah, I know we'd discussed how we would facetime so she could meet everyone. But still. It kind of hurt that she wasn't here.

I shut my suitcase and took it into the living room.

At least I'd been able to get ahold of her this time and she said she would be home soon, that she was just running late. Not like that one horrible day when I couldn't get ahold of her.

I went into the kitchen and tried to figure out if I wanted lemonade or iced tea. I peeked in the cookie jar and found snickerdoodle cookies. I grabbed the carton of milk.

Soon I was sitting at the table dunking my cookies in milk and sulking.

Seriously, Drakos. This is how you're going to spend your time? Sulking?

I started to laugh.

I heard Millie's car drive up and got up to pull open the door. Something didn't compute when she got out of the car.

"Renzo, can you get the stuff out of the trunk," she hollered, as she bent back in and reached over the driver's seat to pick something up off the passenger seat.

Fuck, I've never seen those jeans before. They were red, skintight, and looked incredible.

She turned around. "Renzo. The trunk? We don't have much time."

Her hair. It's different.

"Renzo. I need you to get my suitcases out of the trunk. The Lyft is going to be here in twenty minutes, and I need to grab something out of our bathroom and I have to tinkle."

Suitcases?

"Renzo, snap out of it!" She sped by me and went up the stairs.

What?! Did she just smack my ass?

"The suitcases!" she yelled over her shoulder.

I went to the trunk of her Mini Cooper and found three rather large suitcases.

What the hell? Is she staying at my place while I'm out of town?

I pulled them out of the trunk and brought them inside.

I waited impatiently outside the master bathroom door. When I heard the sink tap turn on, I opened the door.

"What in the hell is going on?" I demanded.

She turned her head to look at me. Her hair *was* different.

A lot different.

It was a cut that framed her face, and made her look softer, less angular. It was lighter, too.

I think.

"What? Do I have lipstick on my teeth?"

"You look amazing," I whispered.

Her gaze turned soft. "Really? You really think so?"

I reached out and pulled her toward me. "Every time I think you can't get any more beautiful, then you up your game and knock my socks off."

"Renzo, I love you so much."

"I love you too, Millie. I'm going to miss you while I'm in Missouri, Cariña."

She laughed up at me. Her beautiful violet eyes were dancing.

"Honey, haven't you figured it out yet? I'm going with you."

Epilogue

I'd been in contact with Renzo's mom for the last couple of weeks, after the 'fashion-show' at Trenda's house. It was at that point I knew I could make it to the wedding. If. And there were a lot of ifs. If certain things could be taken care of.

First, I had to talk to Doc Evans. I had read up on flying on airplanes and how some people would take a prescribed medication to relax before the flight. I knew I would probably need one before getting into the airport. He and I got something figured out for the flight to Missouri and the flight back home.

I also figured I would have a better chance of being relaxed if we had better seats on the plane, so I booked us first-class seats together on his flights. I never canceled his flights because he would get a notification and know something was up.

Second, I had to talk to Renzo's mom about where

we were going to stay when we arrived. She was so sweet about everything. Renzo was supposed to be staying at Gustavo's house in the spare bedroom. But she said that place was bedlam on a good day. She looked around and said she found a really peaceful hotel for us to stay at. She talked to the concierge and we could get a suite on the top floor, so it would be quiet.

She told me the entire itinerary for the wedding events. Jenny had been right. There was a bachelorette party, a rehearsal dinner, a barbeque the day after the wedding, and a baby shower for Nia since everyone was in town. I told her there was no way I could go to a bachelorette party, and she laughed.

"You'll have more fun staying home with me, Renzo's dad and my mom, Nia and a couple of the others. We plan to order in Mexican food and watch Game of Thrones. Mom hasn't seen it, and everybody at the rehab center has been telling her about it, so she's dying to watch it. Christos is going to die of shock when he realizes how much sex and nudity is in it."

Sharon had been a dream. She had tackled every single one of my problems, and I knew this wedding week would be a success.

All the way from the airport to his parent's house, Renzo kept glancing over at me. I hadn't been very talkative once I had taken the pill that Doc Evans had prescribed, but now I was coming out of it.

"Are you sure you're okay?" he asked for the twelfth or thirteenth time.

I rolled my eyes. "I guess time will tell."

He gripped the wheel tighter. At least he stopped asking me that question.

We were now driving in a quiet neighborhood and the houses were getting bigger. That made sense, since the Drakos would need a big house. When he made the next turn, quiet was a thing of the past. It was obvious which one was Drakos' house. There were cars, adults, teens, kids and toddlers spilling out of the big white house on the corner.

"I'm going to have to park a block over," Renzo mumbled. "I'm not dropping you off, because in this case, it would not be the gentlemanly thing to do."

I let out a weak laugh. He was right about that.

He turned a corner and found a parking spot and stopped the car. He pulled out his phone and pushed in a number.

"Mom? It's Renzo. I've got Millie with me. We just drove by the house. When did you rent it out to a fraternity?"

I couldn't hear what she had to say.

"That'd be good."

He hung up the phone and turned back to me. "We're going to go check into our hotel and then come back to the house."

"Wait. I don't want them to change things just because I'm here. That's not fair," I protested.

"Gustavo's house is less than a mile away. Then there's Polly's and Duke's. Both of them have swimming pools. Everybody will be more than happy to expend some energy elsewhere before coming back over to mom and dads for dinner."

"Are you sure?"

He reached over and grabbed my hand. "I'm sure."

When we got back to his parent's house forty minutes later, there were three cars in the driveway. I couldn't tell which cars parked in the street belonged to the Drakos household. The garage door was up, so that was how we entered the house. Renzo didn't even knock, he just opened the garage door and walked into the kitchen.

"We're here!"

"Good, I need help peeling potatoes." I recognized Sharon Drakos' voice and grinned.

"Bring Millie in and let us meet her," somebody said.

At least it was just one voice, and not a dozen. What's more, it sounded friendly. I held onto Renzo's hand really tightly as he pulled me into the kitchen.

He bent and kissed the woman, who was washing her hands off at the sink.

"Mom, this is Millie."

"Millie!" She came over and hugged me, and I fell

into her embrace. She felt like a mom. Even better than
Little Grandma. Not as good as my mom, but so very
close.

"Mrs. Drakos—" I started.

"You call me Sharon, or you call me Mom. Those
are your two choices."

"Okay, Sharon. Thank you for all of your help. I'm
so excited to be here."

I watched Renzo as the penny dropped.

"How come I'm thinking my two favorite women
in the world have been collaborating behind my back?"

"Because you're not dumb," a handsome man said
as he came up behind Renzo and wrapped his arm
around his back.

"Dad," Renzo smiled. "This is Millie Randolph.
Have you two been conspiring?" he asked me.

"Nope. Just me and your mom."

The older man had eyes that looked like Renzo's.
Very dark, wise and kind. He held out his hand, and I
took it. "Millie, it is a pleasure to meet you."

"You too, Mr.—"

"Call me Christos."

"Okay Christos. It's a pleasure to meet you."

"Where is she?" a woman yelled. "I want to meet
her. Get out of my way, you big oaf."

"Don't go in there guns blazing. Show some
decorum."

I giggled.

A stunning brunette wiggled past Christos and

blasted a hundred-watt smile at me. "Millie! You're here! I can't wait to hear all about your orchard." She pulled me in for a tight hug, and it didn't bother me. I knew she was Angelica, but there was not one thing about her brash manner that bothered me. She was just kind down to her bones, and I soaked in all of her goodness.

"I can't wait for you to see my orchard too," I grinned into her cleavage.

"Angel, step back. You're suffocating her," Renzo laughed. He pulled me back from Angelica and turned me toward another handsome man.

"Millie, I want to introduce you to my brother, Bruno. He's the guy who got me on the plane to get back to you so fast."

"The one with the country music stars?" I asked.

"Yep, that's him."

I held out my hand. Bruno gave my hand a gentle squeeze. "It's nice to meet you, Millie. I'm glad to see you're doing so well. You handled yourself really well during that hostage situation."

I blushed.

"Hey!" a man yelled from another room. "There's no way to squeeze in, and since I have the bride beside me, I think she gets priority. Renzo, get your scraggly ass out here, and introduce us to the woman who is obviously too good for you."

I laughed. "That's Jase, I presume?" I asked Renzo.

"You'd be right."

"Oooooh, scraggly ass. That's a good one," a high little voice said. "Justin is going to be so peeved when I call him a scraggly ass."

Another high voice, this time a girl, said. "Jase didn't call him a scraggly ass. He said he had a scraggly ass. Lachlan, you need to get your insults right, otherwise they aren't effective."

I looked up at Renzo and he was actually biting his lower lip to stop him from laughing. I looked around at the others in the kitchen. They were all doing the same. Bruno and Christos moved out of the way, and Renzo ushered me forward. Then I saw the most beautiful family on earth. A large dark man, with his arm around a small shapely strawberry blonde, with a boy and a girl standing in front of them, locked in a debate about what the best insults were.

I want that.

Renzo bent down and whispered in my ear. "What? I couldn't hear you."

I hadn't said that out loud, had I?

I shook my head and smiled. "Hi everyone," I said.

"Hi Millie," Jase said as he stepped forward. "I'd love to introduce you to my family."

"We're not your family yet, Jase. We're only your engaged family. After the wedding, we'll be your real family," the little girl said.

Bonnie squatted down in front of her daughter. "Amber. Do you love Jase?"

"Of course," the little girl said. She was clearly outraged.

"Does Jase love you?" Bonnie persisted.

"Yes."

"Are we here for one another, no matter what?"

"Yes." Both Amber and Lachlan said at the same time.

"Then we're a family already. Saturday is just icing on the cake."

"Will there be pie at the wedding, or only cake?" Lachlan asked.

"There has to be cake, so mom can smoosh it at Jase," Amber said knowingly.

"Millie, you have now officially met, my soon to be wife Bonnie, and our travelling side-show, Amber and Lachlan."

I tried not to laugh. I really, really did. But it just burst out. Then I heard everyone behind me laughing, so I didn't feel so bad.

"Grandma Sharon, is there cherry pie?" Lachlan yelled.

"There will be for dessert. Renzo, come help me peel potatoes."

Bonnie sidled up on one side of me and whispered in my ear. "Welcome to the circus."

Renzo lifted our linked hands and kissed the inside of my wrist. "I'll see you later. Bonnie, I'm counting on you to keep her safe."

"I promise."

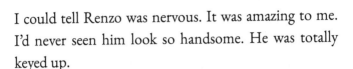

I could tell Renzo was nervous. It was amazing to me. I'd never seen him look so handsome. He was totally keyed up.

"You're going to do great." I told him as we got into the rental.

"I just don't want to fuck up," he said as he got behind the wheel.

"You won't."

I fiddled with the radio on the way to the church and I was so relieved when we met up with his parents. They were able to assure my hero that he would not let his brother down. I was seated in the second row, which was great because I got to watch my man in his tux. Now that he was standing up in front of the church, he was as cool as a cucumber. Jase turned to him and said something, and Renzo responded. Jase laughed, and I saw him relax. Yeah, Renzo was the best man in the world.

The wedding march started, and we all stood up. There was only one bridesmaid, and I couldn't remember her name. I think it was Shannon. But then came Bonnie. She was being escorted up the aisle by Lachlan and Amber.

When the Reverend asked, "Who gives this woman away in marriage?"

Everybody in the church waited to see what the twins would say. It was a crapshoot, and I was surprised that Bonnie was allowing it. Then they opened their mouths and said in unison, "we do."

That was the point I had to get the Kleenex out of my new purse. I was smiling, but I was crying.

Hours later at the reception, I realized that even when my parents were alive; I hadn't smiled this much. There was so much joy, love, and laughter with this family. Renzo was lucky to be a part of this.

"What cariña?" Renzo asked.

"I said I love your family."

"They love you," he whispered into my ear. "Would you like to dance?"

"I would love to, but I've overdone this trip. I would end up really hurting, and there is another dance I would like to do with you later tonight."

His laughter sent tingles down my spine.

"It was wonderful of your sisters to arrange a table just for the two of us." I told him again. I still couldn't believe they had done that. We had seats at one of the large tables with Bruno and Angelica and a couple of others, but Polly and Elani knew about my anxiety with crowds so they'd also arranged for us to have this table to secret ourselves away from the crowd. They were so thoughtful.

"Yes, it was," Renzo agreed. "So, my family didn't scare you away?"

"No, like I said, I love them," I assured him.

"They love you, too. But not as much as I love you, Millie."

I smiled.

"You've had such a hard life," he said.

"So have you." I reached up and brushed my fingers down his cheek. "I'm so thankful that Sharon and Christos found you."

"So am I. I think that was destiny."

"It was Renzo. You deserved to have a good life." I picked up his hand and kissed the inside of his wrist. He chuckled.

Then his eyes turned serious. "Millie, the greatest gift that destiny handed me was when Irv asked me to go help at your orchard."

I went still. He couldn't mean that. Not really.

"You hold my heart and soul in your hands. I want to live with you, grow old with you, just be with you, the rest of my life."

"But..."

"Don't you want the same?" he asked gently.

"With every beat of my heart. It's just sometimes I still have a problem thinking I'm worthy. But I'm getting there. I'm really getting there."

He flashed me his toothpaste smile.

"Will you marry me, Millie?"

He reached over to the vase of flowers on the table and pulled out a blue ribbon. At the end of it was a turquoise blue velvet box. He opened it up and showed me a blue stone, surrounded by black diamonds.

"It's a sapphire that exactly matches the color of your eyes," he whispered.

"It's beautiful," I breathed.

"Will you marry me?" he asked. "Will you be my wife. Be my family?"

I held out my hand. It was trembling. He slipped the ring on my finger.

"Renzo, didn't you know? We are already family. But yes, I'll marry you."

～

Their Stormy Reunion, Book 3

How can I trust him not to break my heart again?

MICHAEL

I fell in love with Fallon when I first saw her in Mr. Vandeboe's class in our junior year. I knew she was destined to be mine. But a year after we graduated from East Tennessee State, she had our wedding all planned — and it made me want to break out in hives. I loved Fallon, but I felt trapped. Spending my life with her was too big of a step, but how could I get out of it without breaking her heart? The answer is—I can't, and then I make the worst mistake of my life.

FALLON

I fell in love with Michael the night of our senior prom, when he took my innocence. He showed me a world filled with care, love and passion that took me to the stars. I knew after college all our dreams would come true. We'd go back home to Jasper Creek and start a family. Then one gut-wrenching moment turned joy into ash. Devastated by his betrayal, I ran away the day before our wedding.

Now I'm a different woman. I came back to Jasper Creek to help my mom take care of my dying father. The town considers me a pariah for leaving the golden boy at the altar, but I don't care. Michael and I know the truth, and that's enough. So why in the hell is Michael following me around town, insisting he wants another chance? Has he lost his mind? Worse—why does my foolish heart want to give him that second chance?

Get your copy of Their Stormy Reunion (Book 3) Now!

About the Author

Caitlyn O'Leary is a USA Bestselling Author, #1 Amazon Bestselling Author and a Golden Quill Recipient from Book Viral in 2015. Hampered with a mild form of dyslexia she began memorizing books at an early age until her grandmother, the English teacher, took the time to teach her to read -- then she never stopped. She began re-writing alternate endings for her Trixie Belden books into happily-ever-afters with Trixie's platonic friend Jim. When she was home with pneumonia at twelve, she read the entire set of World Book Encyclopedias -- a little more challenging to end those happily.

Caitlyn loves writing about Alpha males with strong heroines who keep the men on their toes. There is plenty of action, suspense and humor in her books. She is never shy about tackling some of today's tough and relevant issues.

In addition to being an award-winning author of romantic suspense novels, she is a devoted aunt, an avid reader, a former corporate executive for a Fortune 100 company, and totally in love with her husband of soon-to-be twenty years.

She recently moved back home to the Pacific Northwest from Southern California. She is so happy to see the seasons again; rain, rain and more rain. She has a large fan group on Facebook and through her e-mail list. Caitlyn is known for telling her "Caitlyn Factors", where she relates her little and big life's screw-ups. The list is long. She loves hearing and connecting with her fans on a daily basis.

Keep up with Caitlyn O'Leary:

Website: www.caitlynoleary.com
FB Reader Group: http://bit.ly/2NUZVjF
Email: caitlyn@caitlynoleary.com
Newsletter: http://bit.ly/1WIhRup

facebook.com/Caitlyn-OLeary-Author-638771522866740

x.com/CaitlynOLearyNA

instagram.com/caitlynoleary_author

amazon.com/author/caitlynoleary

bookbub.com/authors/caitlyn-o-leary

goodreads.com/CaitlynOLeary

pinterest.com/caitlynoleary35

Also by Caitlyn O'Leary

PROTECTORS OF JASPER CREEK SERIES

His Wounded Heart (Book 1)

Her Hidden Smile (Book 2)

Their Stormy Reunion (Book 3)

OMEGA SKY SERIES

Her Selfless Warrior (Book #1)

Her Unflinching Warrior (Book #2)

Her Wild Warrior (Book #3)

Her Fearless Warrior (Book 4)

Her Defiant Warrior (Book 5)

Her Brave Warrior (Book 6)

Her Eternal Warrior (Book 7)

NIGHT STORM SERIES

Her Ruthless Protector (Book #1)

Her Tempting Protector (Book #2)

Her Chosen Protector (Book #3)

Her Intense Protector (Book #4)

Her Sensual Protector (Book #5)

Her Faithful Protector (Book #6)

Her Noble Protector (Book #7)

Her Righteous Protector (Book #8)

Night Storm Legacy Series

Lawson & Jill (Book 1)

Black Dawn Series

Her Steadfast Hero (Book #1)

Her Devoted Hero (Book #2)

Her Passionate Hero (Book #3)

Her Wicked Hero (Book #4)

Her Guarded Hero (Book #5)

Her Captivated Hero (Book #6)

Her Honorable Hero (Book #7)

Her Loving Hero (Book #8)

The Midnight Delta Series

Her Vigilant Seal (Book #1)

Her Loyal Seal (Book #2)

Her Adoring Seal (Book #3)

Sealed with a Kiss (Book #4)

Her Daring Seal (Book #5)

Her Fierce Seal (Book #6)

A Seals Vigilant Heart (Book #7)

Her Dominant Seal (Book #8)

Made in the USA
Columbia, SC
01 July 2025

60194864R00183